A CAST AWAY

G.A. SMITH

Print, eBook and Cover by
N.D. Author Services [NDAS]
www.NDAuthorServices.com

ACKNOWLEDGEMENTS

JUST SO YOU KNOW

It is with great thanks that I mention UCC here for giving me both the time and the resources to focus on this project. Without it, I'm unsure if this would have ever been finished.

Along the same lines, I want to very much thank Judy and the rest of the folks at Willamette Pass Inn for putting me up and also putting up with me for those two weeks up in the mountains, where nothing could intrude on my solitude, and where about two-thirds of this got done. You've got the perfect place there for more things than you imagined. Thanks also for checking in on me from time to time to make sure I was still among the living, and that if I wasn't, you had more coffee.

I want to say thanks as well to my early readers who took a chance and invested their time with this, and for all their important feedback and encouragement: Di Francis, Barb Hendee, David Miller and Melinda Benton, among others. However, a very particular thank you to Christy Keyes, who stayed by my side, from a great distance, when I was up in those mountains alone and unguided in winter and who helped me find my way through the flurries.

To all of you, you have my gratitude.

Finally, let me say that even if this is the wrong place to do so, this story is dedicated to Larry and the UCC Nine. May you continue to be remembered by us all, and may this little thing of mine be just a small bit of that remembrance.

TABLE OF CONTENTS

Acknowledgements i

Earlier 1

First Summer 3

Chapter One: Trauma, Therapy, Lies and Aliases 5

Chapter Two: The Man in Black 15

Chapter Three: Purple Loosestrife 21

Chapter Four: Wiley and Chuck 27

Chapter Five: Kenna's Curl Up and Dye 33

Chapter Six: Getting to Know You 43

Chapter Seven: Life is Trauma 51

Chapter Eight: The Danger of Gophers 63

Chapter Nine: The Register Guardian Herald Clarion
    Bee 71

Chapter Ten: I Get a New Job 81

Chapter Eleven: An Hour of Perfect Beauty 85

Chapter Twelve: Gil's Good Gas 93

Chapter Thirteen: The Dream 99

Chapter Fourteen: Stacy Grips grip 109

Chapter Fifteen: An Unexpected Cut 119

First winter 123

Chapter Sixteen: Fighting Words 125

Chapter Seventeen: Ice Fishing 133

Chapter Eighteen: Lost in the Snow 143

Second Summer 155

Chapter Nineteen: Hollis in Springtime 157

Chapter Twenty: Hollis at Dinner 167

Chapter Twenty-One: Miracles 173
Chapter Twenty-Two: The Broken Road 181
Chapter Twenty-Three: Commiseration 189
Chapter Twenty-Four: On Assignment with Jeff and
   Chip 193
Chapter Twenty-Five: Kenna Tells Me 201
Chapter Twenty-Six: The Game is Everything 213
Chapter Twenty-Seven: Del's 227
Chapter Twenty-Eight: Suspicions About Hollis 241
Chapter Twenty-Nine: Grasshoppers 249
Chapter Thirty: The Fire 259
Chapter Thirty-One: To Feed Three Thousand 279
Chapter Thirty-Two: We Make It Through to Another
   Day 287
Chapter Thirty-Three: After 293
Chapter Thirty-Four: I Meet Death and Live to Talk
   About It, Again 297
Chapter Thirty-Five: A Brief Meeting With Extreme
   Fall 307
Second Winter 317
Chapter Thirty-Six: Jeff and Chip Hit the Slopes
   (and Other Things) 319
Chapter thirty-Seven: Huggin and Muninn 331
Chapter Thirty-Eight: The Consolation of Philosophy
   in Winter 349
Spring 357
Chapter Thirty-Nine: The Hope of Spring 359
Chapter Forty: A Cast Away 369
Chapter Forty-One: Elegy 371
Later 383

EARLIER

I tried to tell you once, I really did.
I will try again now.

First Summer

CHAPTER ONE:

TRAUMA, THERAPY, LIES AND ALIASES

A T FIRST there was a strange sort of recognition of what was going on in that room, of the sounds next door, but it didn't happen right away. Thinking back now, if I let myself, those first few dull thuds were like the sounds of a fist against the wall, or maybe even the sound of a heavy stone dropped into an empty well if you can let yourself hear it, and those first sounds represented at least two deaths, maybe three, and one was my best friend.

The recognition didn't happen right away. I had time to make a joke in my own classroom on that first week of classes, with a room full of captive freshmen finishing their first week of college. I said something about how my best friend, who was teaching that class where the strange noises and laughter were coming from, that it sounded like he was having some time over there with his students. And then there were more sounds. More fists against the wall. More laughter. I turned my head toward the wall behind me with another joke on my lips and saw the clock.

It was exactly 10:41 a.m.

At that moment, I realized those sounds weren't laughter at all. They were screams: the sounds of terror. It's a sound that's visceral when you know it, and I hope you never do, and it does something to you that you can't resist. It did to me. I started yelling, "Get out! Get out! Get out!"

A scramble of bodies raced by me and all was confusion and senselessness. Outside the door was a woman lying on the concrete, damaged in a way I can no longer see because now she's only a blackened silhouette in my mind. I know who she is. I know her name.

And then I was running and running and running, and I can't tell you what I was thinking at that time, looking at the faces of the terrified eighteen-year-olds around me. We ran to another building and then a room with no windows and locked the door and slid a file cabinet against it and then we waited. And I waited with something inside me that couldn't come out.

I knew what was happening in my friend's classroom and I wanted to tell someone to go there and help him, just help him, and I wanted so badly to say it, but there was no one to say it to. And I wanted to scream but I couldn't. I didn't know how.

Later, and I have a difficult time understanding later from now to yesterday any longer, we came to know that the killer had only a few minutes to slaughter nine people, one for each of the minutes left in the class before the state police, just two minutes away, arrived and ended things. And yet, while I can't speak for anyone but myself, there is never an end to such things.

That's all I can say about that for now.

. . . . .

There are only a couple of ground rules here, and if you're okay with that, then we can go on with whatever it is that this is.

The first rule is you're reading something from someone you don't know at all, and the person writing this is pretty darned screwed up. No, I don't mean like "Hey, I'm sorry to hear about that," or something else that we say because we're pretending to be alive and a viable, meaningful part of life and living and just getting on. I mean that most people can't understand what I'm saying when I say I'm screwed up and not at all okay. And that's good. That's really good. I'm happy for you, in any way that I remember what that means.

The second rule is you must allow me the opportunity to lie when it suits me, and this also applies to the first rule. I can only say these things through deflection, and that's how it's going to be. Are we okay for now?

. . . . .

Nine months went by, and I believed I was doing okay and just fine and I was okey-dokey, especially because everyone around me on a daily basis was certainly not okay, and I kind of thought by comparison I was okay, but no, no I was not.

One day I was out in the very large garden that I had built over the years, sitting in a chair with my back to the shed I'd also built. There were honeybees and bumblebees drowsing in the penstemons and petunias and lupines, red, blue and white, and hummingbirds' wings cut through the air with a sound like electric wires singing. The hot air was just beginning to cool as the sun slowly made its way behind the ridge of the valley to my back, and squadrons of swallows filled the air, swooping and diving, flashes of iridescent blue and green against the white oaks of the far valley ridge and the pastures shot through with patches of blue camas and orange buttercups.

Above the valley ridge in front of me, cumulus rose in a crescendo of clouds and formed an enormous wedge, like a ghost ship cleaving the sky, and all around me the air vibrated with bird song. Long ropes of vines with melons and cucumbers trailed along the garden paths, and tomatoes and peppers and eggplants hung down like Christmas ornaments from raised boxes. The bluebirds watched me hopefully, waiting to see if I'd rise and disturb some earth for them, and a humming-bird paused momentarily, suspended in the air ten inches from my face, and cocked its head back and forth as I looked out, and then sped on its way.

I didn't see any of this, however, because I was thinking that there was a very sharp knife in the shed just at my back and if I could rouse myself enough I could get up and get it, come back and sit down, and cut my wrists and very likely bleed out before anyone noticed. I didn't do that, however, because I didn't seem to have either the energy or the will to get up and go into the shed, and besides, I had already bled out: everything was gray and I could see nothing.

Okay. That's enough of that.

·　　·　　·　　·　　·

After a few more episodes along the same lines, and a series of threats from my wife, Joanie, I went to see somebody. Her name was Linda, and after several months she said to me, and I'm just paraphrasing here, "Wow. You're pretty messed up. If I were you I'd just, you know, hang myself or jump into a pool of lava or something like that."

She has this bedside manner that sticks with you, and she is not the sort who sits back with a notebook and passively nods her head in commiseration.

She was saying this because I kept saying things like "I don't know about that" when she pointed out something to me, or "I think I'll just figure that out later," when she said I should take a long hard look at something.

Finally, one day she put down her notepad and she said with kind of a look on her face which once I'd have been able to interpret but couldn't just then, "Why don't you just ignore all the things I've been helping you with for the past months and just, you know, run away from it all?"

I thought that sounded pretty good, and so I went home and said to Joanie that Linda had advised that we go away and never come back. Joanie was surprised to hear this, but said she was getting tired of eight months of Oregon rain and then four months of drought, and so we started doing some research about where we should go.

"Someplace quiet," I said.

"Someplace dramatic," Joanie said.

We looked at maps. We'd already lived in many places before, and it was hard to decide.

"Remember the times we traveled through Montana?" Joanie said. "The wild horses we saw?"

"I do," I said, "and having a steak at the Golden Steer in Madison."

"I wonder if you can still get mixed drinks to go there?"

"The Big Hole and the Beaverhead and the Missouri and all the rest," I said.

"And remember how you liked fishing the Clark Fork?" she said. "And Flathead and Glacier and the endless trails."

"And waking up to the sun coming over the Rockies?"

And we smiled together, because that was happiness and that's where we wanted to be. Who wouldn't? So, it was Montana, and that was that.

We moved ourselves and our three dogs to Dobbins, Montana, in April that year. It's right up near the Big Rockies and is more than dramatic, it's a place you wish you could see yourself. We saved up and had all our stuff sent to a little house we bought on five acres in what passes for a development in Montana: a rancher decides he'd like some extra cash and sells off a morsel of his part of the state. Four houses show up. It's a development.

Anyway, we moved in April because we thought it would be nice to move during the spring. No one told us it was still winter in Montana. So, we actually arrived in our little wagon in a blizzard.

We did get a few looks from people in trucks and SUVs as we navigated mountain passes in blinding sideways snow. I grew up in Nebraska, and I can tell you that the trick about driving in a white-out is to just ignore it. You just keep driving and pretend it's not happening. You do that because if you didn't you'd realize pretty fast how incredibly stupid you are to be out driving in weather like that. Besides, Montana was waiting for us.

When we pulled into Dobbins that afternoon we found the Safeway and loaded up the back with as many supplies as we could cram in around the three dogs because we figured we might not get out for a while. There was no way this little one-horse town had a snowplow. I also grabbed a snow shovel and tied it to the roof of the car. Once we got everything loaded we headed out to our new home.

We plowed through some drifts on country roads and then we found what we hoped was our place be- cause we couldn't see very well, and I gunned the drift in the rock driveway and got us up fairly close and that was as good as it was going to get. We got the dogs and our supplies inside. I tried the garage door, but it was frozen shut, so that was that. I'd dig us out tomorrow, assuming the snow let up.

The good news was there was firewood in the garage. We got a fire going, opened a bottle of wine, fed the dogs, and sat down on some furniture wrapped in plastic.

"We made it!" Joanie said. We clinked glasses.

"Welcome to paradise," I said.

It didn't stop snowing the next day, or the day after, or the day after that. We didn't have television hooked up yet, but we had plenty to do with just getting every- thing unpacked from all the stuff that the movers had deposited in the garage.

At some point in the process of me asking "Where should this go?" we stopped for a break and I said, "I want you to call me by my middle name whenever we're around anybody else."

"What? Why?! There's no way I'm going to call you 'Alyeska'. It's a crazy name. What was the matter with your parents anyway?"

"I just want to start over is all. I just want to completely start over somehow. Isn't that okay?"

Joanie sat silent for a minute.

"Okay. But just if there are other people around. And I'm calling you 'Al'. Get used to it."

I figured 'Al' wasn't so bad. I could live with that.

And then Joanie said, "Do I get an alias too?"

"It's not an alias! We're not running from the law or in a witness protection program. It's just a, well, sort of pseudonym. It's my middle name, not like something I made up."

"I want an alias too."

"It's not an alias. Can't you just be Joanie, a.k.a. Joanie?"

"I'll come up with one and let you know," she said. "What about 'Uhura'?" She began straightening pictures we'd hung earlier, muttering to herself. When I came in the room from time to time I could hear her say things like "Esmerelda," with a flourish, and then, "No. Maybe 'Arwen'," with a romantic tone. I went back to the garage and unpacked things.

Anyway, a month later, spring arrived, which lasted for three days, and then it was summer.

.   .   .   .   .

DAYS AND NIGHTS

There are some other things I'm going to need to say. If you just want to skip these and stay with the story, you should be all right.

I couldn't tell Joanie what I was thinking and why I lied to her I just couldn't because I don't know why except that I knew I had to go away I just knew it and even though I knew I was coming home to lie to her and change everything I thought it would change everything and that's what I wanted more than anything and then that night later after we'd talked about it more and had decided I thought that was good because that's about as far as I was willing to think. I just can't think or don't want to is what the problem really seems to be.

CHAPTER TWO:

THE MAN IN BLACK

AFTER JOANIE and I had been in Dobbins for a few weeks, we were standing behind the house, looking up at the Rockies and hurting our necks doing so, and we both sort of sighed and smiled and the smiles said, "Yep. Worked out pretty good, huh?"

Dobbins has no K-Mart, and has no McDonald's, and has no Walmart or any other sort of mart, and it has no obese children whose idea of food is French fries and sometimes I actually consciously think of this and thank God that such places still exist in our country. We have no snowplow (way too expensive, and besides, you've got a truck or a horse or a snowmobile, right?) and people here want, more than anything, to just live. You know? Just go ahead with their lives without worrying about all the silly stuff that you might think is important but which in no way affects your life. It's good. It's real good.

And yes, after a few weeks we said to each other about six times, "But how can I get so-and-so? There's no place for two hundred miles that sells it!"

That's when you remember that whole internet-thing, and it doesn't matter what goat-path you live on, those folks from UPS and FedEx are just fearless crazy people, and yes, they'll deliver. It's especially fun watching them plow down the streets, such as they are in winter, and jump out with your box of goat milk or dog vitamins or whatever. They know the routine: this is Dobbins, and you need to make it here, or else move somewhere a little more like something on TV.

. . . . .

Joanie and I and the dogs quickly found ourselves just amazingly pleased to be here. We'd wander through town for no reason, saying hello to everyone and anyone. "Hi, nice to meet you," and it was all so very nice. One day we were walking along like that, holding hands because that's kind of the way we are, and we saw someone coming down the sidewalk toward us and...have you ever done that? You know, when someone is walking on 'your' side of the street and you feel like maybe you'll just cross the street right then instead of encountering them even for small talk? It was like that.

Well, it was actually more than that, because the person walking toward us looked like a very bad storm, even at this distance, and we're new here and we looked at one another and wondered, maybe, is this actually okay or not, because frankly, I don't really understand what okay is anymore because not so very long ago somebody showed up in the classroom next door dressed in body armor and with multiple assault weapons and killed everyone in sight and so my concept of normalcy has changed a bit.

And so even though this was just a very large man walking toward us who appeared very angry and dangerous, we didn't know what to think or do, or what was proper or perhaps just, well, misunderstanding. But I tell you, I never, ever want to misunderstand people again like I did a year ago when I could have imagined aliens landing on campus before I imagined what happened.

Joanie and I in fact did not cross to the other side of the street, but if there was a next time, maybe we would. Instead, we just got out of the way and stood next to the curb as best we could.

Some thirty paces off you could get a look at him. He was tall, very tall in my mind, maybe six foot six or better, and he was built. He was neither skinny nor heavy, and given his size he exuded a sense of raw strength. He was dressed in dark jeans and a black shirt and wore a black, flat-rimmed cowboy hat which hid at least some of his face as he seemed to not necessarily be looking forward, but rather mostly down, and perhaps he had grown used to people getting out of his way. But as he approached, you could see his expression more and more clearly. He struck my sensibilities in an almost physical way, and I'm going to have to tell you, based on my recent experience, I was afraid to be in proximity to him.

As he passed us, Joanie said, "Good morning," and he said nothing at all, but his left hand went to his hat rim in an arc that maybe, if you were being generous, signified the touching of his hat as a means of acknowledging your existence. After he had passed, he turned into the local diner.

"What the hell was that?" Joanie said.

"Don't know. Don't care. Let's see what's in the drugstore."

Even so, a few days later I stopped in at Del's one morning, our only place to eat in town (unless you count the hot dogs at Gil's Good Gas which, frankly—sorry for the pun—are really good) and got a cup of coffee, and then sat on the bench out front, and it really is The Bench because it's the only one. I sat there basking in the early morning Montana sun, and to tell the truth the sun is different wherever you go, and it really was the "Montana sun" and not one that you can have anywhere else.

I know that sounds crazy, but it's not. "Our" sun has to do a bit of work to get where it's going. It's like the people who live here. They have to get up in the dark if anything is really going to get done that day, and it's the same with our sun. Oh sure, it has to first, several hours earlier, wash up against the beach on the east coast, and then kind of walk up and down the Appalachians, and then of course it's smooth sailing from there. No problem to just stride across Iowa and Nebraska and Kansas and the Dakotas. But then it reaches the Rockies, and now it's serious business.

Now the sun has to just sort of man up and you can kind of see it taking a bit of a break and considering, "Do I really want to do this all over again? It was such a pain yesterday." But it does. It stands there, maybe back around Spearfish, and then gets a really good running start and by golly, up the Rockies it goes, grunting and panting to drop down upon a little guy, sitting on a bench, enjoying the day's first coffee. Like that. Except for the fact that this little guy looks up and sees this very large dressed-in-black guy on the other side of the street, who is also illuminated by our sun.

This is going to be one of those confessions you just don't want to make as we go along here if you're still with me, because of meaningless concepts such as "objectivity" or even "manhood," but I have to tell you that even seeing this guy from across the street was, I don't know. I think I'm trying to say that I was kind of scared or something, because I saw four other people get out of his way, and they were locals who must have known him, and because it was summer now, it could have easily been tourists, and my mind bumped over that idea and why that would be very bad. Because, I have to tell you, I could somehow feel this guy from across the street. I'm not kidding. And that idea of him running into that particular tourist, who had that particular attitude, and who would not yield his ground, and I sat there imagining a broken neck, and quite surely it would not have been The-Man-In-Black's. Not a chance.

This guy, and I'm remembering back to another day of having seen a killer, is not the same. He is not some crazy killer, because I can just somehow feel that. He is not that one who has somehow lost his mind and imagines that by killing others he can somehow be fulfilled. And yet, he has killed, and I know it. He is angry in a way I cannot understand. I am glad he is on the other side of the street.

I drank my coffee, and our Montana sun washed over Dobbins.

Days and Nights

For the longest time I have had the ability to plan my dreams while I'm preparing to sleep. I'm not kidding.

I would simply decide in advance what I was going to dream, and then I would. All night. Any time. I'd just tell myself I was going to dream about fishing or hiking maybe, and then I would. I'd somehow roll my closed eyes back up into my brain and there was the dream and that was that. I'd fall asleep in no time, too. I don't dream like that anymore.

There's something else there. I don't know what it is. It's like the sound of cicadas, or a branch scraping against a wall. Something. It can be loud and it makes me think of other things that were not in my plans, and I cannot sleep like I once did, and I don't know why.

Instead, whatever I dream about is bad, very bad. I'm walking one of the dogs and somehow the dog drowns or is hit by a car, even though that can't happen. Joanie and I are walking and a tree falls on her or a house nearby is on fire and Joanie runs in and doesn't come back. I'm fishing and then I'm drowning. I cannot sleep. I don't know why.

I want to sleep again.

CHAPTER THREE:
PURPLE LOOSESTRIFE

THE WORLD is filled with very bad things. I have of course understood this all my life, but largely in an intellectual way. Yes, there have been personal tragedies, and more recently I have been so close to things I cannot understand that my mind had to just run away into a little box and cower there in order to feel somewhat okay. And that is something I don't wish to talk about at all, for my own selfish reasons.

Even so, I understand that of course it's not just me who has to face these things, but that we all do, all the time, each day. Everyone does, and some just meander through their lives, like myself, and wonder, "Why me?" and then other people take action. They're prepared. They're saying, "Oh, no. Not me," and they have a plan. That's why I have to tell you why flowers can kill you, and why you have to kill them first. It's your only option.

. . . . .

There was this day, when Joanie and I were driving back home from town, a few miles or so, during the four to six days of early summer before it becomes blazing hot, and on the horizon we could see smoke. Naturally, this was not good. You now live in a place that has giant pines in all directions, and images of

Smokey Bear glowering at you in order to remind you of your moral responsibility not to kill everything and everyone around you by being stupid, and if that's not enough, then there are signs everywhere saying "Fire Season Is Coming" and there could be a fiery end to all things: "Do You Have Defensible Space?" So, smoke is usually not a good thing.

However, as we got a bit further from town, we saw various individuals with miniature flame-throwers strapped to their backs, no kidding, igniting the plants in the ditches that habitually surround everyone's property.

"What in the world is everyone doing? Why are they burning their ditches?" Joanie said.

"Oh, I forgot to tell you," I said, "but I heard in town earlier that Tuesday was Crazy-Day in Dobbins, like that episode from Star Trek."

As it turned out, people were burning the ditches in order to kill, among other things, an invasive plant called Purple Loosestrife. Now, you might be familiar with the Garden of Eden story about how sin comes into the world just because there's this apple, and you may also have heard of Pandora's Box and how she just, well, she just *had* to look into it.

If you're familiar with these stories you may have noticed that both stories involve a certain level of "entrapment," as we'd say. Even so, just listen to the word a bit, "Loose-Strife", and there you go. Eating an Apple? Opening the Box? That's nothing. In this case, you should have known better just because of the name: "Oh, what you got there? Oh, some Death Weed? Hey, just put that in the salad okay?" You got some Purple

Loosestrife on your property? You'd better get out there and do something about it, because if you don't, you are going to Hell in a hand basket for sure. Now that is the nature of Evil in the world.

I am not the sort of person who has ever considered Evil as something that needed my attention more than, perhaps, on some occasions, my vote. I would, like almost anyone, like to believe that I am a "good" person, though I suppose we'd quibble about the qualifiers for a bit. I'd like to think that, whether or not I intended it, I was at least something of a role model for my students for the past thirty years, at least in some area or another, and that I had been a good man and husband, and that, consequently, my life had some modicum of meaning when all was said and done.

I have had to readjust my thinking about the nature of Evil, and where it comes from, and what, if anything, one might do about it and how to stand up to it and genuinely be the Upright Man you've always thought you were ever since that day when The-World-Fell-Apart when I was left with no certain reference points. But, by golly, after talking to people in town I was going to become the Deacon of Death when it came to Purple Loosestrife.

Here's the deal. This flower is so darned invasive that it actually pushes out grass. Grass! You know, like God's number one thing He always liked? Grass is the most common plant on the planet, and certainly God meant something when He ordered it that way.

This thing is just as it's named: it releases "strife" on any ecosystem it's introduced to. Kudzu? Child's play, because you can actually eat that stuff. Loosestrife?

Livestock jumps away from it. Cattle. Sheep. Hogs. Horses. Nobody can eat the darn thing.

Meanwhile, it's wiping out all the things the animals can eat. You have to kill it, before it kills you and yours. So anyway. Joanie and I learn this and we are on the watch for it, just in case, because you never know when something, even a little something, is going to come and ruin everything.

.   .   .   .   .

One morning, Joanie and I were wandering the property with the dogs, and we saw a beautiful little flower by the house that made us think of lupines up in the mountains. There are no other flowers on our property. There are none. I have this feeling that this is because I've perhaps done something awful in my past and I am being punished for it, but that's just me so don't overly concern yourself about that.

So, this was really one nice flower, and given its singularity, we pulled up our chairs and sat by it. You know, both to admire it and keep it company, because we're generally friendly sorts and like to say hello to new arrivals in the neighborhood. Well, we were sitting there, admiring Our Flower, and the problem was that Joanie has several degrees from the university in, I don't even remember them all, but they involve things like -ologies of one sort or another, which in this case was very bad. If only she'd studied an -ish or an -ing, we could have just carried on. But she was looking at it then with her University Mind instead of the one that I'd been using which was my That's A Nice Flower Mind.

And of course you know the conclusion of this, that we had discovered the Devil Flower in our midst.

However, as opposed to what you might think, this caused four days of discussion concerning the moral dilemma involved. And really, I have no energy left for moral dilemmas.

On the one hand, it's just the one flower, and yes there's the definite possibility that it might spread and then the next thing you know you're setting your yard on fire. On the other hand, it is a real pretty flower and it has done us no harm whatsoever, and it's not as though poison ivy is growing in the yard.

And yet, what would happen if neighbors spotted it? You can kind of imagine people putting up ugly signs in your yard or something, or maybe commando-style rushing in with a flame-thrower while adopting a scorched-earth policy. But then again, it's just the one flower, you know? And it's up by the house where no one can see it. Why just kill something?

Several days later, in the kitchen, Joanie said, "You gonna do it or you want me to?"

"I'll do it," I said, and went into the yard and dug up the flower.

At dinner Joanie said, "Sorry about that. I hated to have to kill it."

"Oh, I didn't kill it," I said with my mouth full of salad. "I put it in a little pot in the garage. We can put it here in the kitchen window and just hide it when company comes by."

DAYS AND NIGHTS

A quick question: what's the safest place you can think of? That is, what would you consider to be a place that you could actually get to in a time of crisis where absolutely nothing could hurt you and you'd be safe? I know a place like that, but I can't tell you about it. Not yet.

CHAPTER FOUR:

WILEY AND CHUCK

W E'D ONLY BEEN in town maybe five weeks when it became obvious that we were going to need a second car. Our little wagon was no match for the rock-covered roads, and I could only imagine what it was going to be like trying to get around during the winters, which I understood were pretty bad, and we'd already seen what "spring" was like.

I decided that what we needed was a good old pickup truck, maybe something like I always imagined that was about six feet in the air and had giant knobby tires on it. So, given there was pretty much only one of anything in town I found myself at Wiley's "Wreck-A-Mended" body-work and used car sales emporium. I didn't know what made something an emporium instead of a store, but I figured I'd just think of it as a used-car dealership and not tax my mind any further about it.

When you pull into Wiley's one of the first things you notice is the beautiful symmetry of things. On your left hand is a pile of what might have once been vehicles at some point in time. You have to assume this, because here and there in the mish-mash of rusting metal you can see what you're pretty sure might have been a headlight or a bumper, but really, it's hard to tell.

It could just as easily have been an old hair dryer from the '50s. But, given the two trades that Wiley apparently involved himself in, you have to figure that these mis-shapen piles of scrap that filled a quarter-mile of otherwise unoccupied pasture must be at least one half of the equation.

Then, on your right, what you see is perhaps ten things that are in fact recognizable vehicles of one sort or another, which easily must qualify as the "mended" ones, though one might have wished for a better physician and a better treatment plan for their future well-being.

I sat there in the car and considered my options. It was either Wiley's or drive two hundred miles and maybe find something better. So I figured, well, let's just see anyway. I could always make the long drive if that was the only other option.

Between these two sets of human invention was a Quonset hut of unknown age and of questionable repute, and there was a sign in the window that said "Office", so I pulled up and parked, and started to walk over toward those vehicles that appeared as though they'd been in running order at least at some point in their lives.

I happened to be making my way toward the first vehicle when the voice behind me made me jump partially out of my skin and whip around to face someone who reminded me of a lumberjack who hadn't been back from camp and into civilization for a long, long time.

Even so, Wiley, or perhaps Mr. Wiley, was decked out in some coveralls of varying colors and blotches, the holes in which exposed a person to quite a lot of pale flesh and body hair, and over this was draped a plaid shirt that might have once been red and black, and perhaps whole, but which was now more of a screen to partially shade oneself from the harsh summer sun. He wore an unlaced pair of boots, and perpetually wiped his hands with a shop cloth. He had a blocky, square head, topped with short-cropped gray hair, and an expression that suggested a sort of sadness about a world that bore down on him quite heavily.

Assuming this was indeed Wiley, I ventured that I thought I'd have a look around if that was okay. Wiley, as I found out later, was extremely fond of his vehicles and insisted he tell me about every one of them.

"Each one has its story," he said. "Some are sad, and others more inspiring."

Well, okay, he had me there. I figured that if nothing else I might hear a yarn or two and spend the morning with a story-teller, even if I didn't buy anything.

Wiley led the way to what he referred to as "The Corral," and given that I'd said I wanted a truck he took me to the "truck section" and offered an extended arm as if to say "There they are" of the five vehicles with air still in their tires.

Wiley approached the first one, a Ford of indistinct years and pedigree, then turned to me and said, "This is Chuck."

I had to think about this for just a second, no doubt looking like I was either an idiot or perhaps just hard of hearing.

"Chuck?"

"Yes, this is Chuck. At one point in his life he was Charles. He was the sort of Charles who inspired one to do good deeds and to watch out for one's fellow man."

"Was?"

"Charles, that is, Chuck," Wiley said a bit sadly, "fell on difficult times. You see, there was the new wife, and then quickly afterward was the first baby, but as it happened, it was twins, you see. And so Charles was proud at first, but then realized that there was no way he could keep up with the family growing so quickly. You see?"

Well, now that he said so, I think I really did see.

"But what happened to him?" I had to ask.

Wiley sighed deeply, and looked away for a bit.

"What always happens when you just can't keep up. You start taking risks, maybe even gambling, trying to keep up a front for others, and yet you know it's all a lie. You start sneaking around, doing what you want, and none of it's ever good in the end. And then he just fell in with the wrong crowd."

Wiley took a deep breath and let it out.

"What I think, just to say my own piece in the matter, is that Chuck would like another chance. Just one more chance. And I don't fault him for that, do you? Who wouldn't want just one more chance to make things right again?"

I couldn't at all disagree with that. I reluctantly and slowly moved from Chuck on to the next pickup in the Corral.

"This is Festus," Wiley explained, as we viewed a Dodge of some years and some very obvious experience with life, replete with all its ups and downs, particularly the latter.

"Festus?" I asked. "Like in 'Gunsmoke'? The sheriff's deputy?"

"No," Wiley said, "rather the Greek god of Fire and the Forge, Hephaestus."

"Well, that doesn't sound good at all for a truck," I said.

"It is, but it isn't, "Wiley said, and sighed deeply again.

And you know, I'm not sure I even want to tell you about what happened with Festus and Aphrodite and how he made beautiful things, but was still sort of crippled and ugly himself. No, I think I'll just pass on that. And maybe also on Richard and Carl and Fred. Anyway, I walked back to Chuck.

"Go ahead and kick the tires," Wiley offered. "I'm sure he feels as though he deserves it."

I didn't, but I got inside and the key was in the ignition, so I stomped the clutch and turned it over and it started up fine. We drove up and down the road a few times, and Wiley imparted some of the nuances of the truck—uh, Chuck—like how to roll down the window without it getting stuck, and things like that. And then Chuck came home with me and he was mine and I was his. A second chance is a good idea after all.

DAYS AND NIGHTS

I yelled at Joanie today about I don't know what. I apologized later and she hugged me.

I yelled at one of the dogs today and I don't know why and later I apologized and he licked my face.

I woke up in the middle of the night shouting something and scared everyone and woke them up, but we all got back to sleep after that.

CHAPTER FIVE:

KENNA'S CURL UP AND DYE

WHENEVER YOU MOVE somewhere new, there are certain essentials you need to figure out right away. You need to know where your doctor is, your dentist, your auto mechanic and your grocery store, pretty much in that order as soon as possible, just in case of an emergency. As it happened, there was only one of each in town, and so these were all easy decisions. As it also happened, however, there were two places in town where you could get your hair cut, and so I had to make a choice about that.

So, when it came time to get the pate pruned a bit I figured I'd walk up and down the two blocks that made up downtown and check things out. I went first to Bob's, because they had a barber pole out front and for some reason that reassured me until I started to think about the historical nature of the pole, symbolically wrapped around with snakes dedicated to healing, and ancient goddesses and cults and then later medieval leeches and blood-letting into bowls and just had to take a deep breath to stop thinking crazy things like that for no reason at all, and so sort of just stopped in and sat down while other people were getting their hair cut, being noncommittal and all, you know, just looking.

And Bob's seemed just fine to me: nice, calm, clean-looking sort of place, where three elderly gents sat reading newspapers, waiting their turn for what I assumed was Bob, doing the honors, snipping away at another fellow's head. And Bob, if that's who it really was, also seemed very calm and quiet, and also attentive to what he was doing, and had this very staid look on his face as though very quietly and deliberately concentrating on his task.

Or so I thought. That's when he stood back and shouted, "And then she just left me! Just like that!" And that's also when he took his scissors and stabbed them a couple of times in the arm of the empty chair next to him.

The fellow in the chair said, completely unalarmed, "I know, Bob. It's hard on a fellow, ain't it?" And the other three gents looked up from their papers and magazines and grimaced a bit and shook or nodded their heads and returned their attention to said readings.

Bob, meanwhile, appeared to have regained a bit of control, and clenched and unclenched his hands a few times, then sighed deeply and resumed his follicle treatment. It's right about then that I stood up and turned around a few times as though lost, and maybe I was, and seemed to think maybe I should find the door if only I could decide where it was. Bob didn't look up from the head he was concentrating on, but apparently had noticed me nevertheless, which made me squirm just a bit.

"Hi," he said. "Be right with you," and before I could think very much about how he might possibly be with me in some future setting I said, loudly, "I shouldn't have had that burrito for breakfast, um, yesterday," and I stepped quickly to the door and exited.

And so, that only left the place across the street and down three doors, called Kenna's Curl Up and Dye. As I crossed the street, I saw two ladies leaving the shop and they were laughing and jostling one another as though they might have had a couple of drinks and were headed off to an even better party somewhere. I had to smile about that, but because I am male, and they were not, I couldn't get any idea as to whether or not they had just had a haircut and what the results might be. Do I need to explain that further?

Anyway, this was my only other choice, and because Bob's seemed like more of a risk than I wanted to take, and because blood-letting there might not really be a thing of the past, I thought I'd at least check out Kenna's.

When you walk into Curl Up and Dye, you notice nothing but Kenna herself, a single barber's chair, and then chairs along walls in all directions, and an occupant in every chair, mostly women, or in this case, all women. There is of course a mirror to go along with the barber's chair, but this is behind the person in the chair. The reason for this, as I came to see right away, was because Kenna was regaling her audience who sat in all of the available chairs, and so of course she needed to face them. The woman in the chair didn't seem to mind that she couldn't see what was going on, so I assumed this was standard procedure.

Every person in every chair and from every angle was watching and listening to Kenna as she recounted a particular episode of when she was in the Army:

"So, one of the exercises we had t'go through was 'What would happen if the Enemy dropped some gas on us right there in Germany?' They had a name for this, but that's not important. What they did was, they set us out our protective suits and you had to get them on like real quick and do it real smart, or else you'd regret it for sure. And so me and this other fella we're getting our stuff on as fast as we can and we check each other out to make sure everything's okay and all, and we say 'Yes, you are good to go,' and then we had to walk into this room and then they turned on the gas for real and we had to stand there for a couple of minutes. Well," she said expansively, "the fella I was with he apparently didn't have his mask on just-so, and so after a coupla minutes he tears out of the room."

She paused for effect there until someone from the audience could ask the question: "And was he all right, Kenna? How'd he do?"

Kenna had not been cutting any hair at all that I saw during this time, but it hardly seemed to matter. Everyone, including myself, wanted to know what happened to the other guy.

Kenna seemed to believe the suspense had now reached the proper pitch and so she went on.

"Well, after the green light came on showing me I was done then I left and ran down the hall to the latrine to see how he was. Let me tell you right now that he was comin' out of every or-i-face a person has, all at the same time!"

There was no applause here, but rather laughter from some quarters and giggles from others, and I'll admit, I was smiling at that too for some stupid reason. However, from one chair, a lady whose name I understood later was Maude said, in a small little voice, "But you were supposed to check him out before he went in, right?"

Kenna grinned then, and said, "You got me there. Never could stand that little weasel. Never did give me the time of day."

And then the house came down with that, and everyone was laughing so hard there was no room for anything else. And I figured the performance must surely be over for the day. But it wasn't.

I have just realized that I haven't said anything at all about Kenna or anyone else in the shop, and just went right along to the story I walked into, so I'm going to have to back up a bit. So, there's Kenna. Kenna I'm guessing is about six feet tall, with light red hair that she has rolled up into a sort of bun-pony tail that ends up looking like a Mohawk of some sort. Frankly, given the venue, her hair is in absolute disrepair, but apparently no one minds that: you know, the auto mechanic with no grease on his clothes would seem kind of disreputable to me somehow.

She has, well, an angular face and high cheekbones that somehow don't all seem to go together in a way that I can't describe, and yet you'd be very foolish if you didn't say she was pretty even so. Anyway, she was wearing overalls and a T-shirt of indistinct color, and plastic flip-flops.

She was waving her scissors at least in a way that didn't remind me of Bob. I had no idea what her accent was. It wasn't local, and perhaps was an amalgam of wherever people live who grow up without helping verbs. I know, but I'm biased about that sort of thing.

So, the lady in the chair was now apparently finished and she got up and Kenna said, "Just leave the cash on the counter!" really loud, as if the woman was maybe hard of hearing, which apparently she was because she just walked right on through the door without looking back, and someone said, "I'll go get her," and followed her out the door.

Kenna just shook her head and said, "Lucy. Is she ever gonna wake up again?"

This got a few looks from members of the audience, but no commentary. Then, much to my surprise, she looked at me, standing there, and said, "Sir, I believe you are next. How would you like your hair done today?"

I had better say first that I wasn't expecting that, and just sort of looked in every direction at everyone else who was there, pretty much everyone in town except for the gents at Bob's maybe.

Kenna said, "They're just visiting, sir. I got time for you."

You realize of course that I was just getting my hair cut, and of course not much could go wrong there because you know it just grows right back out again whether you want it to or not, so it's a bit hard to describe my nervousness. I cleared my throat a little and then said, "Oh. Thanks."

Then I took my place on Kenna's stage, facing her audience.

Kenna first said to me as I sat in the chair, "Sorry about that last story, sir, but if you come into a beauty parlor you're bound to hear some kind of graphic things."

I just sort of mumbled something then, but I don't

remember what that was. I couldn't quite wrap my head around beauty parlors and graphic stories, but I'd become educated in time.

"So you are new here, right? I haven't seen you around before."

And I admitted that this was true and gave her my current name. I also managed to ask if she was indeed Kenna, because I didn't yet know, and she said she was.

I said, "Kenna is a really nice name. I haven't heard that one before."

Kenna paused then from her first few snips and said, "Yep. There's a bit of family history there. See, my daddy was really fond of the name 'Kenneth', and the way Mother explains this is that the reason they had six kids was because Daddy kept trying to have a boy, just so he could name him Ken. But no such luck," she said with a grin. "Six girls! All of us! So, anyway, when I came along Mother tells him 'That's it. No more. You'd better name her Ken or else rename the dog!' So, that's how I got my name."

Once that was explained to everyone's satisfaction, except perhaps the woman with the small voice who had spoken up earlier and who just shook her head, as if remembering some long-ago tragedy, Kenna directed the conversation outward.

"So, Dreama, what you been up to anyway?"

This was said to someone sitting right in front of me who wore a sweatshirt with the arms cut off at the shoulders and which said "ARMY" in big green letters.

Dreama grimaced and said, "Well, you know ol' Johanson, the principal at the high school? He calls me up and says can I come by because he's got something serious to discuss about Athena. So I'm all worried that somebody's been bullying her or something because, well, you know, and I ain't going to stand for no bully-ing, let me tell you."

It's just about here that I might mention that there's a reason Dreama's sweatshirt is cut off at the shoulders: she has arms that any body-builder would envy. If it's okay, and I hope it is, to use the word "burly" when de-scribing a woman and not mean anything by it other than an estimation of her strength, then burly it is. Dreama has short-cropped, iron-gray hair, and if she did service in the Army as I suspect, then I'm pretty sure our military is still putting righteous fear into our enemies. She is powerfully built, and the tasks that come on a daily basis in Montana are likely child's play for her.

Kenna asked, "And so what was it anyway?"

"Well, what it was," and now Dreama was getting a bit worked up here and all I could think about was Bob twenty minutes earlier, but Bob with maybe a cannon, "what it was is that he calls me in and says 'I think your daughter has been cheating on her essays.' And he shows me some boy's essay for something and shows me hers and I tell him it's the other way around, he's been cheatin' off her!" Dreama put her hands together and cracked her knuckles.

"So then what?" Kenna asked.

"Well then he says, 'But Dreama, see this word here? Athena doesn't even know what in the world this word is, let alone how to spell it.' And so I reached across the desk and grabbed him by the tie, and right across that desk he came! Ha!"

This produced much laughter at the expense of Mr. Johanson, but Kenna pressed: "And then what?"

And Dreama looked down and shuffled her boots a bit and said, "Thirty days public service. Huh."

"What do you have to do?" asked the woman with the small voice.

"Oh, just burn ditches and all," says Dreama.

"That's not so bad," said Kenna.

"No, it isn't, and I want to get me one of those little flame-throwers for myself anyway. I noticed Johanson's place might have a patch of Purple Loosestrife growin' right up next to his house." More laughter now.

"Well, he's got *some* kinda strife," Kenna said, and brought down the house.

DAYS AND NIGHTS

One night, I woke and saw Gripper sitting up just looking at me. I don't know why. He got on the bed between us with his back to Joanie. He licked my hand as if to clean a wound, but there was no wound there. Not there.

CHAPTER SIX:

GETTING TO KNOW YOU

WHENEVER YOU MEET "newness", of any sort, there is an adjustment period. Sometimes you get lucky and this period is very brief, and then other times not so lucky, and adjustment takes all your patience if it's going to happen at all. There seems to be in us a sort of natural reaction to anything that isn't a well-worn part of our current and ongoing experience. You can react to this variously, but really there's pretty much only embracing this new thing as something that will enlarge your life, or else you reject that thing and run away back to "normalcy", which of course is very comforting. This can involve almost anything. Even inanimate objects.

·   ·   ·   ·   ·

Well, Chuck and I hit it off at first, but then we had some "issues" as people like to say these days, which is not a word I'm fond of because it ought to mean something like the next installment of *National Geographic* arriving or something similar. Anyway. For the first week, Chuck and I strolled around together and all was well. Then, at least based on Wiley's description of

Chuck's past, he seemed to be backsliding on me, whereas I had put my complete trust in him.

This was not a good way to begin a relationship, as many who have attempted the art of dating will tell you. For example, if you are out on a date with someone during your first week of having met, and you suddenly flop over on the floor at the café and start having conniptions and making odd, sort of quasi-demonic sounds, then naturally that's going to put a bit of a damper on the possibility of a second date.

So, what I'm trying to say is that Chuck started doing strange things for no apparent reason, and I had this bad feeling that he wasn't happy at all with his new arrangement, and so I wasn't either. Far be it from me to put someone into indentured servitude or something similar, and I had thought that it was I who was doing the favor toward him, but that's not what I was getting in return.

And it wasn't the little things either, the sort that we all just normally overlook in a relationship, like the funny way someone grips their coffee cup or the fact that the passenger-side window took two, sometimes three hands to roll up properly. That goes with the territory as far as I'm concerned. No, this started with a version of flopping over on the floor and making demonic sounds, and I was just not prepared for this in all kinds of ways, which perhaps I can explain a bit more about later.

So, Chuck and I were taking a ride from the house down into town, which is several miles from our place. It is a good, well-rocked road, and relatively even for this part of the world as it drops down into the valley, and so I was confident that this didn't overly tax Chuck's sense of involvement in our venture. You know, I'm being sensible, just checking out our relationship and sort of saying, "See? I'm like this a lot of the time. And what are you like?" We're just getting to know one another.

So anyway, Chuck coughed. That's it, coughed. It was like a clearing your throat sort of cough but that was all, and then Chuck rolled to a stop. I stopped then too. Not just literally, but emotionally and intellectually. The first thing I thought of was Wiley, and what I might say to him in the future about having hooked me up with Chuck, which I admit was petty and reactive on my part. Then, the better part of my humanity kicked in and I was concerned that poor Chuck was somehow under the weather and I hadn't known. I got out and popped the hood and looked at Chuck's vitals.

Now, this is actually the bad part that I know some of you don't want to hear about. At least it is for me. This is the part when, in any relationship, you have to acknowledge that you're completely ignorant of certain things that any normal human being would simply take for granted. I suppose a comparison might be that you said something completely stupid that actually caused your date to cry, by which you can kiss that goodnight kiss goodbye, and then don't even have the wherewithal or presence of mind to produce a handkerchief to at least blunt your bluntness. Like that. So, I was looking under Chuck's hood, pretending that I knew what I was looking at, and I had no clue whatsoever.

Now look, my education has afforded me certain skills that you may not fully appreciate. If ever you needed me to quote some Dante and why his vision in the Seventh Circle of Hell is significant for the overall theme that he's building in four-part allegory, then I'm your man. If ever you needed five, maybe six dead languages interpreted for you, not a problem. I can elaborate on two hundred authors of great literature on call, and explain in great detail how a composition for your next biology paper should go. But why did you make your date cry when all you did was tell a story about a family vacation, and what does that big block of metal under the hood of a vehicle actually do? Nope. Sorry. Completely clueless. Isn't that what marriage counselors and mechanics are for?

So, I looked around, hoping to see some sort of obvious wound, because if it was some sort of mental thing with Chuck, then it'd be the blind leading the blind of course. Nope. No gaping wounds that I could see that needed pressure applied while the medics arrived. No obvious need for a defibrillator.

I called up Joanie and said where I was, and Joanie knows all kinds of things from studying all those –ologies at the university, but because, like myself, she'd never studied an –ing, then she really couldn't offer any meaningful assistance. So, she came and got me, and someone else came and got Chuck and trundled him away in a wheelchair over to Wiley's and we went back home to await the prognosis.

Wiley called a bit later to say that Chuck had merely been suffering from a relapse into some sort of chronic listlessness that was a holdover from a traumatized childhood and adolescence, but that he was now right as rain and fit to come home. Something like that. So, we went and picked him up, and he seemed just fine.

However, during the next three weeks, Chuck gave out on me three more times, thankfully not when I was out on some deer trail of a road while I was fishing, but still. I got some tools from Coastal that I thought might come in handy, and a big roll of duct tape which was more my speed for automotive repair. Even with the tools, I drove around nervously, just sort of expecting the next seizure that Chuck might have.

During this period, however, I got to know quite a few people in town and the surrounding countryside, though not intentionally. This was as a result of people stopping to assist me when Chuck broke down, and who called Wiley or a tow truck or actually fixed him because they knew something about engines.

The silver lining of all this is that I had a renewed sense of faith in my fellow man. We were all in this to-gether, no matter what Life threw at you. And that's the way it is in small towns, where everyone knows when you're in trouble and is willing to take the time to help you out.

And that's why, when I saw a black pickup pulled off on the side of 81 with its hood popped open, I pulled in behind in order to offer any assistance that I might, such as it was. I got out and walked up alongside and pretty much just saw shoulders and a black hat bent down into the engine compartment.

"Hey," I said. "How's it going?"

There was no reply for a moment, and then the hat and shoulders extricated themselves and stood up. It was The Man-in-Black!

If you don't know what the definition of "visceral" is, please stop for a minute and look it up. I am completely embarrassed to say that when I recognized who it was I almost yelped and ran back to the safety of Chuck. I didn't, but I felt that way.

This guy just emanated danger and anger in a physical way that only a complete idiot couldn't sense. Up close, I could see he had mismatched eyes, one blue, one, well, gray close to being almost black. His angular face might have been described as "handsome" in some other context, perhaps minus the scowl, the thin-lipped expression, working toward a sneer, and the furrow of his brow, and the absolute intention behind the eyes that left nothing to one's imagination about this interruption.

"Seen you around," he said.

"Yes," I said. "I don't know anything about engines, but if you want me to make a call? Give you a ride...?" I ended weakly, as if I were apologizing for bothering to offer to assist him.

"I don't need anything," he said with a voice that was utterly flat and with no emotion of any kind to it, looking back down at the engine compartment.

And has that ever happened to you before? You know, you say to someone, "Sure I'll help you move that piano out of your back bathroom. Oh, not a problem," and then they say, "Oh, no. Got it covered," and you just sort of feel something relieve a great burden from you? It was like that.

I started to walk away then, gladly, but I offered, "Name's Al."

As I turned to go, I thought I heard from the head in

the engine compartment something like "Hollis", but I wasn't sure.

Chuck, reliably, thankfully, took me away from that place.

DAYS AND NIGHTS

Joanie decided she will make up a bed in the spare room so that she can sleep at night.

I saw a familiar face in a window yesterday and I stopped in surprise at first and then smiled and stood a while and the light seemed to shift and there was nothing there. It wasn't a big thing to me, and I forgot it twenty minutes later, and then remembered it when I was in bed, with my eyes closed I think, I'm pretty sure, but the face was different and covered in blood and became unrecognizable and I sat up screaming and no one heard me and so that was good.

CHAPTER SEVEN:

LIFE IS TRAUMA

THROUGHOUT MY LIFE I've considered some things pretty foundational and as such these things would never change. These might be as far-ranging as my faith, my abiding love for Joanie, and headed downward on the nether end of things to the decision never to wear a tie unless it would hurt someone else's feelings not to. Nevertheless, even with such fundamentals firmly in place, I'd like to think I have an open mind about things, and if incoming data should prove my assumptions wrong, well then I should at least be open to the possibility of revision. That's reasonable, isn't it?

For example, I have opinions about things. Lots of things as it happens, and as a fairly sentient being I'd like to believe that these opinions are founded on knowledge and experience. If something comes along that just simply says, "You were wrong," then fine, I'll take it under advisement and give it some serious consideration and then, maybe, possibly, change my mind about it. It could happen. I'm sure it's happened before, such as in the aftermath of That Day, just as an example, wherein I discovered that the world was not in fact Safe or Sane or The Way I Thought It Was. Yes, I am completely open to revision if it isn't overly intrusive in some more fundamental way.

. . . . .

Chuck and I continued our strained relationship throughout the summer. We'd be doing fine for a couple of weeks, enjoying one another's company, and then, with no warning, he'd dump me and leave me on my own. Joanie and I were actually growing somewhat used to this. When I'd leave the house she'd say, "Good luck!" like maybe in the same way someone once said, "God speed, John Glenn!" which of course he really needed, given the circumstances. And that's how it was.

"Got your phone with you? You know, just in case?"

"Yep, got it with me."

And off we'd go, me never knowing if we'd get to our destination or not, or if we were ever coming home. So, it was on one of these occasions, in my private thoughts as we were going along, that I began to wonder if perhaps, possibly, I had made a poor choice in bringing Chuck home with me after all.

I know! I know I was the one who said second chances were important, so you don't have to get all indignant on me about that. But, Chuck had had many chances, and this was Montana. You need to realize what I'm talking about. You break down on almost any road other than 81 and there isn't going to be anyone coming by for the next month. You get behind this peak or that ridge, and no, your phone isn't going to work. Even out in the Great Flat where someone might see you from a hundred miles away, if there was anyone, and there's not, and where satellites seem to think

"There's nothing there. Why bother?", your phone isn't going to work, you're just going to sit there, day after day, until the random driver finds you and your bones and the later autopsy shows that at some point you tried to eat the tires from your vehicle. So, yes, I was reconsidering my choice because new data had come in.

Anyway, so what happened was that Chuck was taking me along some long-ago logging road because that's where I wanted to go, and I assumed he did too because it was going to be a very nice morning in which he got to enjoy the wonder of the Montana landscape and I was going to do some fishing. And just about howevermanymiles we were up this mountain road Chuck coughed once again, and rolled to a stop.

And I already know what you're thinking: that perhaps if I had been a little kinder or more understanding, this wouldn't have happened at all. And if you're thinking that, then you need to take some deep breaths and reconsider, because from my own perspective right then, Chuck had it in for me from day one and had been simply waiting for his chance to do me in for good.

I sat there for about two minutes just sort of in awe that I might be somewhere where no one would ever find me and that there was no possibility of getting back down to anything that might pass for civilization without substantial food and water, and if truth be told, some idea about how to survive outside when it still got down into the 30s at night.

Okay. I had made some new opinions about things. And one of them was Chuck. I got out and popped the hood, but this was of course simply something to do for a few minutes because my mechanical skills with vehicles ended with putting the key in the ignition. I started looking under the hood for no sensible reason at all except for keeping the word "panic" out of my mind. Just get busy thinking about something, anything at all, as long as it isn't dying at night at 5200 feet in the air where it's going to get down into the frozens on some road where there's no chance at all of someone coming by for six weeks and which you know from experience can't support a phone call out, despite the fact that everyone on the planet feels oh-so-very-"connected" because they have a silly three-hundred-dollar phone.

I started looking under the hood, and yet I knew I should be looking for firewood and shelter, and getting some water somewhere, but I just didn't. Instead, my head just sort of *blinked,* and I got the tools that I bought at the Coastal, and my handy-dandy red shop cloths, and I walked into the dream that I was going to fix something.

I got into the engine compartment, I mean, really, climbed in off the ground, and started looking around for no reason whatsoever, because I had no clue what I was looking at.

It's a combustion engine, right? So I know that means something. Uh, it combusts because uh gas is sent to the carburetor, and then it goes into the engine somewhere after that, and then things happen inside. Okay. I will investigate the carburetor. I know, I'm not sure why because it never came up in Homer's *Iliad,* which sustained an entire culture for 4000 years, but somehow I know what that is and so I see it only has two screws, so how bad can that be? So, I take it off. The problem is that once it's off, and I look at it, I have no idea if it's okay or not. I shake it a bit. That's always a good idea, isn't it?

I put it back on, so I didn't forget how to do so. I started looking at other things. There appeared to be a tiny, tiny filter in a plastic tube that either went into or out of (how can I know?) the carburetor, and I looked at it, and it, too, was only attached by two screws, so heck, I took that baby off too, because if I didn't then I was pretty much done and then that word "panic" was going to resurface and that just couldn't happen. Because, really, all I had left was duct tape, and that might only come in handy if I needed to re-attach a limb on the fifty-mile hike back down out of the Rockies.

I got tired then, thinking, because I suppose I couldn't keep on thinking of things like engines, because somewhere, back in that little box I keep in my head, there was something else that wanted to get out and I didn't want that, and so, well, I just sort of lay there in the engine compartment for a while and did what I always do these days: I just somehow stopped thinking. I'm unsure how a person can do that. I don't understand it. But that's what happened.

That was why I missed the sound of a vehicle coming up the road and slowing, as it passed me. I looked up and saw a black pickup truck that somehow looked familiar, but frankly I had lost cogent thought at that time, and so I watched it slow and then accelerate and move on up the road and out of sight.

And when it was gone, I roused myself and wondered what I had just done or not done, and this is an issue with me these days: What should I have done or not done? Could I have saved lives? Could I have been a hero? Could I have just died along with everyone else? If so, who cares? What am I doing now? I am unsure.

I got up and down, and walked around a bit. I tried to get my head back to thinking again. Finally, it occurred to me that what goes up must come back down, so the truck must come back down, right? Maybe I should lie in the road to make sure they stop? Uh, maybe not. Bad idea. I think instead I'll stand by the open hood of the truck, and pretend that I'm deeply involved in it.

Yes. That's what I'll do. I have shop cloths, I reminded myself. Yes. Perfect plan. And yes, after forever, the truck came back down the road! I was saved! Except now I recalled where I'd seen the truck before.

He extricated himself from the cab of the truck, after he had stopped, because he had to. He had to sort of put his head out first, followed by shoulders, torso and then legs. Nothing else would work. He did so without effort. He stood at least six and a half feet tall, with mismatched eyes, dressed only in black, and looked at me.

"We meet again," he said, without any tone of voice, or any expression on his face.

"Hey," I said. "Name's Al. I think I may have stopped for you once."

"I recall," he said. "Hollis," he said without any inflection whatsoever.

People often say, "I have mixed emotions about such-and-such." Sometimes I think I know what they mean, and then other times not, because most of the time they simply mean "I need to make a decision," or something like that, and not really "mixed emotions". Honestly, if you had "mixed emotions" about something, that would be kind of strange, wouldn't it? Really, what would it be like if you felt fear and joy at the same time? That would really be something, wouldn't it? So, that's what it was. Really.

Here he came: walking toward me, and I tell you I'm not imagining this, my fear, because he just had this anger and danger rolling off him in a way that you'd know even if you had your eyes closed, and I saw and felt that, and at the same time I was thinking this might be my only chance to get back down off this mountain before nightfall, and I had mixed emotions. That's how it really is.

Hollis stepped to the engine compartment without looking at me. In fact, from his expression, he was studying the engine to the point that I was utterly excluded. Naturally, this was a good thing, because I wasn't going to be helping.

"Check the carb?" he said after a bit, without looking at me.

"Yes," I said.

"How'd it look?"

"I don't know," I said.

"Why?" he said.

"I don't know what it's supposed to look like."

His eyes narrowed a bit.

"I see you've taken the fuel lines apart, and so how's the filter?"

"I don't know. I don't know how to check it, if that's what it is."

Hollis looked around at my tools and the shop cloths for a bit. Then he stopped. Then he turned to me, and I have to tell you, there was something burning inside this guy that had to get out and you really, really didn't want to be around him. When he looked at you, there was no emotion at all in him, and you felt like giving any back would be meaningless, like telling a grizzly how beautiful it was before it ate you.

Hollis looked down at me and said, "Al, that's your name, right? What are you doing here anyway? You don't seem to know jack about an engine, or really anything else, do you? Montana isn't a place you want to be."

Well, now I was nervous. I mean, what do you say? 'My therapist told me to run away to someplace where nothing ever happens so that I can heal up a bit? I'm not supposed to think about my fears or depression for a while?' Something like that?

I righted myself slightly, still one elbow on the engine compartment, doing my very best impression of a manly sort of guy who is nonchalantly about to say something wry and terse, and said, "I'm just here to get away from it all, is all."

Hollis stood up from the carburetor and stretched to his full height and looked at me with those mismatched eyes a moment and said, "Get away from what all?"

Now, I don't mind a direct question or two when it's something I can reasonably answer, like "What's in the omelette?" or "Did you bring the dog in?" and that sort of thing, but this was different.

I decided that the stupid thing to do was tell the

truth, and though it pained me to default to what was comfortable, I did.

"I, uh, now that you ask, well, I'm trying to get away from trauma for just a bit."

This took Hollis a bit of time to process, with a very thoughtful and confused expression on his face that probably usually sent people and the rest of God's creation scurrying out of the way, during which I set down the useless socket wrench and wiped my hands on a certified engine repairman's red shop cloth, all the while looking for something important on the ground. Hollis wasn't buying it, however.

"I don't get it," he said, pushing back his hat a bit. "I mean, how do you run away from 'trauma'?"

Now it was my turn to look confused.

"Like this," I said. "Here I am. No more trauma. Just like that. I left it behind where I came from."

Hollis looked down on me for a minute, but it seemed like twelve, and then he started unbuttoning his shirt. Okay. Let me just run this past you. What circumstances can you imagine where two men, pretty much strangers, are talking about something and then one of them begins taking off his shirt? Yes, I know. None of them are going to end very well.

Hollis finished unbuttoning, and then given the size of his frame he sort of angled and stretched out of the shirt one elbow and arm at a time and held the crumpled shirt in one hand. Let me tell you right now, that if I thought before that Hollis was a pretty darn imposing fellow, once he had his shirt off I thought that this might be what it was like if you ever faced an angry moose, and you're pretty sure you'd really like the moose on your side in a fight, if that was at all possible. For that matter, Hollis was probably the entire side of somebody's army.

And besides that, Hollis's chest and torso and arms were a patchwork of scars. He looked like some mad surgeon had taken out all his practice work at stitching up wounds on just one subject.

Hollis looked down and pointed at one and said, "Right there is where an elk gored me when I walked up to it and thought it was dead, but it wasn't. And so lesson learned."

And then he seemed to look around through some of the others that maybe deserved a special narrative and pointed and said, "That one was hauling wood over Waldo Falls one winter so I wouldn't freeze to death in my cabin, and I slipped on the beaver dam up above and fell thirty feet onto a branch," and he turned around and showed me the scar on his back where the branch had gone all the way through.

And then I couldn't help myself and started asking, "What's that one? And what's that one?" and that went on for a little while, while Hollis explained each one, and then finally I pointed at a really nasty, red-looking, scalloped-shaped pucker of flesh just right about where his heart would be.

Hollis was quiet about that for a minute and then said, "Remember when beer cans had pull-off tabs? Well, I put this one in my shirt pocket and then slipped on a rock coming home from the bar and it just cut me something awful when I hit."

I couldn't help myself then and just doubled over laughing. Hollis laughed a bit too, I think. He showed some teeth and kind of made short snoring sounds that I hoped were an indication of laughter. Then he closed up even that small slit of his mouth, and he put his shirt back on and looked at me again like I was a map he was trying to read.

"Life is trauma," he said. "You can't get away from it, wherever you go. Just follows us around."

And then he got a screwdriver and did something meaningful with it, and I watched.

"Do you have duct tape?" he asked later, "because this filter is shot and all you need to do is tape the two ends of the fuel line together."

DAYS AND NIGHTS

One night Tan slept on the bed with me and later she started to howl in her sleep. I rolled over and stroked her until she stopped and then she seemed to go back to sleep. Later I woke up shouting something about I don't know what it was just nononono and woke my-self up. Then I lay back down. Then I felt a paw drape itself around my neck.

CHAPTER EIGHT:

THE DANGER OF GOPHERS

W HAT IS a little bit disturbing about living in Montana is that there's always the possibility that you might get shot, accidentally mind you, in your front or back yard, such as they are. No, this isn't because of radical extremists of some sort, which by the way all live across the border in Idaho, everyone assured me, but because of the existence of gophers.

Given my personal circumstances, where I'd have believed an alien invasion might have taken place before it ever crossed my mind that there'd be a mass shooting at my school and I'd be in the middle of it, I for one thing never thought before how easily a gopher might get you killed, and on top of that wasn't this exactly the kind of thing I thought I was getting away from?

I never really understood this before now, but gophers are actually the bane of all organized civilizations. The reason? They make holes in the ground. You can just sort of see the ancient Egyptians moving gigantic blocks of stone to form the pyramids when suddenly the chief task-master calls a halt to their gargantuan efforts: "Gopher hole! Five minutes break.

Wally! Get up here and fill in that little bit of blasphemy right now!" It's like that.

They make holes, and those can be deadly. Your cow steps into one, or your horse, and that's a broken leg and that's all she wrote about that. So, you absolutely have to do something about that, as a good citizen, just like whenever you see some Purple Loosestrife you have to kill it, wherever you are and no matter what you're doing. Public responsibility comes first.

.   .   .   .   .

Our neighbor, Delmer, whom I've never met but can sort of make out in the next parcel over, is a fastidious lawn-mower. He seems to be on the mower a lot, even though there are times when he's riding it, and at this distance I still expect to hear it, but can't hear the actual mower-blade going. I assume he's keeping the Purple Loosestrife at bay, late in the year, and so good for him.

Every so often when I'd stand on the front porch, however, I could hear a gun shot, and then see a plume of dust in late summer in front of the mower as Delmer moved through his acreage. He was hunting gophers. This was fine, I suppose, as an exercise in civic duty, until it was September, and the ground was then hard as shale. And that's when I came to know that standing on the front porch was a way to die unexpectedly.

So, there's Delmer, riding around on his lawn tractor, blasting away to left and right every so often with a hand gun. I noticed the plumes of dust coming up off his place, and then heard the shots a split-second later. It wasn't long, though, before the first ricochet came my way as a little bit of a "zing" in the air next to me.

That's when I thought crouching down on my front doorstep was maybe a good idea. That's also when Joanie came out the front door at asked what I was doing squatting like that and why was I throwing rocks at the house?

"Get down!" I said. "It's Delmer! He's shooting gophers!" Joanie crouched down with me then and I explained the incoming fire.

"What do you mean throwing stuff at the house, anyway?" I asked.

"I just heard what sounded like someone throwing a rock at the house outside the living room window," she said.

"Let's get back inside," I said quietly. (I have no idea why I did so. I mean, the enemy wasn't likely to hear us over the lawn tractor and gunshots.)

"Stay low!" And we sort of crouched on into the house and closed the door. Then, through mutual agreement we went into the kitchen because it was at the back of the house and seemed safer.

"So what are we going to do?" Joanie said. "Go over there and tell him to quit shooting at us?"

"You kidding? Tell somebody to stop shooting gophers? Around here? You crazy?"

"How long is gopher season?"

"I don't know. Probably over soon, don't you think?"

So, what we did was, we stayed inside whenever Delmer was "mowing". That's what we did. We're not stupid.

. . . . .

I know you'll think I'm making this up, and I'm not, but the week following we saw signs up in town announcing the annual Gopher Shooting Festival. Yes, this is true. "It's all good fun!" the posters read. Now given that the list of social activities in town was a little short, Joanie said we should go.

"You never know. We could learn something."

I wasn't sure what we might learn about dead gophers, but it was way past time to do a little socializing with our fellow Dobbins-ites, so we headed on down that Saturday to the big to-do.

Some of you know what I'm talking about, and the rest of you will have to just visualize it, but small-town festivals all across the country are largely the same, with minor variations. There will be food vendors, and crafts, and group activities, and information booths, and entertainers, and music and maybe even a parade of some sort if you have enough people. Well, that's what this was like, minus the parade.

Here and there you could pick up pamphlets about gophers and how they breed like, well, gophers, and why they're not just a nuisance but the bane of all organized civilization, as I pointed out earlier. The food vendors, well, yes there were in fact folks selling jams and such, but one of the big events was the cook-off competition, which as you may have guessed involved the best gopher recipe. I passed on that, and I'm not even going to try to describe gopher-on-a-stick.

Of course, the main event was the family shoot-along, which was interesting but somewhat dangerous to watch. This occurred in a nearby pasture which just happened to be teeming with the rodents, and so the competition was of course to shoot and retrieve as many of the little thugs as possible. Joanie and I as non-combatants moseyed over to the killing-field to watch.

There didn't really appear to be any rules about where to shoot and when, and so a sort of predictable crossfire ensued and family groups, as well as individual mercenaries, roamed the pasture shooting this way and that. Fortunately, most of the cries coming from the field were shouts of recrimination: "That's not fair, Johnny! I was just aiming at that one!" and that kind of thing. Meanwhile, I sort of put Joanie and me slightly behind a couple of other onlookers, well, just in case. I'm thoughtful that way. Besides, I figured most folks around here were pretty tough, and could likely take a bullet and not even notice.

As the proceedings, well, proceeded and the bodies of rodents piled up, we were treated to a running commentary from the onlookers around us:

"That kid can't hit a bull if it was standing still," somebody muttered. "He's six! What've his folks been showing him anyway?"

"They're just doing it all wrong, is what it is," someone else lamented.

That got my attention: "How so? Is there a better way to do it?"

"I just use a golf club," he said. "Number five iron, usually."

When the mayhem finally ended and the toting up of bodies had concluded, there was a presentation to the winner. People gathered around and the MC who was to present the trophy (which was a smallish affair with a gopher on top) hushed the crowd and said that he felt that it was only right that last year's winner present the trophy, because he was in fact in attendance.

As it happened this was the fellow who had explained

about using a five iron, and he stepped up to do the honors. He handed the trophy to a wiry little kid who had his side-arm properly holstered. I believe he had two dozen as the winning total. Somebody shouted "fore!" and the fellow laughed a bit at that, but clapped the kid on the back and told him he'd beat his record for sure next year. I decided right then that I was never going to play golf with the locals.

DAYS AND NIGHTS

One very beautiful and hot summer day I had absolutely nothing to do and pulled a cold beer from the fridge and a lawn chair from the garage and went into the yard to just sit back and look at the Rockies for a bit. Joanie was in town and the dogs were way too smart to be out in the sun, and so it was just me and a cold bottle sitting in the summer sun. It was very hot, and eventually I closed my eyes against the sun and lay back with my bottle on my chest.

I was so very comfortable that my mind just wandered a bit, and then it came to the box in the back of my head where I keep all the things that I never want to see or think about ever again. It's a wooden box, maybe three feet long, ten inches wide and deep, and it has a lid on it. It is made of pine. It is a rough box, and not sanded or adorned at all. It is a very quiet box. I like it that way. So, you know what I did? I thought maybe I'd just have a little look-see, you know, just a quick peek. So I did. I opened the box just a bit, but couldn't see anything at all. It was just all dark in there. I think I chuckled a bit about that. I opened it a bit more, and still nothing. So, what the heck, I opened the lid the whole way.

When reality returned I was on my hands and knees in the yard crying until I realized I was crying and so stopped crying, and perhaps screaming at some volume, because I don't recall. I lifted my head, and even from this level and vantage point and distance I could see Delmer on his back deck looking over in my direction. So, you know what I did? I crawled around on my hands and knees, pulling up pieces of grass, and throwing them off to the side, in a pretense that I was merely weeding the lawn of nonexistent weeds.

After a bit, when I figured that the coast was clear, I sat back in the lawn chair, and closed my eyes, and then I went to the garage and got my driver and four three-inch brass screws, good ones, and I put a good long screw down in each corner of the box.

CHAPTER NINE:

THE REGISTER GUARDIAN HERALD CLARION BEE

O F COURSE, after a while it became clear that I was going to have to get a job. The problem there, as Hollis had so nicely put it on that earlier occasion, after having spent my adulthood as a college professor I didn't really have much in the way of transferrable skills. It had already been determined that teaching at this time was not a good idea, and besides, the nearest center of higher education was several hundred miles away. Even so, I figured that having a Ph.D. in medieval literature and languages probably hadn't damaged me beyond all redemption, and I could in fact read, write and add numbers when forced to. So, all totaled up I had three skills that might do someone some good somewhere.

The problem was where? My therapist had suggested somewhere along the line that maybe I should write for a while as therapy, which is all well and good for mental health (unless you ask a professional writer), but that wasn't going to bring in any cash. Finally, I decided that maybe I'd head down to The Paper and see if they needed any help with anything.

As it happens, the tri-county newspaper is published right here in our own little town. It's called The Register Guardian Herald Clarion Bee, or something like that, but thankfully everyone just calls it The Paper. On the one hand, this makes it much easier to refer to, but on the other hand it takes a bit of getting used to in casual conversation. For example, at Del's you might hear someone say "Did you hear about the elk Wally shot in The Paper?" or maybe "I think I saw that Rusty Williams died in The Paper." That kind of thing. You start to think maybe "Paper" is a deadly weapon or maybe the name for a particularly nasty neighborhood somewhere. I eventually came to understand this is just a basic grammar problem, but I'm not about to try to tell anyone about direct and indirect objects in a sentence, so you just get used to it. In no time at all I picked up the knack myself: "Did you hear about that mudslide in The Paper?" I have it down pat now.

So, down to The Paper I went. The offices are actually located just a bit out of town off the highway, in what must at one point have been a manufacturing building of some sort. It's a concrete block affair, with rusting corrugated tin roofing. The windows are quite small, and there aren't many of them, and it gives the place a rather disreputable look. This, in my opinion, is perfect for a newspaper, in the same way that it is fine that Ahab has a peg-leg and Richard the Third is portrayed as a hunchback of some sort.

Anyway, Chuck and I pulled up and found a door, and it wasn't locked, so I figured it was probably okay to let myself in. Once inside, I discovered I had made a mistake. The building appeared to be empty, except for piles of refuse and some rusting, unidentifiable machinery of some sort. I looked around, and was just about to turn around and leave when I heard a yell from off to my left. I wandered that way, took a left and a right, and down toward the end of a hallway saw a light, so I thought I'd see. In a moment, I beheld the heart of our journalistic endeavors in this corner of the world.

What I saw were two thirty-something guys playing basketball with a wad of newspaper and a tiny little hoop stuck on the wall up about eight feet. One guy, who was maybe a few inches shorter than the other, had the other's arm behind his back with one hand and his other across the fellow's chest. "Foul! Foul!" the guy in the half-nelson yelled, all the while aiming for a hook-shot at the rim.

The struggle lasted a few more moments until the taller guy launched his shot and, miraculously, it went in.

"Good shot," I said, and I meant it.

The shooter turned around, nonplussed, and said, "That's nothing! I made one from halfway under the desk over there yesterday."

"Quit bragging," the other guy said, and he picked up the wad of paper and motioned as if he were dribbling it around like a basketball, then spun and made a jump shot which rimmed just short.

"Dang!" he said, shaking his head.

I introduced myself, and sat in the corner and said I didn't want to interfere, but I guess the game was over, because the two then each occupied two desks, side-by-side, and so I pulled my chair over and sat down again.

"How can we help you?" said Jeff, the taller of the two, and maybe the better shot.

"Well, to be blunt, I'm looking for work and I wondered if you had any needs here at The Paper."

Chip, the slightly shorter of the two, asked, "Well, maybe. What do you do? Have you worked for a newspaper before?"

And just a split second before I said no, I considered that I had been the faculty advisor of two student papers at one time, and so I simply said, "Yes, a couple."

"That's great," said Jeff. "What kinds of things did you write?"

Well, they sort of had me there, until I remembered that I had in fact contributed a couple of pieces to a college newspaper back in the day, and in high school I covered local sports a time or two.

"Oh, I've done sports, and also copy editing and layout, but I mostly wrote columns of various kinds," I lied.

"Oh! A column!" Chip exclaimed. "That'd be great. We've never had a column before, have we, Jeff?" he said and turned with a smug look at his partner.

Jeff reddened just a bit and said, "Just briefly. But it never really took off."

"No, it didn't," Chip said. "I guess no one really wanted to read about insects after all."

This was obviously a sore spot, at least with Jeff, so I added quickly, "Oh, I was thinking more along the lines of 'local color', you know. Pieces that maybe had to do with people in the area and what they're up to and all."

Jeff said, "Yes, that sounds reasonable. Why don't you put something together and bring it in for next week's issue?"

And so that was that. All I needed to do now was actually write something.

I asked Joanie that afternoon what she thought I should write about.

"What about somebody who's got something interesting going on?"

"Like what?"

"Oh, you know, anything. Like somebody who builds pyramids out of hay bales, or who has an extensive barbed wire collection. Like that."

That actually didn't sound too bad, except I didn't know anyone who had anything interesting going on. I thought maybe I'd go ask somebody if they knew anybody who was "interesting". So, the next day Chuck and I took a drive into town and I sort of just walked around a bit looking for someone I knew well enough to ask about it.

Unfortunately, I didn't see anyone right away, so I sat on The Bench outside Del's and thought about it. I could go over and ask Kenna, but then I'd be there for an hour, and I had a suspicion who Kenna might tell me was the most interesting person in the county, and she could be right about that, but I figured I'd keep that as my ace in the hole. I had a notebook with me, and had a list of "maybes" in it, but none of them really jumped out at me. This was going to be my first ever column, and so I wanted it to be especially good. I was looking down at my list when a shadow enveloped my notebook.

I looked up, and there was Hollis, looking down on me, dressed pretty much all in black, with his typical expression which was an imitation of an onset of bad weather.

"Morning, Al," he said, and I'm not sure how the words got out because he didn't actually seem to move his lips, because that might have possibly marred his normal look of utter disdain for the universe.

"Oh, hi Hollis. How's it going?"

"Fine," he said, which was pretty good for Hollis.

But then it struck me, maybe I could ask Hollis if he knew anyone interesting.

So I said, "Are you in a hurry, or heading somewhere? I just wanted to ask you about someone and I thought you could help me out."

"Del's," he said and just walked away, down a few yards and turned in.

I had a pretty bad feeling about this, because if there was anybody in this world I didn't want to make mad, or even give a hint of the impression that I was somehow, even ever so slightly impinging on them, then that person was certainly and far and away Hollis Granger. Even so, I stood up and followed.

So, Hollis was at a booth by the window having coffee, and I sat down opposite and got coffee as well. Hollis was looking at his coffee without looking up, maybe scrying the future in it somehow, or maybe just trying to make me nervous.

"Hi," I said again, and I explained to him what I was doing and why and would he maybe know someone who was "interesting" that I could write about?

"No," he said, and he looked up with those mismatched eyes and this time for some strange reason I didn't look away.

"Hollis," I said, "you asked me this not so long ago, so I hope you don't mind if I ask you the same thing: what are you doing here? Are you from here?"

Hollis snorted and simply said, "No."

"Do you mind if I ask what you're here for then? I mean, you asked me, and I told you."

He looked at his coffee again, and then said, "Okay." And he said: "I'm not from here. I grew up in Kansas. Farm boy. Normal kid. Played basketball in high school. Then I decided to go to war."

"What? I mean, with whom? War?"

"Are you stupid, Al? Where you been living anyway? Iraq, Afghanistan, wherever. Just another place where you try to kill people before they kill you."

Now I was quiet. "You're a combat vet? How long have you been here?"

"I got back after maybe four tours somewhere, they all look the same, and so I guess I've been here three years."

And I had to ask and I had to know, and so I did, and Hollis, an Army Ranger, went on about thirty minutes about that, if you can believe it. And I was just quiet, and no one interrupted us, and if anyone came by they just looked at Hollis as he talked and they moved on.

"Why here? What do you even do here?"

"Anything I can," he said. "I ride fence and watch the herds and run off the wild horses if they're getting spunky. I had to shoot at a grizzly last year, but I didn't kill it, just scared it off. I'm done killing things. Last year I spent the winter with the herds down low, livin' in a wagon. Two years ago I helped some guides with tourists' elk huntin' and carried their kills down the Rockies." And he went on from there, and I was quiet. Real quiet.

I don't know why, after all that he'd said, but I just came back to the most basic question again.

"So why are you here?"

And that's when I saw that I had asked the wrong question completely, because his face clouded over like the thunderstorm-to-be and he was angry. No, not like you and I get angry, I mean angry. Like I-might-just-eat-barbed-wire-to-distract-myself angry.

"Hollis," I said, "I'm sorry, I didn't mean to..."

"Just shut up," he said with some venom. Heads turned in the diner. "Just shut up."

And I shut up. And then we both just looked at our coffee for about two minutes.

"You know how I said you can't run away from trauma," he said, "like I was trying to explain to you before? That's what I'm trying to do, got it?"

And I just looked down at my coffee and said, "Hollis. All those scars you showed me the other day. You didn't get a single one of them out here, did you?"

Now he was quiet, but then: "Some. No. I don't remember. Except the pop-top. That did happen here."

And I couldn't even laugh about that. I just couldn't find it anywhere.

So I said, "Hollis, you're probably the most interesting person I've ever met. Would you mind if I wrote about you?"

And Hollis, who had had both hands flat down on the table top, looked up and then cracked his knuckles and said, "Okay."

DAYS AND NIGHTS

When classes resumed after the shooting I went back into the classroom and began teaching, several different classes a day, for weeks and then months. In all of that time I have no idea what I said or what I was even teaching.

CHAPTER TEN:

I GET A NEW JOB

So, I TOOK my story down to Chip and Jeff a couple of days later and they looked it over.

Chip said, "I like it," and Jeff said, "I don't know. It seems kind of heavy for our paper," and then Chip said, "Play you for it."

And of course this was not how things should go, especially with the worse shooter backing me, but Chip winked at me and said, "Let's do it!"

And so it began: my possible income being determined by two grown men attempting to throw wads of paper into a "basketball" hoop. Jeff grabbed a piece of old newspaper and wadded it and handed it to Chip, who apparently agreed that it was official weight and size and then tossed it back to Jeff.

"You first," said Chip, and then to me, "Might want to get out of the way."

And so the game was on, with my life potentially hanging in the balance. Jeff went first, and he "dribbled" the ball around a bit, with his back to the hoop, faking moves to the left and then to the right, while Chip jumped up and down behind him, calling insults about his prose style and fact-checking deficiencies.

"Four and a half calfs!" he said, and I don't know what that meant but it must have gotten under Jeff's skin a bit because his first hook shot went wide.

"Ha!" Chip exulted, and picked up the wad of paper.

They exchanged positions now and Chip looked down at his feet and pretended to bend slightly as if to remove an obstacle from the field of play, and Jeff looked down briefly and that's when Chip made his move for an easy lay-in.

"So," Jeff said, his mouth a slit, "that's how it's going to be, huh?"

This time, then, after they'd exchanged places, Jeff just did a fade-away jumper that Chip was powerless to defend, and the score was tied.

After this, Chip retrieved the "ball" and as if by mutual assent now both combatants focused on "defense", which was essentially trying to bear-hug one another to prevent a shot from being made. Scores were made, however, to my surprise, and as I learned later, the rules were you only got ten shots per game (I suppose this was to allow some work to get done later in the day), and so the game was coming to a close.

The score was tied, and Chip had one go left. I couldn't really do it, but I really wanted to say, "C'mon Chip! You can do it!" but I couldn't, and so instead I watched nervously from the bleachers. Chip began his usual dribbling of the ball, and then faked a turn around and instead moved away from the hoop and toward the desks. Jeff was paralyzed by surprise. I was too.

Chip jumped up on a desk and said, "Watch this," and threw the paper wad with one hand in a long arc that crossed the room, caromed off the ceiling, and fell through the hoop.

"Woo hoo!" I shouted. "That was great!"

Jeff stood looking at the paper wad, then the hoop, then the ceiling and finally Chip, retracing the shot in his mind.

"That was awesome, buddy," he said. "Just pure awesomeness."

He went over and gave Chip a hand down from the desk. Chip was grinning like a coyote pup over its first rabbit, but hey, it really was a great shot, after all.

He turned to me and said, "Congratulations on joining The Paper."

Chuck and I picked up some wine on the way home for the celebration.

.   .   .   .   .

A couple of weeks after that first column came out I was coming out of Del's with my mid-morning coffee and had just sat down on The Bench to complete my routine, when I looked across the street and saw Hollis on the opposite sidewalk. He was walking along as usual, head down and seemingly oblivious to anything around him.

Coming toward him from the opposite direction were a couple of Dobbins's local matrons whom I had seen from time to time in Kenna's place, and I continued to watch, expecting at any moment for them to stand to the side and get out of Hollis's way, as any sane person would do. But they didn't. Instead, as Hollis was just about on top of them, one of them said something to him which I was way too far away to hear, and Hollis pulled up short and looked up from his usual reverie.

I could see the ladies talking to him now and they each said a thing or two and then one of them reached out and patted him on the chest! And then they made their way on down the sidewalk chatting to themselves, while Hollis simply stood there looking straight ahead. Then he turned around and looked in the direction of where the two ladies had gone. He slowly turned back toward his former trajectory and then he spotted me looking straight at him. He stood there for another moment just looking at me, and then he touched the brim of his hat and stalked away.

DAYS AND NIGHTS

During the days that followed the shooting I only wanted to sleep. I slept completely dreamless nights. Sometimes I would sleep some hours during the day too. It was the only time when there was any relief. It was as if I had been wounded and only sleep could heal. And then there was waking, and the horror of recognition again. I couldn't function when awake. Then one day, this reversed itself, and all my nights were downing in something nameless and shouting.

CHAPTER ELEVEN:

AN HOUR OF PERFECT BEAUTY

ONE REASON we chose to live in Montana was the landscape. To say it's "dramatic" just doesn't quite cut it. It's like living in a calendar photo. It's inspiring. It makes you glad to be alive. You don't want to sleep while it's there, waiting for you to look at it, feel it, breathe it in, and just be in it. Yes, you put up with the tourists, depending on where you're at, that's a given, but even that's kind of enjoyable, watching the vehicles with all the different license plates passing through, loaded down with canoes and kayaks and camping gear and horse trailers and whatnot.

In fact, one of our favorite pastimes was people-watching down at the Safeway. Just get yourself a basket to blend in and wander around looking at people buying stuff while they're here on some sort of wilderness adventure. My favorite is when you see a group of guys who've shown up for their fly-fishing vacation. There's four of them, all wearing very expensive "outdoor" clothing with brand names designed to tell you just how expensive their clothing is, wandering down the aisles, collectively trying to decide what will constitute a five-day menu. There is confusion, many opinions, and more confusion.

One wants only organic orange juice and wonders how you make eggs Benedict after all. Another is searching food-like things that come in boxes, hoping to find something that one just puts over coals. Nothing is going in the cart, however. Then, they find their way to the meat department. Okay. Now they're in business. Steaks and burgers and ribs find their way into the cart. One fellow goes back and grabs six large cans of baked beans. This, suddenly, is recognizable food.

Somebody remembers barbecue sauce and goes off to find some. Somebody else remembers burger buns, and he heads off too, and brings back paper plates as well, and plastic utensils, and he's greeted with great admiration. Another remembers that there is such a thing as frozen hash browns, and that perhaps some might be wanted for breakfast, along with some eggs and sausage. Several boxes of those, and six cans of Dinty Moore stew, two dozen eggs, three pounds of sausage and they're set. Almost.

They head to the beer aisle. Now the debate begins again, not about what sort, or does anyone prefer wine, but rather quantity.

One of them steps to the fore, dazzling the others with pure statistics: "There's four of us, and we'll be out five days, so that's five cases, right? Ten twelve-packs, right?" Some nod in agreement but others seem to find his mathematics dubious.

"Better make it seven cases," one fellow suggests. "Got the drive home, of course." Complete consensus now, and their shopping is finished.

. . . . .

I got started fly-fishing back in my doctoral days in Washington long ago, and so Montana was sort of returning to paradise for me. As often as I could on those amazing summer days of June through September I would find some stretch of moving water and cast away almost everything else. Those days have been among the best in my life. The rivers here are famous, and so of course you have to share them with others, but that's okay. Just to be here is a wonder, and as time goes by you find your own secluded spots and can get away from almost anything, and just drift away like a Pale Morning Dun on a glassy pool.

However, just to say, you can die unexpectedly while fly-fishing. I know. I'm sorry to bring it up. But I just can't shake Hollis's stupid observation about how trauma just follows a person around and how you can't really get away from it, no matter how far you run or how much you want to hide and try to avoid it.

. . . . .

On one of those blessed days when I woke way before the sun was up and Joanie was still asleep and I grabbed the thermos of coffee and headed out the door without even waking the dogs, Chuck and I headed down some ways with turns and dips that I had become familiar with even in the dark and then pulled off a mile from the river I wanted and parked in a little gravel pull-out just big enough for one car which also had a sign on the barbed wire, in tiny little print, which said that the owner of this particular ranch wouldn't shoot you if all you wanted to do was hike a mile through the woods to get to the river and do a little fishing, or something like that. It was written in draconian legalese, but that was the upshot. I congratulated myself once again for having translated the Great State of Montana's official verbiage, and said goodbye to Chuck, telling him to take a rest, while I headed off for a few hours.

It was late June and in about two hours it would be blistering hot. The sun was still below the Rockies then, and so a mile-long hike in my waders was just a bit of getting the chill out of my legs.

I like walking in the dark here. The trail is mostly smooth and flat, and the woods crowd around you like a giant hallway as if you'd just left the bedroom sleep-walking into a pleasant dream. There is no sound at all in that hour before dawn. It is utter silence except for the scrunch of your boots on the earth. It is a time for thinking about whatever it is your mind wanders to, and I have schooled my own thoughts in such a way that I can actually think about nothing at all if I like, and I do these days whenever it's possible. I'm not sure what you think of that. Maybe just think of it like needing to go to sleep when you're really, really exhausted and the only comfort is somewhere and something so pleasant and so wonderful that it just is, and it asks nothing of you but to exist. No thinking required at all. Maybe like that.

I had timed things perfectly, as planned. The sun was just now struggling above the peaks to let enough light down onto the molten-silver river that lay in front of me that I could see enough to tie on a fly and wade into the water, through the rocks, and stand alone in the glory of this place, water rushing all around me the color of air.

I could tell you what fly I tied on, but I won't. That's part of the deal. Instead I'll just tell you that my first so-so cast resulted in a swirl I could barely see in that light, and a lifting of rod and line and a rush of life like a bolt of electricity from fish-to-man that is probably something like what happens with a defibrillator that I never want to know about. Like that. It was a good fish, they all are if you know what I mean, and I carefully brought him to my feet to spend the briefest of time possible admiring his beauty: that silver shot-through-with-red-and-black-spots marvel of God's creation. And then with a flick, the hook was removed, and back he went to his own little piece of paradise. And so it was, several more times as I made my way upstream.

I wish I could tell you how good it all felt. I wish I could actually find the words to describe it. It is the best sort of therapy a person can have, I believe. It is peace that just sort of fills you up to the point where time slips away and all you might otherwise worry about does too.

And it was right about there, at that particular point of my own conscious reckoning of the beauty and grandeur of the world and my place in it, that I heard something crashing through the woods right behind me, as I stood on the bank trying to tie on another fly. This was not the sort of sound made by a clumsy angler. This was the sound of something quite used to crashing its way through any sort of obstacle it might ever wish to. I was frozen to the ground. I couldn't think or act. I knew there were grizzlies here, but really, why now, why here, why me? It had been such a lovely hour of life.

I stood and waited, and a moose crashed through the brush to stand seven feet from me. She did not see me at once, and then turned her gaze to meet my own. Okay. I'm pretty sure that everyone knows what a moose generally looks like, even if you live in Los Angeles, and of course you've seen them on television. Let me tell you what it's really like. She was six feet tall at the shoulder, and her head and neck of course added up to a nine-foot-tall being looking down at me, not even with surprise, and certainly not fear, but with utter disdain. I could see every hair on her body. She was magnificent and frightening in ways I could never describe.

I could not make my mind fire enough to say a silent prayer of hope that she was not trailing a calf, or I'd be a goner for sure. She looked at me, and I could see in her eyes that she was deliberating whether or not she should go to the messy trouble of exterminating me, or just get on with her busy day. She "huffed" at me, and among humans this might have also involved a hand gesture, and then she walked into the river, easily swimming across the killer-currents further out, made the other bank and paused. She did not look back. There was no need to see if a threat followed, because I had been weighed and measured and discounted.

I noticed, fleetingly, that my feet were wet, which was odd, because I had my chest waders on.

DAYS AND NIGHTS

Sometimes, during the worst of it, I thought about killing myself. I thought about various ways to do so without even much trying. I could just fall into the river, or turn the steering wheel just as I approached a concrete underpass, or just sit down and cut a wrist and then fall asleep. I never did these things. I didn't have the will for it. I went from being alive to just being dead, and there were no angels to show you the way.

CHAPTER TWELVE:

GIL'S GOOD GAS

THERE CAME A TIME when I was running out of easy ideas for my next column for The Paper. I hadn't yet done one on Kenna. I was kind of saving her for a rainy day, so to speak, because I was certain she'd give me a lot of material to work with, even though I actually didn't know her all that well at that time. I went in to town to ponder this over coffee at Del's, but stopped in at Gil's Good Gas on my way.

When Chuck pulled in and parked, it struck me that Gil's Good Gas was likely one of the most remarkable places in town, but that I had simply gotten used to it as time had gone on. First, as with most other things here, it's our only gas station, and second, it is a museum to an era gone by that most people wish hadn't.

The thing is, Gil, who's maybe thirty-ish now, inherited the gas station from his father who had passed away maybe ten years ago or so. At that time it was a "regular" gas station just as you might find anywhere in the country. And also at that time, Gil was dead-set against running a gas station for the rest of his days. He had just graduated from UM with honors in anthropology, and his dream was to go to graduate school back east somewhere and get his graduate degree in archaeology and paleontology and leave this little chunk of Montana and pursue his dreams across the planet in exotic and dangerous places. As I understand it, his mother stood in the way.

Now I only know this second-hand, but I have it on good authority (Kenna) that during the reading of his father's will, upon learning that his father had bequeathed him the gas station and that it was his dying wish that his son "follow in his footsteps" (as Kenna said), that he said some rather inappropriate words, I believe two, and got up and walked out of the lawyers' offices and slammed the door on his way out. This in turn sparked a three-week-long silence from Gil's mother, who, if you ever met her, didn't need to be a combat veteran like Hollis to know how to best go at your adversary.

In summation, the accused party (Gil), in order to have any peace at all, had only two options: he could 1) pursue his dreams as an anthropologist and archaeologist and head for parts unknown, thus leaving the aggrieved party (his mother) to fend for herself, or 2) he could abandon his dreams and stay in this one-horse town and end up selling gas for the rest of his life. Gil decided he would do neither and both.

What Gil decided to do instead was pursue both anthropology and archaeology as they applied to gas stations. The first thing he did was unearth everything from the fifties that he could possibly come by. He had the newish steel/aluminum pumps taken away and replaced them with glass-topped, filtered pumps from a Phillips Museum in Canton, through which you could actually view the darn gas you were buying. I have no idea what this might have cost him, but his mother backed him in this, and she had gotten the savings (Kenna said), and so they went all in. At the same time that the pumps were dug out and the new ones installed, Gil placed an oil machine with varying hoses for different viscosities and brands of oil as well, along with water lines and air hoses. Then he tore down the old awning and replaced it, after months of study, with an old Texaco one he had actually gotten delivered and refurbished from a relic along Route 66 somewhere in Nevada.

Gil spent every night for a year reading and viewing pictures and talking to people on the phone, and emailing people, and then he tore down the office building and built an exact replica of one from the fifties, all done in gleaming chrome. He had emblems of various oil companies everywhere, all very tasteful, including the aforementioned as well as Sinclair, and Esso and all the ones that no longer exist.

To stop at Good Gas is, well, when Joanie and I first arrived and we pulled in, we thought we'd traveled back in time sixty years. And we didn't want to leave. We wanted to look at everything for hours and hours. It was just amazing. It made you feel good to get gas.

However, you need to understand that Gil was an anthropologist first. This was his first love: understanding people and where they had originated and the nuance of how environmental and economic and social pressures shaped how we were and what we've become and how we are. He applied this knowledge in very noticeable ways. You need to visualize Gil's Good Gas beyond the archaeological aspect of it, its sheer physical presence, as pleasing at that may be, and instead try to understand it as something designed by a very thoughtful man to appeal to you, and your very humanity, no matter what's happening in your life right now. Gil's is therapy.

When Chuck pulled in that day, there was Gil, dressed in a very smart khaki uniform, with sharply creased pants, crisp shirt pockets freshly ironed, the corners of which were quite clearly level with one another, a Texaco Star emblazoned above his chest, and a lieutenant's hat that looked like it could steer through fog without a lighthouse. He was attended, immediately, by Simon and Theo, also dressed in this fashion. They descended upon you, and if you hadn't been here before then you might think the local militia (which is across the border, in Idaho of course) had just suckered you into a very bad day. But no. Their beaming smiles and salutes tell you instead that you just pulled into the very best fill-up you ever had in your life.

"Good day, sir!" Gil said. "Good day, Chuck, you wonderful old guy you!"

"Good day!" Theo and Simon said. "What does Chuck want today?"

And when you step out of your vehicle, you notice that there isn't a stray piece of hair on the concrete, let alone actual debris, and everything is as crazily impeccable as Gil and his assistants are.

And before you can say anything at all, Gil has the hood popped and Simon is checking your oil, and Theo is checking your tire pressure, and Gil is shaking your hand saying, "Thank you for coming. It's a pleasure to have you here today."

And then Theo said, "Chuck's left back tire is down 1.7. Can I do it?"

And I said, "Whatever Chuck wants, Chuck gets."

This makes everyone excruciatingly happy, as well as myself.

Simon, almost disappointed, but still with a smile, said, "Oil is good, sir. May I check your odometer against my last check?"

There's no way I'm going to say no to that, because that would absolutely ruin the drama that you've just driven into, but didn't know you had.

Later, you might meet Gil at The Office or at the Safeway when he's off stage, and you'd find him in jeans and flannel like everyone else, and might, perhaps at first, be surprised that he has foot-long hair which he keeps tightly bobbed and tucked away under the hat when he's on stage, and Theo and Simon as well, being the sort of teenagers they are, here and there around town, and not at all sucked out of *Leave It to Beaver*. It's fine. They're "off", you see? But the performance, that's everything, and it's all a person can want, and you get drawn into it right away, even as a stranger passing through town who might wonder "Just what the hell was that?" and yet go away thinking, "Well. That was very nice, now wasn't it?"

And this is all on purpose, you see? Gil has studied this down to tiny motes of what makes us tick, and he knows a whole heck of a lot more than Madison Avenue about what people want. And what you really want, I believe, is not to be wherever you are or doing whatever it is you're doing, because instead what you want is Gil's Good Gas. There isn't anything better than that.

When Gil and Simon and Theo were finished, and Simon was just then absently rubbing a sheepskin cloth over Chuck's hood, making him feel all warm and comfy, I said, "Hey. Would you guys have a few minutes sometime to talk?"

DAYS AND NIGHTS

Later on, something new: anger. I have never been an angry person, even at those times when perhaps I should have been. I just really don't do angry. And then suddenly I was angry all the time, about almost anything and everything. I wouldn't have wanted to live with me. I want it to stop. I want to be me again. I can't make it stop. I'm trying.

CHAPTER THIRTEEN:
THE DREAM

IT IS WORTH telling you what dreams are, in case you hadn't figured that out. Myself, I'm still working out the details. Dreams are of course these things that happen both while you're asleep and then also while you're awake. The ones that happen while you're asleep, those are tricky. In the old stories, this was how you'd know if God wanted you to do something important, like maybe go on a quest for something, or perhaps Great Truths were revealed and you were intended to bring these things to others, or maybe you had a genuine epiphany, and suddenly understood your true purpose in life.

Alternately, they're the place where we work things out, good or bad. We feel or think these things and then they get played out somehow, like a film with live-action, as if they were somehow real life in some way. They're odd things, and symbolic somehow, and we're supposed to figure them out with our waking minds, or else not. Sometimes we laugh about them, and other times we make sure we never, ever tell anyone about them.

Sometimes they inspire us, and other times we flinch away from them, horrible ugly things as they might be.

Waking dreams are a whole different thing. These are things that occupy one's mind in the waking world, and are probably described as easily as wants or needs, and they're things you don't currently have, or perhaps you think you don't, but want for some reason. These are the ones we all know about, but maybe don't talk about. For some of us we might want wealth or maybe to meet someone to love, or something silly like a car or a new refrigerator or whatever. We might want what's trivial, or important to us somehow, and we can get caught up in it if we're not careful...just walking in a dream, even when we're awake. Waiting. Hoping. I know what I'm talking about here.

.   .   .   .   .

Law enforcement in Dobbins is Walter. He belongs to the State Patrol, and is a Sheriff by rank. Walter grew up in Missoula, and played football in high school, and was on the wrestling team, and went off to college, and he never wanted anything but to be a police officer, and then to move on to the FBI to solve the really serious issues in the country. He had everything a boy could have growing up, and when he knew his dream was to become a member of the upper echelons of law enforcement he pursued it like a bloodhound. It would never escape him.

In college, he played football and was quite good, but he was even better in his classes because he had the dream in front of him the whole time. It never left him. He'd be out getting a burger with some of the guys and a car would come careening down the street on a Friday night and Walter would jump up and say, "Did you see that?" and everyone else at the table was just eating their fries and laughing and Walter wasn't hungry any-more, just itchy. He wanted to solve things and Make a Difference and he was ready.

The truth be told, Walter was so focused on the dream that he almost missed seeing Veronica in the hallway on his way to class, but he didn't. When he did see her, he was so absolutely thunderstruck that he dropped his books on her feet as she sat on a bench reading. He was so shocked when she yelped in pain that the dream temporarily went out of his head.

After the exclamations and awkwardness, Walter dropped to his knees and removed Veronica's shoe and massaged her foot, never looking up at her be-cause he was afraid to, because what he'd seen in just about four seconds would mean a serious obstacle to his dream. Veronica's foot was fine, and when Walter managed to find the courage to look up he saw Veron-ica smile at him in a way that he had never seen or un-derstood before. She was so very beautiful. It was a dream he never knew he had. Two days after gradua-tion they were married.

As it happened, Veronica grew up in Dobbins and persuaded Walter to get a job there if he could. And, as it happened, Walter was so darned highly regarded as a candidate that when he graduated he could sort of almost write his own ticket, and with a bit of persua-sion directed in the proper channels by his ranch-owning parents, he got the gig in Dobbins. But, you have to realize that Walter now had a brand-new dream, one that would occupy his every waking thought from now on. He wanted a family, and so did Veronica, and that meant he wanted it with all he had.

You need to understand that Walter was so very good at his job that he could keep the dream just a little bit off to the side as he dragged down a tourist on the road doing something foolish, or near someone's property, or when he had a domestic dispute, or investigate a robbery or find out who was behind some foolish vandalism. He could do it. But he couldn't do it for very long. Not for a single day, I mean.

He'd be listening to some couple who, for whatever reasons, had just about had it up to here and that's when the lawn tractor had been doused with gasoline and then that was when Mister-Knows-Everything got what was coming, and then the shoving got started and somebody's head hit the cabinet and then there was a whole lot more shouting and things said you could never unsay and Walter would step in.

And he'd look at them and talk to them and threaten them and sit down on the couch with them—and no I don't need any coffee—and listen, and all the while he'd be thinking of Veronica, and can't we maybe have a boy or a girl? A girl would be so amazing! A boy would be so good! Think of all the things we could... and then he'd have to write a ticket, or threaten someone with county lock-up, or actually have to run them over to Missoula for the really bad things. And he could never, ever get it out of his head, not even for thirty minutes.

Now, I'm not so very sure about how to say this, but Walter and Veronica tried hard to have children, but it didn't happen. Okay, fine. Kenna told me. She said that Walter and Veronica were trying "like weasels", and I guess I understood what that meant. Apparently, when–

ever Walter was off duty, then he and Veronica were trying like crazy to have children. Now, mind you, Kenna talks to a large audience each day, but I won't say that that's where the rumors came from. Not exclusively.

The story is that they tried and tried and tried, and the first time I ever saw Walter, pulling up to Del's to go in and quick grab a coffee, he struck me as a little tired, if you know what I mean. So I guess they were giving it their all, hoping that they could finally, after three years, get their family started. And Walter's dream would not let him go.

The problem with this kind of dreaming is that you just never wake up from it. It's just right there, staring at you and you're looking back, day after day. Like I said, Walter was functional during this time, but apparently not wholly so. He'd stand on the sidewalk and watch a young couple go down the walk with their stroller and then he'd sit on the bench outside Del's and just watch them walk into infinity, which just happened to not be his own infinity, and then he'd get mad about it and stand up and look for something to Set Right, because that by golly was his job. And that was how I first met Walter.

.   .   .   .   .

Chuck had taken me down into town to stop at Daffyd's so I could peruse his ridiculously expensive flies and perhaps buy one or maybe even two. I'd gone in and spent half an hour looking, and Daffyd and I had talked about the rivers and this and that and where I'd been going and which tourists he was going to guide that week and that was that. I spent three months of income on three flies and headed out the door.

When I walked out, I saw Walter sitting on Del's Bench on the opposite side of the street, and he seemed to be looking out toward the Great Beyond or whatever it was that he did. You see, I didn't know at the time that he had a dream right in front of him, or else maybe I'd have done something different, or maybe not because I might have thought he was distracted enough that it wouldn't matter. But I didn't know Walter then. So, I just looked left and right and walked across the street.

Right then I made eye contact with Walter for no particular reason, and I could see from there something just change in his expression, as if he'd just been woken from a very pleasant dream to discover there was actually a skunk under the bed and he'd better do something about it. His brow went up and the corners of his mouth went down and he stood and strode right out into the middle of the street and stopped me there.

He said, "I don't know you, but I've seen you around, and you are just about one bad driver away from being dead, you know that?"

He put his hand into his back pocket and pulled out a citation pad and was just about to ask me my name I guess when a logging truck came down the road and blared at us and we both jumped because we hadn't seen it and I said, "Maybe we should get out of the road?" and Walter jumped left and I went right and was back in Chuck in no time and he took me on out of town.

And then one day the news came, like the wind parleying between the new leaves on the trees, touching each other and everything else, and it spread like fire in tall grass: Veronica was pregnant. That must have been in September, because it was at the end of May, and almost Montana spring, when she delivered at the hospital in Missoula.

Now, here's the thing about dreams that I've discovered. When you want something so badly, so much so that it takes up all your waking moments because you just can't let it go or just don't want to, the dream you want so much just sort of bends reality. This is a bit like how particle physics works, which even Einstein couldn't figure out but had to acknowledge: particles actually take on particle or wave form simply depending on human observation and consciousness of them. Yep. Neils Bohr once said that if you think you know what particle physics is all about, you simply don't understand it. In any case, I think Walter and Veronica bent all of quantum reality around their wants and dreams, because Veronica delivered triplets.

When summer came thirty days later, Walter had built a stroller. First, you have to really understand Walter. You do realize of course that he's been living the dream all his life and that it's all come true, just one thing after another after another, and so now he sees the next one, just laid out in front of him like the end-less horizon waiting for the sun to rise. So. We aren't just talking "stroller" here.

Walter goes out to the garage and dreams it, like Lathe of Heaven or something. He sees it. He first imagines three seats side-by-side, and revels in the idea of the sheer audacity of it. However, as a sane and thoughtful man he also imagines having to run senior citizens off the sidewalks, such as they are, with the contraption. So instead, he imagines and plans and engineers on paper and then into reality a stretch-limo stroller. He puts six big knobby tires on it with independent axles because of course in Dobbins you're going to need them more often than not, and he creates three seats with sheepskin cushions and three-point seatbelts. A minor dream. No problem seeing it through.

Chip and Jeff did a story of course on Walter, Veronica and the triplets, and had a big picture of Walter with the kids in the stroller-tank four-wheeling through somebody's pasture. They were the talk of the town for a long time, and I guess still are. Young women wanting to be mothers still come by and see Veronica and ask for tips or maybe if she'd just touch them for good luck, and the guys ask Walter if he'll buy their lottery tickets for them.

Me, I just want to ask Walter how to dream, because I think I might have forgotten.

DAYS AND NIGHTS

The thing is, when you discover that you have a head wound, and maybe you never do and I suppose that also happens because it almost happened to me and I'm sorry if that's how it's going for you right now, there really isn't anything you can do to return to interacting with anyone else in the same way as you might have before. It would be different if you had a cast on, or maybe like Hollis who has his entire body crisscrossed with scars, each one of them telling a different story that none of us would ever wish to hear told in a first-person narrative in great detail and at the time of their inception.

If you had a cast on, or those very visible scars, then you'd at least imagine someone somewhere would kind of give you a break sometimes. I mean, I'm hoping they wouldn't tell you to walk faster to keep up with their pace when you were hopping along on your crutches with that full-leg cast on. That would be pretty mean of them. Of course it would. But when there's no open wound to see, that's really different.

Nobody says or asks: "Oh. Mass shooting. I understand. Lose some people? Best friend? Others? Ah, gotcha."

No, and you can't even wear a T-shirt to say so.

Joanie is so mad at me sometimes and she says I have no sense of humor anymore and I say I'm sorry and that I'm trying to get better and she is mad and says that I should just hurry that up. I can't show her the hole in my head. I can't even say it.

I wonder now about the idea of loss. I suppose for a lot of us, if we're lucky and you know what I mean, it happens with our parents. And the way this goes is that it creates a hole that cannot be filled. You don't say, "Oh, well, that was bad. I should go get some new parents." No, it happens and then that's all there is and then that hole can never be filled again. It can't. There is no caulk or glue or stitching to make the hole not a hole. There is nothing to fill the hole. The hole is a hole and will always be a hole. And when you have a hole in your head, and no one can see it, there isn't anything you can do about that.

CHAPTER FOURTEEN:
STACY GRIPS GRIP

IN MONTANA there are occupations that only exist in certain parts of the country. For example, there aren't that many places where you'd look in the classifieds and see something like "Ditch Rider needed." A Ditch Rider is someone who rides along canals and natural waterways to ensure that someone isn't taking more water for irrigation or their livestock than is their due, and it's an important and sometimes dangerous job.

A fairly common occupation around the country, though it is one you may never think about, is that of Game Warden. The reason that you may never have considered what occurs during one's employment as a Game Warden is likely because you've never had the occasion of running into one while he or she was exercising their duty and authority. This would be perfectly reasonable in many parts of the country. In Montana, however, being a Game Warden is very serious business because tourists, and admittedly sometimes residents as well, can do some really crazy things while they're out hunting or fishing or even just driving along looking at the scenery.

Just as an example, I once overheard at Del's the story of a fellow who had come out from the East Coast to do some grouse hunting. The story goes that he had had very little luck bagging any grouse, but had discovered that the quail hunting was absolutely fantastic. He had been camping out for several days, and so by the time he was passing through Dobbins once again, he had managed several days' worth of the daily bag limit for quail.

Apparently the fellow was nearly ecstatic over the good luck he had had, and was dying to tell people about it. So, at his first opportunity he cajoled one of the locals into checking out his trunk-load of quail. As it happened, once the fellow popped open the trunk, said citizen was faced with the unfortunate situation of being the person who had to tell the fellow the sad news that his trunk was in fact filled with approximately twenty-four dead meadowlarks, which, as it happens, is our official State Bird.

· · · · ·

Our Game Warden around here is Stacy, and by all accounts she takes her job very seriously indeed. She has developed a sort of legendary status in the area, because even though she's the only one we have and she has to cover an enormous area of wilderness all by herself, she has been said to have been spotted all over the region at roughly the same time. One morning while Joanie and I were having breakfast at Del's, we heard two gents across the way explaining an encounter with Stacy:

"So, I was wading upstream by that point and I kind of caught something funny out of the corner of my eye."

"Funny? How's that?"

"Well, what I thought I saw was a bush moving. I sort of kept looking at it and then just went on my way. I'd gone up just a bit further when somebody said, 'Good morning, sir!' in a really loud voice and I about fell into the river. I whipped around, and there was Stacy, dressed as a freaking bush!"

·   ·   ·   ·   ·

I have actually had several encounters with Stacy. The first occasion was not good at all. In fact, I'm unsure how well things went on any of those occasions.

One morning Chuck was taking me to the river, and you really need to realize that I'm not quite sure where Chuck was taking me, but that's okay. I trust him and I am certain he knows what I want, and even if it's something he wants, I'm usually okay about that too. Anyway, Chuck dropped me off and the sun was almost making its way over the Rockies.

Let me see, in retrospect, if it's possible for me to describe this to you. It is difficult. Here, the sun just now falling down the western slopes of ten-thousand-foot-tall peaks, caped in snow, revealing their majesty to mere humans such as myself, and it looks as if The Almighty has woken and has brought light to a newly created world. Below me, in the valley between the tall pines reaching up from the rocks, is a kind of fairy-world of water and mist, draped in shadows black and green. Your first step forward, leaving the road and the things of Man, is to leave all and everything behind.

As you pass along the path, more and more visible in the growing light, you see buttercups aching for the sun, and purple lupine aching for the rain, and other, tiny white flowers, merely aching to be seen. And slowly the river grows in front of you. There are no words to ascribe a color to it, and instead one must think of something so very alive and familiar-yet-foreign that you cannot grasp its living self. It is beyond you, going on and on and is such a massive piece of life that it's bigger than anything you can imagine, running its course of life across this earth for miles and miles.

And I sat on a boulder before the great river, and for the life of me I couldn't see it. It was happening to me again, even though I had run away from it all, away from all that could hurt me or bend me or make me something ugly and misshapen. I couldn't see any of this at all. At all. And I just sat there on the rock looking out onto God's most perfect creation, and I was utterly blind to it. I might as well have been sitting in a laundromat watching the washer on rinse cycle.

And then I got angry. This has happened to me on occasion, where I remember real-me versus post-me, and, mostly it just wears me out and wears me down but that's okay, it's like erosion, just some natural process I'm guessing. But not here. Not now. Looking out onto the thing that would have, sometime in the past, I don't remember when, have made me so...I don't know...so something more powerful and better and more happy, and I couldn't find it. I just couldn't find it. What was the matter with me? I was empty. I didn't remember anything.

So I stood up and took my vest off, and I threw my rod to the ground and I had, well, a sort of meltdown. Now I know what you're thinking. "Tantrum" comes to mind and things like that. Whatever you want to throw at me here is fine, because maybe that's how it was. A grown man having a tantrum. That's probably it. Anyway, I was walking in circles shouting nonsense at the landscape, and then wore myself out and sat back down on the rock with my head in my hands. And that is when I heard a voice coming out of the sky.

"So you won't be doing any fishing today?" I just sat on the rock, not very surprised about anything any longer.

"No. I don't think so. I don't know. Maybe."

"If you don't mind my asking, what just happened there?" the voice asked from the heavens.

"I don't know. That's the thing. I don't know anymore. Sometimes it just hits me that I'm blind or deaf or just stupid, and I can't be happy anymore, and I don't know why. And sometimes it makes me angry, and then that makes me angry too. And I really don't do angry very well. Makes me ill, actually."

Yes, this was me, talking to voices in my head, in the middle of nowhere, where I've run away to in order to find sanity.

"Want to know something really awful?" the voice said once again.

"Why not?" I said.

"I have a pickup truck parked two miles from here and in the back I have five dead bucks with their heads cut off, and I want the bastards who did that."

"What?! That's just, that's just..." and I stood up and found a rock and threw it somewhere and then I remembered a whole bunch of words that you can never say in the classroom unless it's an arcane exercise in etymology, and then just wore myself out again and sat back down on the rock.

"I hope you get them," I said. "I know you will."

Something about that, the other kinds of awfulness in the world, woke me up a bit and then I realized maybe I wasn't talking to myself like a lunatic and I looked up, and in the branches above I saw a woman in uniform, sitting on a branch, face done in camo, with a very nice set of binoculars resting on her chest. She had a very nice gun resting on her hip as well.

"Stacy?" I asked.

.　　.　　.　　.　　.

The second time I ran into Stacy was like the first time, I guess. I'm going to have to stop there and once again sort of explain myself. You see, the deal is when things happen to me anymore, I no longer seem to behave like I used to. This can be pretty much anything. I step on a nail and maybe an hour later I come to realize that my foot hurts. I pull my shoe off and pull out the nail, absently wondering and not remembering when the last time was I had a tetanus shot.

Conversely, a twig snaps when I'm in the woods and I'm scrabbling halfway up a tree for no reason whatsoever. It appears as though reality is something that I'm experiencing very differently from what I'm used to. It has nothing whatsoever to do with what's going on, I merely perceive it differently, I think. And my reactions follow suit.

So, I broke my normal routine and Grip went with me fishing one morning. Grip is everyone's dream companion. He really is. Grip loves you. He loves to be with you. He loves whatever you and he are going to go do. And if later there might possibly be a snack involved, he could probably love you to death.

He's a big guy, and when he's around, people notice. He's handsome and charismatic, big, black and wolfy looking. He's date-bait, and I know you wish you had him for that purpose, because anyone would follow you anywhere if he was there. And if maybe you didn't want someone there, he's that too. Big guy. Looking at you with those almond-colored eyes that say don't mess around with me. He's your everything-companion. It's really fun that he's going along this morning. I don't know why it never occurred to me before to take him.

On the river, Grip was the perfect fishing companion. I was casting out in the river, never going beyond what I thought was safe. Grip was on the bank, maybe fifteen feet behind me, to my left, very nicely outside my back cast, but I kept an eye on where he was, even so. I hooked my first fish and brought it in and released it, and after I did so I looked back around to see where Grip was, but I didn't see him.

I had a pang then. I panicked. I turned fully around and Grip had been right behind me the whole time, swimming in the river! He was looking at me and probably wondering what the whole fish-thing was, but this water was too swift for a dog to be in because I was pretty planted where I was and it wasn't easy.

I pointed to the shore and told him to go back, and Grip speaks six languages and so I know he knows what I'm saying, but then he just whipped around and started swimming downstream, which was maybe easier because then it struck me that he looked a little tired, and I had no idea how long he'd already been swimming.

And then so there he went and it was obvious now that he was being carried away. I waded back to shore as fast as the current allowed me without going under, and when I got back to shore I threw down my rod and stripped off my vest and went running downstream in my waders as best I could.

I am trying to think. I am trying to run in my chest waders. The two are conflicting. I think, finally, I can't swim in waders to get him, and I can't run in them either, should I spare the time to try to get out of them and then have no shoes on and also possibly lose sight of him? What should I do? I can't think straight. I keep running.

I see him and he's trying to swim, but I think it's more like just keeping his snout above the water, and then there's a stretch where I see a log out in the river, and if I could get there before him, then I could get up against it and nab him. And then I think, I can't get ahead of him, he's too far. I can still get in the water after he gets pulled down, and try to get him out. And all I'm doing is just running and trying to keep sight of him without breaking my leg.

I'm not real sure about my thinking at this point. I will confess that there are times when Past, Present and Maybe get a bit mixed up. I think I am thinking "What I really need right now is God," but I may not have been. That might have come later. Maybe I was only saying to myself, "Ohgodohgoohgodohgod," and I don't remember. I might have been using some Anglo-Saxon nouns and verbs as well. I don't know. I'm just running. And getting tired. And getting slower.

And then I can look ahead a bit and I see someone

getting in the river against the log. That person is taking really careful steps, back braced against the log because to do otherwise is to get swept under. And she is wearing a green uniform, and is getting more and more in line where Grip is coming down the river, weighted down in his heavy fur, just a snout above the water now.

And I can see her look and yell, but I can't hear what she says, and she is just *pressed* against the log now and is almost bent backwards by the current and she has her arms spread. And Grip sweeps in, close, so close, and she turns and grabs him by the collar I guess and then a massive battle begins to determine who will win the day, or who will wind up in Valhalla to fight another day at the end of all things.

And Stacy puts her back to the log and hauls him out, somehow, and Grip is first choking, then okay I think, and she has his collar, holding him up above the water, talking to him, and she and he slowly side-step toward the bank. Stacy has her back against the log the whole time, and I am finally, finally there. I get in, and wade as far as I can, and then we hand him off, and I have Grip and get him to shore where he lies down. I get back in the water and make my way to Stacy, and we grip arms, backs against the log, and we side-step back to shore.

I remember collapsing then next to Grip, to check him out, because I couldn't stand any longer, and he seemed good, but exhausted. Maybe sleep for a week. Stacy kneeled down and had a look and then stood back up. The sun was right behind her and I couldn't see her very well. The light created a nimbus around her head and her face was lost in the light.

"I should write you up for obstructing the river, but my pad's too wet. I also have two more dead bucks, and Bad Guys to find. Have a nice day."

"I'll pay the fine," I said as she walked away.

Grip and I laid there for maybe another fifteen minutes, and then the crazy thought went through my head that maybe Chuck was worried about us, so I got to one knee and managed to get myself upright.

"I think there's a snack in the car that Mom made for you," I said to Grip. That got him up. He has an extensive vocabulary, and "snack" is one word that he knows in several languages.

On the way back I said, "Buddy, you just about got us both killed." I stopped and knelt down and rubbed his head. "How about if this one time we don't tell Mom about it?"

DAYS AND NIGHTS

At the beginning of Chaucer's *Knight's Tale*, two soldiers are pulled alive from a mound of dead comrades. I begin to wonder now what they might have first thought: the glory of being alive, or the slaughter around them that had left so many friends dead?

CHAPTER FIFTEEN:

AN UNEXPECTED CUT

I HAVE HEARD it said that there are consequences to everything you do, and that this applies to both your actions and your inactivity. I don't really know how true this might be, but recently I have begun to think about it more and more, and it disturbs me. I can't think how many times now I've wondered about how things could have gone differently that day of the shooting. I think about things like what if I had had a gun? Would I have tried to run in and save the day or maybe gotten killed myself? I think about what if my friend had called in sick that day, or maybe had taken his class to a campus computer lab instead? I think about taking the job in Oregon in the first place. And I think about running all the time. Just running away and what if I stopped? Anyway, it doesn't seem to matter what you do or don't do, I guess, there will be consequences.

·　·　·　·　·

One morning I had Chuck take me into town because I was overdue for a haircut and I thought that maybe I could get into Kenna's place before the crowds showed up. We pulled up to her place and I was a bit surprised to get a parking spot right out front. Usually I park down the street a ways. I walked up to the door but then saw a sign that said "Closed" and so I turned around to get back to Chuck and I heard somebody say, "Hey, Al. Sorry about that, but I'm closed on Mondays," and there was Kenna coming down the sidewalk.

"Mondays are my days to get chores done," she said as she came up.

"Oh, gotcha," I said. "No problem. I'll just come back tomorrow," and I turned away.

"Hey Al," Kenna called. "Tell you what. I'm not really doing anything anyway. C'mon in and I'll get you done."

Kenna unlocked the door and she put me in the chair and grabbed an apron and got started.

We chatted a bit and Kenna asked about Joanie and if I'd been fishing lately and wondered how it was now that it was getting so late in the summer.

We talked a bit more and then she said, "I saw that piece you had in The Paper the other day. I didn't know you were a reporter or I wouldn't talk so much when you were around."

She laughed and I told her that I had just started for The Paper and that was my first published piece. I said I hoped to have one out each week.

She stopped snipping then and said, "That was real interesting about ol' Hollis. Yeah, that was real interesting. Who'd-a thought he was like a real war hero or something, and gettin' all those Purple Hearts and all? Yeah, that was really something."

And she wandered around a bit then, apparently having forgotten about hair cutting for the moment. Then she grabbed a chair and pulled it up to where I was sitting and she sat down and pointed her scissors at me.

"Yeah, that was really good to know, Al. I really liked that. So you friends now with Hollis or something because he doesn't talk to anybody that I know of." And she looked at me very intently when she said this.

"What?! No! I mean, no, not really. We, uh, met a couple of times is all. That's all."

"Huh," Kenna said. "That's really something then, you gettin' him to actually tell you all about himself. I tried once and he wouldn't even look at me."

Uh-oh, I thought, remembering her story about the guy back during her Army days. I gambled on attempted humor and said, "There're no gas chambers here, Kenna."

She looked at me a bit and then whooped with laughter.

"Nope! No there isn't. Ha, that's a good one, Al."

She sat quiet there for a minute, seemingly not too eager to cut my hair, so I asked, "So what's the deal, Kenna? Why so interested in Hollis anyway? I mean, that is, if it really is interest," I finished somewhat lamely.

Kenna didn't answer right away, but eventually she stood up and stretched and said, "It's just that it's going to be another real long winter, Al, just another real long winter."

And then she got back to snipping.

DAYS AND NIGHTS

I am aware that time has become fractured, and my memories of some things cannot take place in any sort of order. I say this so that you won't expect some sort of coherent story to appear here. There are some things I remember very clearly, and others I do not. I remember an hour or so later sitting in my little study at home when the news trucks started showing up at our little house. They swarmed the front gate, which was closed. They came from all the names you know, and Joanie went out to meet them and came back inside and asked me if I wanted to talk with them, and I cried and said no. She went out and chased them all off, one by one, as they continued to show up again and again.

First winter

CHAPTER SIXTEEN:

FIGHTING WORDS

THE AVERAGE PERSON doesn't really think so very much about day-to-day survival in our country, though this will have to exclude the many homeless for whom the daily necessities are a struggle at best. I have begun to think more about survival strategies these days, though this has been pressed on me unwillingly. I think now that survival is something one must probably have to give real attention to, because you never know what you might have to try to live through.

An interesting fact: in our part of Montana the population diminishes by 75 percent each and every October first. It's true. This is because most people aren't crazy or masochistic. This takes either a simple explanation or a more round-about one, and I'm going for the latter.

.   .   .   .   .

Probably the nicest building in the whole town is a fly-fishing shop just on the edge of town. It is a beautiful log-cabin style building with glossy logs and blue metal roof, and big windows everywhere. It is of course designed for all the tourists passing through, and the prices of things inside reflect this as well. Naturally, I went there often to replenish my flies and swap stories with the owner, Daffyd, who's from Scotland, and whose accent makes tourists drool and they buy even more stuff. So, that first summer in town I made sure to be friendly with whom I considered the most important person in town, second only to Jake the butcher.

As the summer progressed I came in more and more often because it only took me about two days to write my column and then I spent most of the rest of the time fishing as much as possible. Daffyd gave me advice, and in return I'd tell him what I'd been using the day before on a certain stretch and how I'd done, and he appreciated that because he took clients out as a guide each morning and only occupied the shop himself in the afternoons, and so he got a sort of river report each time I stopped in.

On one of these occasions he happened to say in passing:

"You might want to go ahead and get a few of those Duns now, because we'll be closing up September fifteenth."

I had no idea what he meant. "You're going out of business?" I asked. "That's crazy!"

"No," he said, "we always close up each year then."

"Why?"

"Because that's when we move to Florida and open up our shop there."

I still didn't understand. "But what about your customers here?" I said.

"There aren't any," and he looked a bit confused. Then some sort of realization dawned on him.

"This is your first year here, isn't it?" And I admitted that it was.

"Now I see. You have to realize, winter begins on October first."

None of this made any sense to me. I continued to fish and do things with the property throughout September. I mowed the lawn and watered the flowers. Then, that last week of September, the days went from being 90 degrees to 60 by Thursday. By Friday it was 40. On October first there was sleet. And that was that.

. . . . .

Sitting by the fireplace with a Combusto-Log in it, because we hadn't gotten firewood yet because, you know, it was only October, we reflected on meeting the guy who had hooked up our satellite dish back in April when we first arrived. He was very pleased to meet us, and welcomed the idea of "new blood" coming in (I'm guessing he thought we might eventually propagate and add to the limited number of dating choices in the future). We, of course, were very pleased to meet such a friendly person, and he was a real conversationalist when it came to his profession.

"Have you hooked up and good to go in no time. Great thing about where you're at is that you can look at pretty much every horizon except east, because of the mountains of course, and that's good because there aren't any satellites out there anyway. I'm hooking this up low so that you can keep it clean as well."

Joanie had to ask: "You have to keep it clean?"

"Oh, you know," he said, "snow and ice. Otherwise you'll be waiting to see that final touchdown or the last episode of Game of Thrones and it'll just go 'pop' and nothing."

Well, that made good sense to us. But then he paused

in his work and said, "You guys into winter sports? Hobbies? That sort of thing?"

We admitted to our activities, though none of them seemed very much like they had anything to do with winter per se.

He got serious then. "Get yourself a hobby. Really. Otherwise you'll just get drunk and shoot each other."

As October continued, so did the snow and the drop in temperature. The dogs loved the snow, at least that first day. After that, they were miserable. We got that way too pretty quickly. Each day we'd take the dogs around the property for a "run" so they could exercise. I'm certain the neighbors, if they could see us through the falling snow, thought we were lunatics. Here were two figures, dressed as Inuits, making a slow march around a five-acre square, and then doing it again, while gale winds blew snow in ever-increasing drifts, and black figures, which might have been dogs, periodically surfaced and then disappeared again.

By the middle of December, for something to do, we'd drive down to the Safeway and wander up and down the aisles, just to see if they'd gotten in anything new. We'd stand around talking to Jill and Amy in the empty store and talk about nothing. This was bad. You couldn't go outside, because the sub-zero temperatures simply froze your nostrils shut and you couldn't breathe, and thus to be outside for any amount of time would either kill you or require an hour or so of layering on clothing. One day, when I thought I'd run into town to get supplies, and it was 40-below, I hopped onto Chuck's vinyl seat and it shattered like a potato chip. I'm not making that up.

Sitting in front of the fireplace, we again reflected on the fact that we really didn't have much in the way of winter hobbies. We needed one. If we didn't find something to do, there was no way we'd make it through five more months of winter. It was about here that we lapsed into despair, and everything looked pretty bleak, and then we discovered Scrabble.

Joanie had bought the Scrabble board years ago at a yard sale, and it had traveled with us. She discovered it at the bottom of a closet and pulled it out and said we should give it a try. Strangely, neither one of us had ever played that game in our entire lives. Our first forays were mostly about just figuring out the rules, since none came with the board and tiles. We simply settled on some when unusual situations arose, and that was that.

We'd congratulate one another on having made "nice" words: "Oooo, 'cougar' is a good one," or commiserate when a good word couldn't be found, "All I have is 'AI' like in 'artificial intelligence'. Is that okay?" That's how it started.

Then, one game early on, one of us just got smoked on the scoring.

"How the hell did you get 412 points and I only got 172, even though I had both 'organelle' and 'anthracite'?"

After that, it got ugly. Strategy ensued. No way would you play across that triple-word score if it meant the enemy could play on it too. You started to come up with words that you were sure couldn't be extended in order to thwart *your* opponent from piggy-backing on your hard-earned word. If you played "cosmo", the dirty, lousy, son-of-a-gun opponent might make "cosmology" out of it for an even bigger score, and that wouldn't do. Some nights we forgot to eat until late.

Some nights we said, "Open another bottle of wine and let's play best two out of three."

Some nights ended in accusations and recrimination: "You only won because you put an 'er' on the end of 'fish'. Pretty lame."

And some mornings had to begin with an apology. "I'm sorry I played on your triple-word score just so I could get rid of my ten-point 'z' there at the end. That was pretty crappy of me."

We needed a different pastime. Something. It was only December. We had five full months of winter to go.

DAYS AND NIGHTS

I never really understood fear very well, even though I am quite old enough to understand caution and fore-thought and the consequences of not relying on these things. Maybe it was never fear, however, but rather terror, that unexpected thing that can never be a part of your planning and routine. I can vaguely remember that Joanie wanted to get me out of the house for some reason that next day and so we went into town, and Joanie drove and I was inexplicably frightened the entire time we were moving and I gripped the door handle hard and hoped that Joanie couldn't see. We parked and walked into a store and Joanie wanted something there and someone laughed loudly and I grabbed Joanie and said I needed to get back outside where it was safe. We stopped at a restaurant and ordered, and the next table over a group of women talked relent-lessly about the events of the day before, and I told Joanie I wanted to go outside for a while. When I came back she had gotten us another table and we sat and ate I think.

CHAPTER SEVENTEEN:

ICE FISHING

B Y THE END of November Joanie and I started to go online searching for winter hobbies, sports, pastimes, anything. We knew perfectly well we'd never survive the remainder of winter with Scrabble. We looked at the calm and peaceful ("Crochet the winter away!"), and then the sort of dangerous things ("Snowboard the Rockies!"), and anything else that might seem possible. Joanie was all for the dangerous things. That's her all over. Myself, I couldn't see trying to survive winter with a broken leg to top it off. I played the Scared Card and got out of a couple of things anyway.

We swapped ideas, and none fully resonated, but at least we were having ideas this time. We decided it would definitely be an outdoor thing, if for no other reason than we could take the dogs with us. That's when I suggested ice fishing. And because Joanie didn't say, "That's insane!" that meant it was at least on the table, so we started to look into it.

We discovered that there were two basic forms of ice fishing: the freeze-to-death-while-being-miserable sort, and then the go-into-debt sort. We started investigating the latter option, because we figured it might pay off in the end if we both survived the winter with even just a modicum of sanity.

Apparently, as with most things, you can spend as much money on ice-fishing gear as you care to. I mean, what you mostly need are these little-bitty rods, a shelter of some sort, an auger, and a heat source. Joanie also discovered pads that you could lay down on the ice, and that sounded like a good idea for the dogs. So, that didn't seem so bad until we started looking at shelters online.

There were ones that looked like bad pup-tents, and then others in which you might have a wedding reception. We ended up sort of daydreaming about it, and decided that the upper-end ones looked pretty good, and they didn't look too very complicated to erect, which we both thought was an important feature when you're freezing.

"Look, this one even has a window," Joanie said.

So, we put everything together and looked at the total. Hmmm. Not as much as what I paid Wiley for Chuck, but pretty close. The next morning we went into town and stopped at our version of Bailey's Building and Loan.

Strangely, neither of us had ever had occasion to enter our local bank. We had always just maintained our previous out-of-state accounts, and any money we made just got direct-deposited there.

The bank was a nice Montana version of any business. There were pictures of horses and ranchers and trout flies on the walls. The potted plants were cacti. Everybody who worked there wore jeans and plaid shirts, and the male employees had string ties. It was nice.

A young lady I'd never before seen around town greeted us, and we told her we were interested in a "small" loan. She smiled and said that the manager always handled that, excused herself to see if the manager was available, and then came back and led us to an office. Inside was Delmer!

This struck both of us as really odd in a very bad way. I mean, this is your neighbor, and telling your neighbor you need money is hard enough, but explaining what you want the money for might end up in total neighborhood ostracizing.

"Hi Delmer," we both said simultaneously, and then looked at each other.

"I'm sorry we haven't yet been by to say 'hello', but I guess we've been busy settling in. Really like your property," I added, kind of lamely. Delmer smiled and we shook hands and sat down.

"How were the gophers this year?" Joanie asked.

Delmer's business-smile faded a bit then. "Kind of thin, actually. I sort of miss shooting them."

"Oh, but that's good you're getting on top of it," Joanie said with her best smile. "Nothing like a gopher-free neighborhood. Good for everything. And you've sure done your part."

Delmer's smile returned. "Yes, I do my part. It is a good thing, I'll admit. Glad to hear you say so." And then he turned to me. "Al, I've been enjoying your work with The Paper. It is really good to hear about all your neighbors and what they're up to."

"Oh, thanks very much. It's been a real treat to meet people."

"Well," Delmer said, warming up a bit, "I don't know

what you'd think of it, it's just a little pastime of mine, but I've been collecting barbed wire now for over thirty years."

"Really?!" I said. "Wow! I would love to come take a look. I'm sure I could write up a piece on that. Everybody loves barbed wire."

"Yes, I think so too," said Delmer, "except I think the appreciation for its history and intricacies has been lost in these hectic times."

"Oh, I couldn't agree more about that," Joanie added. "Al, it's probably important that you see his collection right away."

"I think you're right, sweetheart."

This seemed to be going okay so far. On the wall I noticed a young man's photo, and he was dressed as a Marine.

"Is that your son, Delmer?" I asked. "He looks like a brave young man."

Delmer swiveled in his chair a looked for a minute. "Yes, that's Scott. We lost him in Iraq. He was very brave."

My mouth opened and I couldn't think what to say, and Joanie shot me a sour look and said, "That's awful. We're so sorry for your loss."

Well, the pleasantries seemed to have ended, and so now it was down to business.

"So," Delmer asked, "about how much were you wanting?" We told him.

"Okay," he said. "Home improvement or something?"

"Ice fishing," I said.

"Ice fishing?" Delmer said, a bit surprised.

"Yes," Joanie added. "It's so we don't murder each other over the next six months."

"Ah," Delmer said.

We got the loan.

.   .   .   .   .

We spent the month of December watching television series that we got through the mail. We were waiting for the ice to get thick enough so that it was safe to go fishing. We watched the entirety of *ER* in a couple of weeks, and then moved on to some others. We practiced putting up the shelter in the front room on three separate occasions, being sure there might not be something that could go wrong. We sat inside it and pretended we were fishing. We were having a good time not-yet-freezing-our-butts-off.

There was no way we could test out the ice auger, of course. We'd gotten a gas-powered one which struck me as a sort of dangerous weed-whacker kind of thing, and bought that locally. We inquired at the Coastal how to operate it, and the fellow took us out back with it after we'd purchased one in order to demonstrate how it worked.

"You really want to be careful using these things, because if you don't, then it'll get all Western on you in no time and then you're coming back in here with one leg and asking for a refund."

We paid close attention. Joanie took notes.

We took the heater out onto the porch and fired it up, and it felt pretty good, even though we were sitting in snow. We got pretty excited about all this.

On January fifteenth, the nearest lake was proclaimed to be ready for ice fishing. We loaded up Chuck in the garage, made food for ourselves and the dogs, got bait from the Coastal, and we were ready.

We played an amicable game of Scrabble, and then went to bed.

The next morning we got up kind of early, though by all accounts there was no reason for doing so for this sort of fishing, and we headed out with Grip and Tan and Finn all crammed inside in what passed for a back seat in Chuck's extended cab. It was snowing like crazy. Nevertheless, we were confident. We had prepared and felt like we pretty much knew what we were doing.

When we got to the lake, it looked like almost everyone who was fishing was bunched up on a certain stretch of ice, except for one or two anchorites who were much further off. I assumed that this was simply Montana need for elbow room, rather than that they knew something more about where the fish were than anyone else. Naturally, we went down to the general area where the other dozen shelters were set up, but not so close as to make anyone feel we were getting in their space.

We had a sled and all of our gear on it, and we hauled it on out onto the ice. I told Joanie that next time, we should harness the dogs to the sled and have them pull it out. They're big dogs, and I could sort of see Joanie mulling it over.

We got to a certain spot and Joanie said, "Here?" and I said, "Looks as good as any other desolate piece of ice," and so we started to get set up.

We were pretty much experts now after practicing, but it still took a while because it was so cold. I augered the holes, we slid the shelter over and I staked it down, Joanie laid down mats for the dogs and our feet, we fired up the heater and started fishing. It was great.

We didn't catch anything for a while, but then Joanie had a bite and then hauled in a real nice rainbow. The dogs went bonkers, barking and circling around while she reeled it in. It only added to the excitement. We stuck it in the snow outside like a fish-sickle. I caught one a bit later, not as nice as Joanie's, but hey, it was fishing. We had hot coffee and sandwiches and the dogs had a bit of a snack with us and then laid down to nap. Joanie smiled at some point, kicking back a bit in her fold-up chair.

"I could get to like this," she said.

"Me too. I know it's not as dangerous as you usually like, but we could always fall through the ice."

And that's about when the wind got up and a ripple went across our shelter. We heard shouting from outside, and the dogs had their fur up.

We peeked out our little plastic window and there, shooting across the ice, was somebody's shelter, with two people in hot pursuit, and they were followed, more slowly, by five or six others. By "hot pursuit" I mean they were trudging on ice as quickly as frozen bodies might take them, which meant the shelter was way in the lead in this race. You need to realize this lake is about a mile and a half long, and if that wind kept up, they'd be going after it for a couple of hours, and it was still snowing pretty good, off and on.

Joanie said some Anglo-Saxon right then, and I was shocked. I had no idea she'd been studying dead languages. What is it about spouses and their secrets anyway?

Then, she took action.

"Open the door! Open the door!"

And I did, as any husband would when his wife is shouting at him to do something, though I had no idea why she wanted to go outside.

"Grip! Finn! Tan! Let's go!" and out they all went.

Right about then the shelter went past us, maybe twenty yards off, and moving way too fast to catch.

Joanie, pack leader, sent up the command: "Get it!" she yelled. "Get it get it get it!"

And the dogs took off, Grip in the lead and Tan and Finn quick behind. Grip got there first, he always does, and barked his head off at the shelter as he chased it. The other two followed suit, harrying the shelter to make it stop.

"GET it!" Joanie shouted.

The dogs ran and circled, but this was new for them: "Uh, Mom wants us to actually, you know, like take it down? Hmmm. That's different. We never get to do that. Usually we just have to make something behave."

Tan got the idea first, and grabbed a tether that was trailing along the ice. She held on, and put her back legs down, and was just a skater along with the shelter. Grip, not to be outdone, grabbed a corner of the shelter in his teeth and dug in. Finn, always the gentle soul, finally decided to help and jumped on top of the shelter, effectively squashing it.

We were quite a ways off now but Joanie was shouting "Hold! Hold!" and then the three of them laid down on the shelter and waited. We got there as soon as we could, and the wind was really whipping now, but the dogs stayed put and we managed to catch up. In a few more minutes, the two probably former occupants caught up with us. They were both dressed like us, that is, wrapped in a death-shroud of outer-wear, and panting pretty hard. One fellow looked at me for a second and then turned to Joanie.

"Those are damn good dogs."

"Thanks," she said.

"They run a bit faster than I can," the guy said.

"They're better on dry ground," Joanie said with a grin. "Come on. Let's get this back to our place and you can hang out with us for a bit and get warmed up."

The dogs were a bit unhappy about having to give up their first kill, but we got the shelter broken down and wrapped up and hauled it back to "our place".

When we were all back in our shelter, the dogs had gotten some extra food Joanie had stashed for them, and everybody had something to sit on, and the dogs settled back down for a quick nap, and one fellow stretched his legs out around the new hole we dug for him and the other guy. Then Joanie got up, went to her duffel bag, and pulled out a bottle of wine.

"Already chilled," she said, and everyone had a plastic cup with some.

The first fellow looked up and said to me, "This is good, isn't it?" I couldn't disagree.

Later that day, later than we thought we'd get home, everybody had a nice meal, the dogs got rewarded with bones to chew later on, and we sat in front of the fireplace.

"That was really, really good today," Joanie said. "I think we're going to make this winter just fine."

I agreed, and suggested small comforts that might go with us next time, and Joanie added some too. We agreed that we'd go again the following week.

DAYS AND NIGHTS

I have been lost and helpless in the past, and am not ashamed to admit it. But not like this. Not knowing if I want to keep living or not. Not knowing if this is somehow worth enduring or not. Unable to think. Unable to believe. Unable to love or laugh. I have heard it said that when the body undergoes severe trauma that it sometimes just shuts down in some way so as to protect itself. I wonder if that is what has happened to me. I don't see. I no longer feel. It's as if that's safest somehow, but I am losing Joanie and self-preservation is coming at a price I cannot afford to pay.

CHAPTER EIGHTEEN:
LOST IN THE SNOW

THE WAY I SEE IT, there are pretty much only three ways the human mind ever tries to interpret cause and effect. It's always the same old question, "Why in the world did this just happen to me?", and then you've got your three basic mindsets that attempt to make sense of the universe. Let me give you an example.

Long ago, when Joanie and I lived in Washington, there was a particular high-mountain lake way up in the North Cascades that we wanted to get to. So, one summer we headed out there, and the final road that you take is a long, long way from civilization of any sort, and that's why we wanted to go. So, on the way out, about halfway up a rather treacherous road, we had a flat tire on my Jeep. Naturally, I pulled off the spare and put it on, but then we had to decide whether we should go on or not, without a spare. We'd passed some very nice places on the way up, so we figured the better part of sanity was to try again at another time, and instead just enjoy one of the places we'd passed. Which we did. Okay.

The next summer, we headed back, and you guessed it, the same thing happened again. Once again we were about halfway up the deer-track of a road before we had a flat tire, and I had just bought new, gigantic and expensive tires earlier that year. We did the same thing. We went back down the road and went someplace else, and still had a nice time. Okay, fine.

Then the third summer it happened again! And that's when I realized the usefulness of my education in dead languages, and I practiced it vociferously on that particular occasion. I put on the blasted *hundheppin* spare tire, I tightened the *draugrlaginn* lug nuts, and retracted the *Hweat! We gardena* jack, remembered some choice words from the *Magna Carta*, and back down the giant mountain we went, once again.

Fine, just fine. But of course it wasn't. So, really, you've only got a few choices to explain what's happening to you.

First, there's the Scientific Mind that wants to explain things to you, because it's very persuasive and is based on tried-and-true Scientific Method. You can largely trust it, and you want to go there first, because, well, you'd like your universe to have rational explanations.

The Scientific Mind says, "There is something in this road inherently capable of piercing large Jeep tires and if we only had sixteen more Jeep tires and several days we could run tests and discover what it is." Perfectly rational, as I say.

Second is the Spiritual Mind. In this attitude toward the universe you understand that the Supreme Being is in charge of absolutely everything and at all times, even flat tires. Here, God is right there, all the time, no matter what you're doing or where you are. This view of the universe is very appealing to me because it pretty much alleviates any need to think about things, because who could possibly understand the mind of God and there's no use wearing yourself out trying. So, this is pretty straightforward: "God definitely does not want Joanie and me going down that road. Period." Why? How should I know? I'm no theologian.

Lastly, there is the Fateful Mind, which would like you to understand some sort of causality in the universe but just doesn't want to get too specific about it. This one just says, "It's bad luck to go down that road," or maybe even, "That road is cursed." That kind of thing.

I'm kind of fond of this one too because it's a sort of one-size-fits-all explanation that applies to flat tires and jars of bad olives of a brand you keep accidentally buying and unpredictable slippery roads and bullets that *don't* hit you while your neighbor is shooting gophers and pretty much anything else.

The issue for me is that I'm ready to embrace all of these attitudes on any given occasion, and there have been times when I've turned them over in my head sequentially and even simultaneously. Yes, you can do that if you really work at it. Anyway, some days just seem to be cursed.

·　　·　　·　　·　　·

Later that January Joanie and I headed out to go ice fishing on the lake. We'd checked the forecast, because not to have done so would have been crazy in the extreme, and yes, the weather was supposed to turn nasty that night, but in the meantime it was going to be a gloriously sunny, though screaming cold day.

We set out that morning, as usual, with all our stuff and the dogs as well. We had a good day on the lake, and I don't recall if we caught anything or not, but because it was January and we weren't stuck inside I'm almost certain it was a good day on the lake. The reason I can't really remember is that I think I sort of stuck that part of the day away in my head somewhere, which is the place I put things that I no longer feel are relevant in some way. Some day I'm going to get in there and then try to get on *Jeopardy* as soon as I can.

By mid-afternoon we figured we'd better get packed up because later the weather was going to get bad and of course it gets dark early this time of year and in the mountains on top of that, and we needed to stop in at the Safeway on the way home.

The sky had clouded over by the time we had packed up, and a few snowflakes were beginning to fall.

"Good timing," Joanie said as Chuck got us back up on the road.

I agreed, and on we went. It's about here that I should confess that I'm one of those people who is often thinking about getting something important done, but then never seems to get around to actually doing it. I mean, I want to do these things, and I know they're important to get done, like that colonoscopy I'm really overdue for, but I don't know. They just somehow don't get accomplished. Maybe it's that whole curse thing.

So, the thing is, pretty much as soon as we'd arrived in Montana people began to tell us how important it was to always have emergency supplies in your vehicle: matches, candles, a blanket and flashlight, water, things like that. Because, if you didn't, one day you'd wish you had done so when your life depended on it.

And yes, I took that to heart, and thought about how I'd make a wooden box with a lid on it and bolt it down in Chuck's bed and fill it with all those important things. I really thought about doing just that. I really did.

Joanie and I hadn't gone too far when the snow started coming down harder than we'd ever seen before. Even though we were still miles and miles from home, we weren't particularly alarmed by this.

"So much for the forecast saying this was coming in tonight," I said.

"Maybe they got the time zone mixed up," Joanie joked.

But, about half an hour later it wasn't funny anymore. It was starting to get dark and Chuck's headlights couldn't let us see very far through absolute walls of snow coming down. Chuck was taking it slow, and we'd all been down this road plenty of times before, but you just couldn't really tell where the road was any longer. At times we plowed through drifts and a pang went through you like an electric charge and you couldn't help but think, "Oh no. Did we just go off the road?" But we hadn't, and kept going.

"I think this is where the curve going north should be," Joanie said.

"You sure?"

We slowed to a stop. "I can't see anything and straight ahead has been working so far."

"Not if there's a curve going north," Joanie said in her most reasonably terrified voice.

"Okay. Let me walk up the road a bit and see what things look like."

"Be careful," Joanie said needlessly.

I got the flashlight, opened the door to gale-force winds, put my head down and started walking up what could only be the road. I went on for quite a while, all the time playing the flashlight around, and as near as I could tell the road went straight on from here. I made it back to Chuck, got in, and we slowly headed onward. I think it was maybe ten minutes later when we reached the curve in the road, which of course we couldn't see, and went over the side and down into the gully.

We were maybe only six feet down, but it could just as easily have been fifty. There was no way we were going to get Chuck back up onto the road. That didn't stop us from trying, however. Joanie got out, and at this the dogs became very grim because they couldn't see her very well, and they always needed to know where she was. Always. I rolled down the window so I could hear Joanie giving me directions, and once the dogs could hear her, then they started going bonkers, wanting to get to her because to them she was obviously in distress.

I rocked Chuck back and forth as best as I could, and managed somehow to get him pointed back at the road, but there was no way he was going to get up the slope. There was way too much snow. We kept trying for about an hour, and then it was full dark and we figured we'd better save the gas until we could see better. Unfortunately, that was likely going to be about twelve hours from now.

Once Joanie got back in and the dogs had settled a bit, she said the words I was dreading to hear.

"What now?"

And I don't know what was the matter with me because in the past I'd have had either three more things I'd have wanted to try, or at least have been able to say, "No worries. We'll be fine," and I had neither. And there had in fact been times like this in the past for us, and I had in fact said those words or done those things. And now it was like I could almost feel something bleeding out of me onto the floorboards and then trickling out into the blizzard.

It was dark. All around us. I stared out the window. I was cursed. That's what it was. I was simply cursed and this is what you got. And you just dragged un-cursed people like Joanie down with you because they were foolish enough to be with you when the curse kicked in.

"Al?" Joanie said. "What do you think we should do?"

I didn't answer. I picked up the flashlight and turned it on and played it out the windshield. I had no idea what was going on. I thought I'd seen something, which of course was totally crazy, because the only thing you could see was the flashlight beam illuminating a steady, sideways blast of snow that was drifting all around us.

And then...no, there was no rescue or something like that, but it seemed as if my mind just kind of went sideways somehow, and I switched the light off and stretched a bit and said, "Guess we'd better put up the shelter, get the dogs fed, and get ourselves to bed."

I know that last sentence sounded like a perfectly normal conclusion, but not for me. Not now. It took us almost two hours to get the shelter set up. We dug out a drift with a piece of cardboard box, and Joanie and I

went back and forth trying to get the shelter put together in the dark (which we discovered was a night-
mare), and then we got it put together at last and then
had to dig the drift out again, and we finally got the
mats in, but then the heater wouldn't light and we tried
it again and again and finally! it lit.

Then we fed the dogs what food there was and left
ourselves a sandwich to split, and we all got inside
with all the gear that looked like it might be either
warm or useful and finally sat down, maybe ten o'clock
now, exhausted. The dogs piled up, and Joanie and I
had our sandwich and some tepid coffee from the
thermos. We got down on the mats then, curled up,
and had a three-dog night.

"Cold," I said.

"Uh-huh," Joanie said. And then I guess we fell asleep.

I will spare you some suspense by saying that I did
not write this down at the time and place the manu-
script in Chuck's glove box so that it might be a record
of why our bodies were found there in the spring. Even
so, rescuing ourselves wasn't easy, but we were determined to do it.

In the morning, we discovered that we were completely covered in a drift, and we had a hard time just
getting the door of the shelter unzipped because of all
the snow pressing against it. It took us half an hour to
scoop out a tunnel in the drift (sideways and then up
when we reached the side of the ditch), and then another hour to clear off the shelter. We didn't break it
down, just in case.

After that, we took a while to rest and let the dogs do
what they needed to do, and we sat and looked around,

trying to come up with a plan. The dogs weren't happy about no breakfast, and neither were we.

Joanie had a plan, however, and we got going at it as fast as we could. First, we dug out Chuck as best we could, and as we had no snow shovel, we did this with anything we had: a piece of bark from a log, the sheet of cardboard from our gear box, our hands, feet, anything. We dug and dug and dug. By noon, we had cleared a path up the slope of the ditch, which wasn't as steep as we'd thought, and about ten feet behind him so we could get a running start.

We found a tiny little cedar tree and defoliated it I'm sorry to say, and laid out every branch and twig and frond in front of and behind our escape route. And then we looked at one another, and we had no more energy left, and so it was time to give it a shot.

Joanie and the dogs got in the bed as best they could, because it was filled with snow, but we figured more weight over the back tires couldn't hurt. And then Chuck got going and he eased back and I could tell he really wanted to do this, and I got him back as far as we could possibly go, and then Chuck decided it was time and off we all went!

There was a lot of snow flying as Chuck smashed into the front of the ditch and started to claw his way up and Joanie was shouting "C'mon Chuck! C'mon Chuck!" and we swerved and Chuck dug in as best he could and we slid back a bit and Chuck wasn't done yet and up, slowly up we went and then...we were on level ground and on the road again!

We danced around a bit after that and hugged each other and slapped Chuck at least a dozen times shouting "Good ol' Chuck! Good ol' Chuck!" and then we eventually wound down after that, adrenaline gone, hungry, tired, looked back at the shelter that had to get broken down and the snow that had to be cleared from the bed to get it in, and we got started.

By mid-afternoon we made our way back, slowly, here and there plowing through a drift, but the road had been wind-swept enough that it was pretty easy going. We were so tired, we didn't talk much now, and I was on auto-pilot driving. I like simple tasks. Mowing. Pounding nails. Driving. You just don't have to think so very much and it's comfortable, comforting. You're just living and going on and everything is okay for now.

And yet, there I was, thinking, "Why in the world did that just happen to me? I mean us. I mean me and Joanie. I mean me and Joanie and the dogs?" And the best I could figure out was that the Spiritual Mind spoke to me and reassured me that Joanie was special and had purpose in life, and thanks for your assistance in getting her back home, but *I'D* have figured out something without you. So, we got home safely, and said a lot about weather forecasts.

DAYS AND NIGHTS

Somewhere during this time I was trying to remember something, and I could just sort of see it at the edge of my mind if you know what I mean, but I just couldn't pin it down. This went on for several days, and there was this unpleasant nagging feeling, something I wanted to recall, but I just couldn't, I just couldn't. It bothered me. At some point I started to wonder if I was merely wanting to remember myself just a little bit, but I had put all that away in the box, and so that might have been it. If so, then I was comfortable with that. No worries.

SECOND SUMMER

CHAPTER NINETEEN:

HOLLIS IN SPRINGTIME

O N JUNE FIRST, after four days during which we went from sub-zero to plus 40, to 65 (which we came to understand was "spring"), summer began again. When it came, it was as if you had somehow, miraculously pulled yourself from quicksand and found yourself breathing hard, looking back at the hole and thinking, exultantly, "That's amazing! I made it! I'm alive and I thought I was dead! Woo hoo!" When you met people again you wanted to hug them as if they, too, had somehow survived a nuclear holocaust: "Hey! Look at you! You're like alive and everything! Nice work!"

It came so quickly that I hadn't even messed around with my fishing gear in preparation to go again. When I finally got everything ready, I told Joanie that I thought I'd go out the next morning, and so Chuck and I drove into town to the fly shop which had just re-opened. I spent an hour there, spending all my money while Daffyd showed me all his new stock:

"And over here," and I can't reproduce his Scottish accent, or I would and make you understand why I'm buying a pound of flies at $2 apiece, "we have the new Salmon Flies for this year's hatch. You will notice that each one has been wrapped with spider silk, extracted on the International Space Station, and that the hooks are plated with 12 karat gold. This ensures the best attraction and retention of the fish."

Or something like that. It's hard to tell when he's selling you something.

I looked up at him. "I just survived eight months of winter, Daffyd, and I live here."

"Oh. Right. Tied in Indonesia, though a really nice wrap. Good work. You won't need them until next month, though. The hatch doesn't come on until at least July second."

Upon exiting the shop after having spent most of my monthly budget, I saw Hollis across the street. He was just standing there, with his hands in his pockets, seemingly staring straight at me. In case he was, I lifted a hand in recognition. I honestly hadn't seen or spoken to him since I wrote that first column, and so I wasn't sure how this might go. He looked at me, and that was it. I don't know why, but right then I thought I'd just go over and say hello.

I was just about to step off the curb and head across the street when a voice said, "Al. Don't do it," and there was Walter.

He had a look on his face that was half dare-me and half I'm-so-sorry-you-are-a-malcontent-and-a-ne'er-do-well. I looked at him, and then at Hollis.

Hollis was turning to walk away, and I turned to Walter and said, for no reason whatsoever, "It's Hollis. He needs me," and I strolled across the street.

I got about halfway across when I just about got plowed down by some folks loaded down with camping gear and hauling a boat and had to jump out of the way. Walter had a conniption, of course, and ran into the street and turned me around by the shoulder and was yelling he'd write me up, and then it occurred to him to go after the drivers and give them a dressing-down and so he went back to his truck, looking over his shoulder, "I'll deal with you later!"

Meanwhile, Hollis stood on the opposite side of the street looking at me, and I don't know. It's possible he was laughing, hard to say. I finally managed to get to the other side of the street without being killed and said, "Hey."

Hollis looked at me a bit and said, "I thought you were trying to avoid trauma."

I just ignored that. That wasn't what I came for.

"Do you fish?" I said.

He looked at me a minute, maybe longer, I can never tell because I can't look straight up like that for long and so ended up looking at his chest.

"Fish? You mean like the transients?"

"Yes, fly-fishing. Like that. I love it. Always have."

Hollis seemed to weigh this in some way, and I don't know what was being weighed, but it took him a bit.

"No," he said, "never have."

"I need you to come with me tomorrow. It's, uh, well... I just know that you can help me out."

There was just the returning stare then, the one I had come to know meant some sort of door had just been shut.

"I don't fish," he said.

Then I got mad. I can't explain this. I had no idea what was wrong with me, but I was just angry, and I don't do angry. And it must have shown, I guess, because all I did was turn away and make two steps before a huge hand clamped down on my shoulder, which just as easily turned me around in mid-stride.

"Where and when?"

I looked up at him again, still kind of mad.

"I'll pick you up. Dark o'clock. Where do you live?"

He looked away, then returned his attention.

"Meet you at the Safeway."

. . . . .

It was dark when I pulled into the Safeway lot, and I didn't expect to find Hollis already there, but there was his black truck and so I pulled up alongside. I got out and came around to his driver's side, and there was Hollis, but asleep, with a flannel blanket over him and a pillow behind his head.

I didn't know what to make of this, but I knew for sure that I wasn't going to bang on the window. I'm not stupid.

I walked back to Chuck, opened the passenger door and said, "I hope this doesn't hurt, but I'm going to close the door pretty hard, okay?"

I slammed the door and then spent a minute or two looking in the back bed as if perhaps I thought there might actually be something in it.

When I looked up, Hollis was standing there, same old Hollis. We got inside Chuck and then headed out. I handed Hollis the thermos, and he poured coffee. I handed him a sandwich Joanie had made for us and he went ahead and ate that with his coffee.

"I got no gear," he said.

"You're covered," was all I had, and we drove in the dark.

I didn't have a spare set of waders that would fit Hollis, so I chose a place where you wouldn't have to wade unless you just absolutely had to. I stopped Chuck on a dirt road and we got out and I said goodbye to Chuck and handed Hollis a rod and a vest. He put the vest on, but it wouldn't close around his chest. I told him that was no problem. I shouldered a day pack and we walked on in.

This place was maybe two miles from where I wanted to be, and I figured Hollis was okay with that. We walked in the dark, under the moon, with the axis of the Milky Way as our guide. At some point, lost in my thoughts, I just stopped and looked up, for about a minute or so, and then just walked on. No comment from behind.

By the time we reached the river, it was just light enough to see. I strung Hollis's rod, and tied on a likely fly.

Hollis said, "What the hell is that?" looking at the fly.

"It's a tiny bit of nothing," I said. "It's what the foolish things want. And the rod? It's just a stick. It has line on it, and the line is what you want to cast."

I stood there a second and stripped some line out and then made a quick cast. "That's it. You just aim upstream and let the fly drift downstream. That's all there is."

Hollis looked dubious, but was willing to try it. I stood back (I mean well out of the way), and Hollis gave it a go. His first attempt caught his pant leg, and I was glad it wasn't his ear, and so I showed him again about holding his elbow in a bit, and then just gently moving that rod back and forth. I think maybe the deal was sort of hauling in Hollis's big frame. He wanted to punish the water with his line at first, I think. Once he got the hang of this, I was pretty sure he could cast to Idaho.

He gave it another go, easier this time, and a bit more attentive to where the line was headed in his back cast, once just kind of flinching out of the way, and I had to mentally smile at the idea of Hollis flinching out of the way of anything. He had two-three back casts, and then laid the fly down in the center of the stream, just as pretty as you please.

"Now what?"

"Keep an eye on your fly, because in ten seconds you're going to have a fish."

He turned and looked at me, and I said, "Watch the fly! Pick up any slack line." Hollis stared at his fly. Nothing.

"Do it again," I said, and he did.

And this time he just sort of instinctively picked up the line without any instruction,

and with no false casts, and laid it back out in the river again.

"This is the stupidest thing ever. No wonder the tourists are fools."

And that's when the fish hit, and Hollis instinctively raised up his rod, and it was hooked.

Okay. So Hollis had a good one on, I mean it looked like a real good one, and he had the rod up like he should and I was standing next to him, and I was pretty excited but pretended not to be.

"Good angle of the rod there, Hollis," I said, because I could see this sort of grim expression on his face which wasn't at all the grim expression I'm used to seeing.

"Keep the pressure on the line so he can't shake the hook, but if he wants to run a bit it's okay to give him a bit of slack."

I don't know if Hollis was listening or not. He was staring at the water, but seemed to be playing the fish well.

I said, "If he jumps, then lift up and..." and that's when the trout made its first jump and holy moley he really did have a good one on. The hook stayed in and the fight continued. This actually went on for maybe two or three minutes, which is really a long time for even a good-sized fish to fight you, but Hollis chose his battles well, I guess. Eventually, he reeled and reeled and the fish came to the bank, a couple of feet below us, and it was a real beauty.

"Do you want to keep it?" I asked. "Or should I release it?" Hollis looked down at the fish for just a second.

"Hell yes I'm keeping it."

So I got down in the water up to my waist and unhooked the fish and climbed back up with it.

"That's a really nice fish," I said.

"Best one I ever caught," Hollis said. And then, "Only one I ever caught. So that's the best, right? First things are always the best, right? I mean, except for getting shot or something."

I had to agree, all the way around.

Hollis caught three more fish and I caught two. I'm not sure if it was solidarity or not, because I was already soaking wet, but he asked me at some point where the best spots would be and I just pointed at a spot on the river and I said, "That big boulder there out at midway. Good holding water behind it. But I can't cast that far."

"You're already wet," he said, stating the obvious.

And then he went in, getting as close to the boulder as he could without getting swept away, and I had a pang of jealousy then, I'll admit it, and he cast away...I think maybe a lot of things.

Standing there, in the middle of the river, I looked down at Hollis downstream and a thought entered my head that I really didn't want in my conscious thoughts at all, but I guess it had been there for a while. It was not a thought that could be accurately articulated, but in retrospect it probably went something like this: I think I just met someone who's more broken than my-self, and maybe if I focus on him, then I can forget about how broken I am.

Yes. I am pretty messed up. Thank God for fishing.

We carried home four fish later that morning, and I said that I'd cook them up for him if he wanted to come by and have dinner. This took Hollis completely off guard. Whatever he was thinking on our walk back through the woods suddenly just went behind a wall.

"Dinner," he said, and it wasn't a question. It was just a statement about something that he hadn't considered.

"It'd be nice, Hollis. Stop by for just a bit, have a meal, say hi to Joanie. Bring a friend if you like."

And as soon as I said that last I wished I hadn't be-cause I had no idea on God's green earth who Hollis might possibly be "friends" with, but he seemed to re-lax a bit and said, "Okay." So, that was set.

DAYS AND NIGHTS

It seems odd to me to become aware that some of the most disturbing things that have happened to me during these past two years are things that actually didn't take place. One night Joanie and I sat outside in some lawn chairs and looked at the stars. There were so many, in huge arcs and brilliant clusters all across the night sky, you couldn't look everywhere all at once, even though you wanted to.

We laughed and exclaimed about shooting stars, and once a huge orange fireball careened against the atmosphere, breaking up, tumbling through the sky as The Maker's fireworks. We shouted and laughed. We sat in awe of it. Later, I was amazed to recall that I had forgotten about stars.

CHAPTER TWENTY:

HOLLIS AT DINNER

I JUST WANT to tell you about that dinner now instead of waiting for later when maybe I can't remember it. I'll confess right now that I forget things, even important things, and Joanie will corroborate that, I'm sure. But really, I'm not sure what happened to my brain not so long ago, but certain parts just seem to be cut off somehow, and I can only remember some things just by association. Unfortunately, when that happens, it's often the bad sorts of things. For those of you who know what I'm talking about, then you know.

It's just a trip to the Walmart and some stupid employee drops a big box of something and you just whip around and go pale and you're looking for the shooter. Or it's the horror movie you've seen three times before but this time you just have to get up and walk into the other room for a bit, just for a breather. Or it's the crash of the unexpected fender-bender nearby and you just want to run and run for no apparent reason. And, once again, I'm sorry about that and I'll tell you about dinner with Hollis. Before I forget.

Just to back up here a bit, merely to inform you that once I got home that morning and told Joanie that I'd invited Hollis for dinner, tonight, and that I apologized for making such a decision without her input, she'd said, quite simply, "Who? What, THAT guy? What were you thinking?! His name is what? You want me to say what? Like you're so full of conversation? And so what, we stare at our plates for two hours?"

I honestly didn't have an answer to those many questions, at least I think they were questions, and could only lamely say, "I thought it might be good. Hollis talked to me that one time."

So, right at six thirty as we'd arranged, and not a moment sooner or later, Hollis's black truck pulled up. I was sitting on the front porch having my second glass of wine, sort of steeling myself I guess, and Hollis extracted himself from the truck. He was dressed as he always was, and I led him inside and made introductions and then we headed out back and parked ourselves on the deck. Hollis had a beer and Joanie and I were having wine.

Hollis said, "This is nice," as he looked around, and we pointed out who the nearest neighbors were and we asked what he'd been up to and what he'd been doing recently, and he said he was kind of between jobs right now and so that line of conversation came to an end.

And there was some further attempt at small talk about the weather and gophers and how I can't keep the deer from eating the flowers, and that didn't go very far, and there was just some additional silence.

And Joanie was swirling the wine in her glass and looking at me, and we didn't ask about war and scars and then Joanie said, "Where are you from originally?" and Hollis said, "Kansas" and I said that I was from Nebraska and Hollis said, "I grew up hating the Huskers," and I laughed and said, "Almost everybody did back then," and then we were on safe ground.

Hollis and I talked football and basketball and he got another beer. We talked about the winters and summers back in the Great Plains and how it's almost as cold and hot there as it is here, and then we talked about fishing and Hollis admitted that it was better than he thought and then we got the grill going and got ready to eat and there were more beers and wine.

Dinner was very good and Hollis said that was the best fish he ever ate and we stretched out in the lawn chairs and hung out a while, and the dogs were napping in the grass, enjoying the cooler evening air. Finn wanted to lie very close to Hollis, and from time to time a large hand went down to rub his fur.

After a while Hollis said that he'd better go and so we made our goodbyes and he headed out and Joanie and I returned to the back yard.

"That went pretty well," Joanie said.

"Yeah. That was nice," I said.

We were stretched out in the lawn chairs again, just watching the sunset.

"Maybe you should see if he wants to go fishing again some time?"

"I meant to ask, but forgot to," I said.

I was kind of distracted right then, and I think I know why, because I sort of felt a thought coming to me again about Hollis and somehow helping him/me in some sort of way and it was a thought I don't really think I wanted to think about and I pushed it away and watched the sun go down.

DAYS AND NIGHTS

I feel a pressing need to tell you about when I went insane. I don't think I can keep this from you any longer. It was the end of summer the year of the shooting. Joanie and I had been out taking an extended drive to the coast, just sight-seeing and enjoying ourselves, and we had a very wonderful time. We stopped in at a small diner in a lovely little picturesque town and had a genuinely wonderful lunch, right on the water, and we both remarked about just how good it was, and we sat at a little table by ourselves looking out the window at the ocean, and we watched sea lions come and go just right next to our window, and it was simply perfect.

It was so very nice. I was so very happy at that moment. We paid the bill and left a very nice tip and hand-in-hand we walked back to where the car was parked and we thought things couldn't get any better than that so we decided to head on back, and I said I was kind of tired, I think, and Joanie said she was too, and so off we went, except I think back, trying to remember, and it started then.

I think I started to feel afraid about something, or maybe I simply felt a little ill. Yes, I think I was feeling ill for some reason I can't explain. I felt myself going out the window as we drove along and I couldn't pull myself back from whatever was making me fade, paler and paler, into something I had never been before, and I pulled over and asked if Joanie wouldn't mind driving because I said I felt a little tired but my mind was slipping out the window and I...thought...very...slowly...but... with...an unnamed fear...that...this is what...it must feel like when you're drugged...and you can just see and feel...your mind slipping...away, so far away. And it went away.

And when we pulled into our driveway I had no idea where we were and I shouted and screamed and cried and said:

"Joanie Joanie Joanie I've been drugged or something and I can't think and I'm going insane just like my mother did."

And I went into the house into the bedroom, my bedroom because there's no one with me any longer, and I slid down by the wall and put my back against it and I had no mind left. I knew I was going insane and had no power to stop it. I couldn't see my mind anywhere though I looked hard for it. It was utter helplessness.

Joanie got down on the floor with me I think, and I think I said the neighbors were watching us so stay away from the windows, and she stayed on the floor and I said I will kill them all if they keep looking at us and Joanie put her hand on my knee and I don't remember her expression because I couldn't see and she got up and I got up and I followed her to the kitchen and she poured a glass of water and I said you're trying to poison me! And I know you aren't but I'm going insane and I don't know why! I don't know why!

And I don't know what happened but I was undressed and in a bath tub and Joanie was on a chair looking at me and I asked why I was here and she asked me how I was doing and I said I was afraid of something and I said that I was going insane but couldn't stop it.

She got me out of the tub and I must have dried off and dressed into something because all I remember was I was on the couch and Joanie was at the other end and I was lying down and she was not and she said, "Do you want to go to bed?" and I said I was very afraid to do that, and she said then lie back and she would watch and I did and she did and sometime later I woke and saw her watching, waiting and I said can you take me to my bed I think I'll be okay and she looked at me and got up and took me by the hand and I laid down on the bed and looked at the ceiling, afraid that I would go mad again, but I didn't and I slept two hours until daylight.

I couldn't think what to say to Joanie the next day. I hugged her and looked down. I couldn't think what to say. She asked if I was better and I said I didn't know but I know I didn't know. And I think that's what happened.

CHAPTER TWENTY-ONE:

MIRACLES

THERE HAVE BEEN many times when I have felt completely lost. Those are the times when I have not been able to look inside myself for answers or strength or direction because there's been nothing there, just an emptiness which I have a difficult time describing. I couldn't think, I couldn't act, and I didn't have the will to do either.

These last sixteen months have felt as though I have been walking blindly, not seeing anything but a gray, cold fog. I wish I could describe it so that you could understand, but like so many things, I will have to tell you about something else.

I need to tell you that the world is alive with miracles and that you'd see them if you could only make yourself be still long enough to see, to really see. It is a state of mind that can escape you very easily, as it has me for many months, except that I have this advantage over you: I live with a miracle whose name is Joanie, and I wouldn't be talking to you right now if it wasn't for her.

I'm going to have to start a little ways back, though, at least to when we were still in Oregon. On that day, when reality came unmoored from all that I had ever known, I called Joanie and said as best I could:

"There's been a shooting. I'm okay. Many dead. They're still figuring it out. Please come and get me. They won't let anyone leave."

By the time she got there, what seemed such a very long time to be without her, the rumors had spread among us all, standing dazed, outside in a warm fall day: It was what I thought. The shooter was in my best friend's classroom, and he had been the first one shot, or so the rumors went. When I saw Joanie pull up, she got out and we hugged.

I said, "Larry's been shot," and we went home.

Throughout the evening the news poured in, and what I feared most became true.

We cried a lot from then on, and there was no relief. A week later, Joanie's best friend, one of our dogs, had to leave us. She was Joanie's best, and had been since she was a pup. We cried again, and again, and there was nothing we could do. I was so broken I couldn't even comfort Joanie the way I should have, but she righted herself, and we moved on as best we could. Joanie, even in her own grief, held me up all that time. I'm unsure what I ever did for her. I have a horrible feeling that whatever it might have been, it was certainly not enough.

· · · · ·

Joanie and I had survived our first winter in Montana and it was the end of May and so it was the four days of spring before summer began. Joanie and I met everyone once again at the Safeway and Coastal and Del's:

"Hey! Great to see you again! Look at you, all alive and everything! Hey, I see you're buying orange juice! That's just amazing!" and like that.

Joanie and I and Chuck are taking a ride. The dogs are with us. We have survived winter and the world is glorious once again. We see every leaf and blade of grass. We pull off and see a flower and Joanie gets the camera and takes a photo.

"A bird! Did you see the bird?!"

It's like that. It's like you just got out of the crypt and are amazed by everything.

Chuck is taking us along, and he is just as happy as can be. We are going slowly, wherever he wants to go, and for no reason whatsoever. I think Chuck likes this almost as much as fishing or carrying something, when he has a sense of purpose. I think he feels the same as we do, that it's good to just be alive and that it's time to simply enjoy the world once again.

Chuck is taking us all over the place. We go up and down mountain roads, we stop and everybody gets out for a few minutes while we look at green grass and fast-running streams, and the dogs are ecstatic that the discontent of winter appears to have gone away, at last. They roll in the grass, tongues hanging out, tasting and breathing in the new season.

So, as Chuck is taking us along some road that perhaps bisects some rancher's enormous segment of the state, Chuck slows and then comes to a stop because we have met an impasse. A very large flock of sheep are on the road, and don't appear to be going anywhere anytime soon.

Joanie and I get out to look at all the little lambs and Joanie takes pictures, and some of the sheep come up and bleat at us and we pet them and talk to them. Then they start crowding around a bit.

Grip sticks his head out Chuck's window and looks at them, smelling the air. The sheep are a bit nervous about this, and back away a bit, making Chuck an island in the road.

Joanie said, "This doesn't look right. Why aren't they behind a fence, or being herded where they're supposed to go?"

"Maybe the rancher is back a bit," I said, "bringing some more along behind. Let's wait and see." So we waited.

And then we waited some more, and before long it started to look like the rest of our day wasn't going to be going anywhere until all these darn sheep got out of the way, and I said so, and Joanie said, "No, I'm not having Chuck push them out of the way, think about the little lambs," and so we waited some more.

"Somebody has to be coming for them, right?" Joanie said after a while.

"You'd sure think so. That's a whole lot of livestock to just be wandering around wherever it pleases."

Joanie started to walk up the road a bit, and then that made the dogs nervous. As I mentioned, the dogs have a set mental distance that Joanie can get between herself and them before they get uncomfortable. If she crosses that invisible line, then they start howling. Finn started first, and then Tan and Grip joined in: a mournful wail of utter despair as Joanie stepped beyond the invisible line of their reckoning. And that cleared the road block in no time at all: 150 sheep, along with all the lambs, scampered down the road about a quarter mile.

When Joanie got back I said, "Well okay then, let's go."

"Something's not right," Joanie said, and we turned back and walked down the road with a cacophony of wails from Chuck coming behind her.

"Hush!" she said, and the moaning chorus stopped.

Maybe a hundred yards along we saw the breach in the fence on our left.

"Do you think you can fix that if I can get the sheep back in?" Joanie asked.

"What? Are you crazy? How are you going to get them in? There's hundreds of them!"

"Can you fix the fence?"

I looked again. "Yeah, maybe. You know, temporarily."

"Okay. Pull it open as wide as you can. Then go open up the truck door."

Okay. I'm a very bad writer and an even worse husband. I have never, in all of this, said anything meaningful about Joanie. I'm sorry. I don't know what it is with me anymore, and I find myself saying that a great deal, especially to Joanie. I don't know. Someday I hope to find out.

Anyway, I'd better tell you about Joanie and the dogs or else you won't believe me. So here's the thing: Joanie spent most of her adulthood, and probably even before that, before we knew each other even as teens, as a serious dog trainer. When we were still kids in Seattle, she was the head trainer at the biggest outfit on the West Coast. She was the Numero Uno Trouble-Shooter and Trainer. Yep.

Even when we went away on our twenty-year-long road trip, she still did professional training, along with her other pursuits, just to keep her hand in. You can look her up on the internet, and everyone knows her name. Anyway, she's like the real deal. Joanie can get any canine on the planet to do what she wants simply by talking to him or her. I'm not kidding about that. The Dog Whisperer? What an idiot that guy is. You should see Joanie go to work.

So, I went back to Chuck and the dogs and I watched intently. Joanie moved on down the road, and waded through the flock until she was on the other side.

"When they start running," she yelled, "let the guys out!"

Then she pulled out her Browning and fired a shot into the air. Oh? I didn't tell you Joanie was armed? I'll have to explain that later, because right then a huge flock of sheep was running straight toward me. I opened the door, and the Black Wolves appeared.

Now you might assume a certain level of chaos here, and there was at first. Even though the dogs thought the sheep were fairly interesting, they really only saw them as an obstacle to get through to get to Joanie as fast as they could. They split the flock right down the middle, between the fences on either side of the road, where the sheep huddled.

Joanie laughed, and I could hear her say, even over all the bleating sheep, "Get Dad! Get Dad!" and the dogs raced back to me. When they got there, I had them sit and wait. They were having so much fun it was hard to get them to do it.

Then, off in the distance, Joanie started yelling and waving her arms, and I understood then what was going on. I talked a bit to the dogs and they got in front of me, then, off to the right, and Joanie was shouting and the dogs were listening:

"Grip! Gogogogogo!"

And Grip pulled the sheep off the fence, and wher-ever he's going, Tan was going too. But I held on to Finn a bit, and he gave me a real look:

"So I don't get to go. It's why I love Mom more than you," that kind of thing. Whatever.

But then the sheep and all the lambs and all of God's green earth seemed to be headed toward me, and I ran to pull the fence open and shouted, "Get 'em, Finn!" and I think maybe he forgave me then, just a little bit, and I yelled, "Right! Right!" and he did! And holy smokes! The sheep funneled right into the pasture with Joanie and Grip and Tan coming along behind.

Joanie herded three lambs in herself, and we got the fence closed up as best we could. And no one ever saw it, except me. Later, Joanie said that it was no big deal, just good training is all. I knew differently, because the mist had temporarily cleared for me. It was a miracle, and I got to see it.

DAYS AND NIGHTS

Once, a long time ago, Joanie and I went on a long backpack trip. Our chosen route through the Olympics meant we had to scale a 7000-foot pass over eight days or else turn back. We had a car waiting on the other end. It was a three-day trip up, and then down the pass for another five days to get out. We had all our gear and food and emergency supplies for ten days, and we were heavy-laden. The first day out, I encour-aged because it was hard going. The second day out, I thought we should turn back, but Joanie said "no", and on we went. The third day out, we looked up at the pass ahead to the other side and there was new snow and we couldn't tell how much, and Joanie said, "Let's turn around, because that's wise," and I said, "That's what we came for, right?" and we went on.

We came to the pass, slowly and very tired, and there was a lot of snow and I said, "I was stupid, we should have turned around."

And Joanie said, "Let's go on, because that's what we came for, right?"

And we did. And we got to the other side and down we went and I don't know if you know what it feels like going downhill with a heavy pack, but it's just as hard as going uphill.

And so we trudged on, and swapped day to day, urging each other on. There was a day when Joanie couldn't make it. I said, "I'll carry your pack." On another day, I was hurt and Joanie took things from my pack and said, "I'll tie that to my back."

We went on. We got to the end, and set down our packs, and looked back up the mountain pass, magnificent and covered in new snow: "That was great, wasn't it?"

And that's what marriage is like, in case you didn't know.

CHAPTER TWENTY-TWO:

THE BROKEN ROAD

I HAD INTRODUCED CHUCK so many times now, without even thinking about it any longer, that people would greet us and say, "Hi Al. Hi Chuck. How you doing?" And I didn't know if that last was directed at both of us or not. I kind of think so.

I had gotten to rely on Chuck to get me anywhere I needed to go, and he proved to be pretty reliable as well. He took me up and down mountain roads in the summers, and plowed through drifts in the winters. Sometimes I thought I might spiff him up just a bit, like replacing the bent antenna or fixing the passenger side window so that you didn't need two hands to roll it up and down, but I never did. I thought he was just fine the way he was.

One morning early I decided to fish a new place on a stretch of a river I hadn't yet had a chance to get to. It was early, like I said, but not dark-early. I wanted to be able to see what things were like there, so by the time we were a few miles out on a windy, rocky road the sun was coming over the peaks enough to let me see how things looked.

The road wound this way and that, following the topography of the river, but I couldn't get a real good look at the river until I pulled off at a bit of a turn-out. I got out and saw the river down below. It was a ways down, maybe twenty-thirty feet or so, but the slope didn't look too bad. I thought I'd give it a try.

I got my gear and started walking back down the road, looking for somewhere it might not be too steep, and after a while I spotted a little switchback trail and followed it down. The river was beautiful. What else?

I hadn't been casting for more than thirty minutes, however, when the sky just turned black on me like somebody flipped a switch. We were in for a really good thunderstorm you could tell, and one place you don't want to be when that happens is standing on a waterway in a canyon. I kept my eye on the clouds, but the fishing was good so I held off for a bit.

I was in the middle of a cast when the first big, fat drops started coming down. That's when I turned back toward the trail, some ways off, but then it really started bucketing down. I pulled my hat down and with my head down like that I nearly missed the trail, but I found it and started trudging back up.

I could barely see, it was raining so hard, and by the time I had struggled all the way back to the road I was completely soaked and it felt like I had five gallons of water in my chest waders.

I turned back to my right, the way I had come, and looked up through sheets of rain and I didn't see Chuck. This was a shocker. I knew perfectly well that the trail I had gone down wasn't more than a hundred yards from where I'd parked, and that was in a straight line, with no curves.

I looked back the other way. No Chuck. This was crazy! Maybe in the rain I'd headed up the wrong trail and come back up on the road further away than I'd thought? I started walking back toward where I was sure I had parked, and the rain suddenly stopped and the sun came back out.

As I went along I looked all around for any landmarks I might have noticed coming in, and after a minute or two, sure enough, there was an old dead tree I'd passed not an hour earlier. So where was Chuck? And then, as I looked up the road a bit it also dawned on me: and where is the little pull-out I parked on?

I got up to the place the pull-out should have been, and it was gone, just crumbled away. I almost couldn't bear to look, but I did anyway, and there was Chuck, maybe twenty-five feet down the slope, resting on his top side, up against a boulder, broken. I just about cried. I was so shocked and angry and sad all at the same time I didn't even know what to do, so I just sat down in the middle of the road and just sat there, I don't know for how long.

After a while I got up and took my waders off and then looked again over the side. There was no way I could get down there very easily, and even if I could, what could I do? I must have stood there looking down for several minutes or more, without even a single coherent thought going through my mind. All I could think was that Chuck was hurt badly, and I wanted to help him, but I couldn't.

I was so helpless it just made me angry all over again. I screamed something inarticulate then and picked up a rock and threw it as far as I could, and remembered a string of swear words I hadn't used for years. Then I started walking around in circles having a conversation with myself that went on like two late-night drunks down at The Office:

"Well, what if I got some poles and placed them... No! That's absolutely stupid! You think you're going to tip him over on the slope? You idiot!... But if I got up on the boulder and just leveraged him back upright somehow, then I could... Shut up! Just shut up!" Like that.

Then I moved on to, "Oh Chuck. I'm so sorry, buddy. I'm so sorry." Then I threw another rock.

After some time walking around in circles it occurred to me that I did have a phone on me, but the chances of it working out here were about the same as a coyote carrying off an elk. Even so, I told myself, the miraculous still exists, I know it does, it's just that I haven't seen it in awhile is all.

I hit the button for Joanie's number and waited one second, two seconds, and it started ringing! When Joanie answered I didn't know what to say at first, I hadn't even thought about it or what I wanted.

So I just said: "Joanie. This is bad. Chuck is in bad trouble. He fell down a cliff. Call somebody, maybe Wiley, ask him if he knows a good towing guy or something who can get Chuck out."

And then we got cut off. It was a miracle to get through, and I simply assumed God now had to get off onto the rest of His very busy day. After that, I found a suitable rock and sat down and waited.

Surprisingly, it wasn't too long before I heard the engine of a big truck coming up the road. It was an old, battered tow truck, like maybe 1960s vintage, and as it came alongside I saw on the door the words "Johnny's Towing", except "Johnny" had been struck out with a line of spray paint and the name "Bobby" had been stenciled in above it. To my surprise, but also relief for reasons I couldn't identify, Wiley got out the passenger side while a very young-looking fellow who couldn't yet grow a beard if his life depended on it joined him.

"Al," Wiley said, "Joanie told me. Let's take a look, shall we?"

And so we did and Bobby, I assume it was Bobby, whistled out long and low.

"Wow," he said.

Wiley clasped his hands in front of himself, and looked for all the world like a medieval friar, if it hadn't been for his semi-obscene coveralls, and said, "My poor boy. My poor lost boy."

I thought Wiley might cry then and I thought I might have to hug him, or he me, but Bobby jumped over the side of the ravine and slip-slided his way down to Chuck and so we were spared that little bit of awkward bonding.

I don't think I was breathing much then, watching Bobby crawl around Chuck's injured body, but eventually he climbed back up. He had a grim look on his face, and I felt like I was in a hospital waiting room being confronted by the surgeon who had some very bad news.

"It's not good," he said, "but maybe not as bad as it looks. I need to get him turned over first, and then I think we're in the clear."

Again, I thought I might just cry at the prognosis.

And then we all heard another truck coming up the road, and to my very great surprise, it was Hollis. And behind him came another towing truck, but this time a flatbed. Hollis got out and walked over to me and jerked a thumb at the other truck:

"Just in case we can get him out," he said, and then he walked over to look down the ravine, and I followed. Hollis looked down for a bit and then turned to me and said, "Man, Al. I thought trouble followed me around."

I didn't think right then that perhaps Hollis had just made a joke, perhaps the first I had ever heard him attempt, because I was just looking down the slope.

Hollis, perhaps knowing this on some level that only he knew, said, "This kid's good. He knows what he's doing. Don't worry." Bobby saw that Hollis was there and walked over.

"Hollis, you think we can flip him?" Bobby asked, just like maybe he and Hollis had done the same procedure somewhere in the past.

"That boulder looks like our lever, don't you think?" Hollis said.

"That's what I was thinking."

"Then let's see."

And Bobby got a chainsaw from the truck and he and Hollis started cutting poles, and another vehicle was coming up the road to become part of the parade of voyeurs.

This time it was a little-bitty sedan, like maybe something made in a place where roads are only big enough for golf carts or something, and now I was genuinely as shocked as I could be right then. It was Jeff and Chip, and Chip had a camera around his neck when they came over to join the proceedings.

"Hi," I said. "What are you doing here?"

"Big story," Jeff said. "Local color, you know."

"Gotta get pictures," Chip said, and so I just left them to it, except for when Jeff said, "Al. Can we get a shot of the grieving family member?"

That's when I remembered that string of cuss words again.

Okay. That's enough of that. Joanie arrived a bit later, and we hugged and she looked over the side with me and told me some comforting words and I said I was glad she was there, and it just reminded me so much of the time when she came and picked me up that other time when all the world had fallen apart that I just hugged and hugged her.

But later, Hollis and Bobby actually managed to get some leverage going with the poles they had cut, and they yelled at us bystanders to get our butts down there and help, and we all did, and then there were three maybe four of us on a pole, and we heaved and jumped up and down and did it again and again, and we finally flipped Chuck back over again onto his wheels.

There was some exultation to this, as you might imagine. But Chuck was in an obviously very bad way, and there was no emergency room for him. The rest of it was merely hauling him back up the slope with the cable, and getting him on the flatbed, and that was all. Chuck had passed.

· · · · ·

DAYS AND NIGHTS

They say that time heals all wounds. I'll keep you posted.

Chapter Twenty-Three:

Commiseration

The next week, I had to go through it all again and again, like some bad memory that would never go away and finally leave me at peace. We had to go into town to the Safeway, and Joanie drove us in. Folks came up to us in the store and said they were sorry for us, and hoped everything would be okay. Jill checked us out without saying anything until she was done.

"I'm sorry about Chuck," she said. "I hope you get on okay."

Amy saw us and patted us both on the back, but didn't say anything, and just looked kind of sad. People stopped us going around downtown to say they were sorry, and what a pity, and sorry for your loss and so on.

But it wasn't going to be okay, because Chuck sat over at Wiley's on one end of the slag, and I had already gone to see, and that's all there was to that. He was so beat up and broken that I could barely recognize him. That's the way this world goes.

The next Saturday, when The Paper came out, Joanie came back from the mailbox with it and said, "Look at this."

On the front page, in giant headline font, the top story read: "Local Tragedy as One Man Loses His Friend in Storm." I read through the Who What Where When of the front page, and then flipped back to the center for the "full coverage".

Holy smokes! There was a full-color photo of Chuck at the bottom of the ravine, and then another with Hollis looking grim-as-usual with his hand on my shoulder, and then another of everyone down pulling on the poles and the triumph in our faces as we turned him over, and yet another of Chuck being hauled back up, and then, finally, dismally, a photo of Chuck sitting over at Wiley's. It was just awful.

Time went on, and driving the wagon around was somehow not much fun. I began to ponder getting a new truck here soon, because we would definitely need one before winter came again, but I just couldn't do it right then. I wrote my next column on Walter and the triplets, because I needed to get back on at least reasonable terms with him, and people seemed to like that one, and so it went.

Then, one day, I stopped in at Del's for no reason other than to get a cup of coffee, and when I was paying I saw a big jar at the cash register and it had the photo of Chuck from The Paper taped to it, and in masking tape on the jar the message read: "Change for Chuck." There were maybe a dozen ones in the jar, and a bunch of loose change. This struck me as both kind of grim and kind of funny at the same time, but I didn't say anything about it.

Later that morning I stopped in at Kendall's, and they had a jar too! This was getting a bit nutty. I slunk out and went back home. However, when The Paper showed up later that day, I found that Chip and Jeff were having a good time with this, too, because they had a photo of the jar at Del's and a little story about "community rallies to..." that sort of thing. I had this bad feeling that I was quickly going to become everyone's joke in town.

On Tuesday I sat on The Bench with my cup of coffee and was just sort of staring out at the new day when a shadow suddenly obscured the light and I looked up and there was Hollis, looking down at me.

"Morning," I said.

Hollis seemed to study me for a bit and then said, "How you doing?" and because I had this bad feeling he meant something more I said, "I'm fine," and left it at that. Hollis stood there another few seconds.

"So, you getting a new truck or what?"

I glanced up at him for a moment and then looked away.

"Thinking about it. I've been looking around," I lied.

"Okay," Hollis said, and then he moved on.

About a week later I very stupidly, yet sort of unconsciously, found myself driving past Wiley's. I really have no idea why I did that, but I did. No idea at all. Closure? I guess they call it that. Personally I think that's a really stupid thing to say, but what do I know? However, as I came up on Wiley's, there was no Chuck. He was gone. Wiley must have hauled him around someplace else to get him out of the way, or maybe strip him for parts. Chuck was gone. He was really gone. Then I drove home and opened a bottle of wine and Joanie beat me badly in a game of Scrabble.

DAYS AND NIGHTS

I still miss him you know. I sometimes think I see him around town and I'm going to walk over and say hi, and then I remember that it's not him. It can't be.

Chapter Twenty-Four:
On Assignment with Jeff and Chip

By the end of July I was resolved to the idea of get-ting a new truck as fast as I could. It was only sixty-four days until winter, and besides, Joanie and I had to share the wagon of course, and this cut into my fishing schedule. On those mornings when the wagon was free, I was always sort of nervous driving it out into the mountains to find a river. It was a perfectly reliable car, but I just didn't feel as safe in it as I had with Chuck, and I kept dreading that I'd cross over a rock and yank out the oil pan or worse. Even when I went out to meet someone for an interview for my column I found my-self on roads that normally I wouldn't have worried about, but with the wagon I took it pretty easy.

I started looking in our local Wooden Nickel, the weekly compilation of classified ads for the tri-county area, and also online, looking to see what was out there that I might afford. I gave up after a week of trying to find something similar to Chuck. That wasn't going to happen. I kept looking, but nothing I saw really ap-pealed to me. I thought maybe people should get Wiley to write their ads for them. He'd sell them all in a heartbeat.

Right about the last day of July, a tiny little car pulled up in front of the house, and out got Jeff and Chip. I got off the porch and went down to meet them.

"Hi guys, what's up?"

"We have a story going on here, and thought maybe you could help us out a bit," Chip said.

"Well, sure, I guess. But aren't you going to write it?"

Jeff said, "Oh yeah, but we just wanted your input. You know. Some day we might need you to help out more is all."

I mentally scratched my head a bit about that, but I wasn't doing anything, and Joanie was out and about that day.

"Okay. Sure. Do I need anything?"

"Naw, you're good," Chip said.

Fortunately, Chip volunteered to sit in the "back seat" of their little car, which was more like the glove box in anyone else's vehicle, because it was claustrophobic enough for me in the passenger seat, with the windshield about six inches away. On top of that, there was apparently no trunk in this thing, and so their camera gear was sitting on all of our laps to make room.

"So what's the story?" I asked as we bounced along the rocked roads that make up most of the county's byways.

Chip, who even though he was in back sounded like he was right next to my ear, because he probably was, said, "A couple of bigwigs in the neighborhood. Came all the way from Casper and then also from Idaho Falls. Going to interview them in the field and study their technique."

Before I could ask any more about this, Jeff laughed and said, "Buddy, you are good, you are real good."

I was confused, of course, but figured I'd find out soon enough, so I just bounced along the rest of the way.

In just a few minutes we slowed down, though, and it was kind of hard to see where we were in this little thing, but it looked like we were at Wiley's for some strange reason.

"Wiley's?" I said.

"Yep," said Jeff.

"Bigwigs at Wiley's?"

"Yep," Jeff said, and there wasn't enough room for me to look around at Chip, but Jeff had a really stupid-looking grin on his face.

We pulled up to the office and extricated ourselves from the car, and just about had to yank Chip from the back. Jeff and Chip got their gear together and then we stood there.

"Um, now what?"

And then Wiley came out of the "office". It took me a moment to recognize him, because he was not in fact wearing his trademark tattered coveralls. He had on a pair of decent-looking Carhartt's and a nice-looking flannel shirt with the sleeves rolled up.

"Hey Al," he said. "Glad you could make it."

We exchanged pleasantries for a bit, and then I said, "Chip and Jeff told me there are a couple of VIPs around, and that we're here to interview them. But they won't say anything else. So what's up?"

Wiley smiled and looked at the other two. "So you didn't say anything at all then? Good. That's good."

And then he turned to me: "Well, I called in a couple of specialists after the money showed up, and they have these mobile units like you would not believe. When I first heard what they could do, well, I had to see it for myself, you know?"

Now I was more confused than ever, but tried to stay focused. I looked at Chip and Jeff, and they just grinned but weren't going to help.

"I don't know what you're talking about, Wiley, and I guess we're here for an interview. What 'specialists' and what do you mean 'after the money came in'?"

Wiley stuck his hands in his pockets and smiled.

"Oh, good. I get to tell the story. So, you know about the stories that Jeff and Chip ran in The Paper? About Chuck and the donation jars?"

I winced a bit, but nodded. "Yeah. Sure. What about it?"

"Well, the two stories got picked up by the *Journal-Star* in Pocatello, and then the *Cheyenne Herald* and the *Casper Register* and the *Great Falls Beacon*, and then from there to Butte and Helena."

"What?! They did??"

And then I turned to Jeff and Chip.

"Well, why didn't you tell me, guys? Congratulations! That's pretty awesome to get reprinted like that!"

Chip said, "That's nothing. Went to the *Chicago Tribune* in two weeks! Yeah, we were pretty excited," and Jeff did an 'aw shucks, it was nothing' look.

"But it gets better, Al," Wiley said.

"People started contacting us," Chip said.

"From all over the place," Jeff added excitedly.

Wiley held his hands clasped in front of him. "Now

boys, who's telling this story anyway? Aren't you sup-posed to be reporting?"

"Sorry, Wiley," Chip said with a grin. "Couldn't help myself."

"Okay, now," Wiley began. "What happened is just as they said. Word got around real fast, and somebody posted the story on one of those internet places, and people started sending money to The Paper, if you can believe it. And a few of the checks they got, well, let's just say I'm glad these fellows are men of integrity or they might'a skipped town." Wiley gave a benevolent smile to Jeff and Chip. I was astonished.

"What? That's amazing! Why would anyone do that? I can't, I can't understand it is all."

"People help people, Al. It's what we do. That's all." Wiley was enjoying this immensely.

"Okay, but then what? And are we really here to inter-view people from out of town?" I asked Jeff.

"Oh, yes," Wiley said. "Like I said before, once the money showed up, Chip and Jeff came down here and we talked it over. I knew some people here and there who are specialists in the field. So I called them up, and they'd heard the story, and so they came here a few weeks back and have been working like devils since then. Josie has a mobile rotisserie, if you can be-lieve it."

And no, I couldn't because I had no idea what he was talking about.

"Never seen anything like it myself. She works on professional racing cars in season, but lives in Idaho Falls. She's like the best of the best at frame work. Phil is a body specialist who just happens to live in Casper, but he's a specialist in antique restoration. I'd show you pictures of his work, but for people like us it's just the stuff of dreams. And there they are," Wiley said as a pair of coveralled people came from around the Quonset.

I walked up and introduced myself and said how glad I was to meet them.

"But I still don't get it," and I looked at everyone. "So what happened?"

Wiley laughed then, a laugh I'd never heard before from him. For that matter, I don't believe I'd ever heard Wiley laugh, about anything.

"Al, Chuck underwent some major surgery and he pulled through just fine."

I was flabbergasted. I was astounded.

"I have someone bringing him around now."

And then I heard the purr of an engine, a very nice engine, and around the corner came Chuck—I think it was Chuck—with Joanie at the wheel. I almost fell over right then, and I heard Jeff shooting photos, but I couldn't take my eyes off Chuck. He was amazing. He was dressed up in Red and Cream, and his chrome shone like daybreak. He was, well, just beautiful. Joanie pulled up alongside with the window down.

"Sorry," she said. "But I only just learned last night and I figured the surprise was worth it."

I leaned through the window and kissed her. "Doesn't he look amazing?" Joanie said.

Then she got out and I got in. Chuck was completely remade. He was bright and shiny and beautiful. I passed my hand over the new paint on the dash, and the chrome instruments. The carpet was all new.

Chuck. I was overwhelmed. I put my head down on the steering wheel and cried for a while, until I heard Chip say, "Al, cry this way a bit. I can't get a good shot otherwise."

Eventually, I got out and Josie and Phil took me around to show what they'd done, inside and out. Chuck was a new man.

"However," Wiley said, "per my advice, I asked that the angled antenna remain, just so you'd recognize him."

I hugged everybody at some point I guess. Probably more than once. And then there came a time when we all just stood there, kind of exhausted.

"Who wants a ride?"

DAYS AND NIGHTS

What's daunting is that even though there is un-looked-for evil in one's life, there is also unlooked-for good. It's just that you can never know what's coming, and I suppose that's how it's going to go.

CHAPTER TWENTY-FIVE:
KENNA TELLS ME

I AM NOT a very keen observer of human nature as I'm sure you've noticed by now. Sometimes I am a bit disappointed in myself about that, but I'll defend myself by saying that I've spent quite a lot of my life looking at things I could actually understand. Most of humanity has not been one of those things, it seems. Naturally, because I'm surrounded by humanity, I try to give it my best shot, you know, but it seems as though I always end up surprised. Maybe we all are at least some of the time, I just don't know. I probably haven't talked to enough people to find out or ever asked them.

It's kind of the way everything seems to me these days: you think you know something and that it's pretty solid, just the way it had always been and always should be, and then something comes along and yanks the rug out from under your feet and then there you go. Things aren't what you thought there were. I realize this isn't very philosophical, but it's just an observation. That's about the best I can do.

· · · · ·

I may have mentioned earlier that Kenna would definitely be one of my interviews because I was just sure she would have something really fun and exciting to relate and that I was kind of saving her for a rainy day, so to speak. And so the day came, at last, but too soon for me because that meant I was pretty much out of good ideas after that. Even so, I told Joanie about my plan to call up Kenna for an interview and she thought that was a great idea, and I did too, except I didn't tell her I had no other great ideas forthcoming. I think by this time Joanie had sort of come to expect that I'd have an endless amount of columns to write for the future, even though there were only 6,000 people scattered around in a county the size of Maryland.

I called up Kenna and said what I had in mind and she agreed, sounding quite pleased over the phone, and said to just meet her at her shop early before she opened for the day. And so that was all set.

On the appointed day Chuck took me on down the valley and into town, and he seemed rather leisurely to me about this, as if maybe he wasn't in any big hurry. Nevertheless, as you know, I have grown to trust his judgment about some things, and so this was fine because it gave me some time to mentally run through my list of things that I usually ask people.

We got down into town and Chuck pulled us in where I needed to be, and I knocked on the door of Curl Up and Dye, and three seconds later the door opened and there was Kenna.

Somewhat to my surprise, Kenna was kind of "dressed up". I don't at all mean to say that she dressed unprofessionally on other days, it's just that usually she seemed a bit more casual or comfortable or something like that. I mean, all the folks at the bank wear jeans and flannel, that's how things are here and it would be odd if it was different. But today, Kenna wore slacks and a print short-sleeved shirt and, well, she looked nice is all I guess I mean to say.

And I said so: "Gee, you look nice, Kenna."

She smiled and said, "Thanks. Going somewhere later, after work."

She led me over to a couple of chairs, and I opened my notebook as we sat down.

"First question," I said, "which I always ask everyone as the first question, is 'Why are you in Dobbins of all places in the world?'"

"Oh, that's easy," Kenna said, as if maybe I was quizzing her or something. "This is where my money ran out, so I stayed."

"How do you mean?"

"Well, that's what I told myself, you see. All right. Let's get this going. So."

And Kenna leaned back in her barber chair while I was sitting on a recliner next to her. I felt like I was maybe a shrink listening to someone's confession, somewhere, for some reason, but I'm the one, again, in the "comfy" chair, and I kind of flinch away from that.

"So, I grew up in West Virginia and there wasn't any-thing for me after high school or anything like that. There weren't any beaus or nothin', or jobs or anything else. Not unless you wanna work the mines and never see the sun again, and that wasn't for me. Watched my daddy die from that. Broken back and then broken lungs, and that's all I needed to know. So, I signed up. Got in the Army like six weeks into summer after graduation. I read this thing that said most of the heroes of WWI and especially WWII came from country places, like where I lived. And I read some more then later about how so very many people from West Virginia had gone off to war, and about all the cemeteries and monuments and the like all over the state, and I figured, 'I got warrior blood in me too then.'"

And she paused and sat back further in the chair, fully comfortable to me, it seemed. "And so I signed up and got going."

"So then what?" I said.

"You know. Boot camp and all that. You know what? I loved it. It was great. Best thing I ever did. Sent me down to Georgia, which is a very nice place, trained me up and then I was good to go."

"What did you like so much about boot camp?"

"Everything! We was on this very strict discipline, up at dawn, eating at such-and-such a time, bedtime and lights out. Working. Learning things. Never lived like that before. It was all good. Discipline is good."

"Well, then what?"

"Shipped me off to Germany! Dutch-land! It was great! Never been in a foreign country before and everything was real exciting and new. Everybody spoke English too, though kind of funny if you know what I mean. At the base I got to do everything. I stripped down and rebuilt pretty much anything you can think of. I was in the engineers, or motors or whatever. It's where you actually got your hands dirty instead of hanging around. I betcha I stripped planes, tanks, trucks, cars, whatever you want. Put 'em back together again as pretty as you please. It was great."

"Well, it was so good, then why did you leave? Could have signed up again, right? Sounds like it was a good life."

Kenna paused for a bit, and then sat up in the chair and readjusted her feet on the bar down below.

"It was Germany, you know," she said wistfully. "I mean, in your off time then you could go wherever you wanted, and I did. I saw cities and mountains and forests and little towns like something on a postcard and I, well, I saw it was a big life out there and I wanted to see it all. Everything!"

"Did you?"

"Well, at first I wanted to, but then I slept on it a bit and figured that maybe the whole world was too big to get to in just one lifetime. So I downsized a bit. You have to understand that until I went off to camp I hadn't been anywhere outside of my little town, and so I got started thinking I'd see America. All of it! After that, I just started saving my money and lookin' at maps. When I got done in Germany, then that was that and they sent me home and dropped me off in Virginia."

Kenna paused then, and kind of looked down and said, "And I guess I was about five, six hours from home then, but I couldn't go back. Nothin' waitin' for me there. What's the point? See some ol' high school buddies or somethin'? Nope, I was on my way and I had a plan. I bought a handful of bus tickets and headed to Miami, which was kind of nice, and real busy, but real hot too, even though they get a nice rain just about every day in the summer." Kenna paused for breath there, maybe.

"After that, it was all West, you know? Went to New Orleans and all, even though it wasn't the right time for Mardi Gras. Saw some of the bayou for a few days, and that was nice but I couldn't stop thinking about alligators and that it was maybe easier fightin' the Russians. Ha!"

She paused again and kind of shook her head, thinking back.

"That was some place, though. I just about stopped there, it was so nice and new and different, but I figured there was lots more to see, so on I went.

"After that I zigged and zagged a bit, over to Texas and then to Utah and Arizona, and then finally got to San Francisco and saw the Pacific. It was amazing. I used to just go out and sit on a bench at the coast and look out on the waves for hours and hours, and then I'd head into town and wander around, just kind of people watchin', you know? I went to all these crazy clubs and ate things I never even heard of and met all kinds of people and it was great, just great. Never seen anything like that before. And boy, I thought hard about just stoppin' right there and findin' somethin' to do, but I had a fair bit of money left and I figured there was still lots more to see.

"After that I just went up the coast and stopped pretty much everywhere I could. Got to Oregon and saw Crater Lake. Hey! Isn't that where you're from?"

I smiled then, and said that I used to live just about an hour from Crater Lake.

"Wow!" she said. "That's some kind of amazing place, isn't it? And when I saw the color of the water there I thought, 'That's just not right,' you know? 'Nothin' can be that blue.' But it was and it's hard to explain it to anybody who's never seen it with their own eyes. And then I just got heart-sick and I had to see mountains, like at home, and up the coast I went and saw all the volcanoes and everything.

"Went to see Mount Saint Helens too and saw a movie about it and that was something I don't think I'll ever forget. And that just made me want to see more and more mountains for some reason."

She stopped then and stood up and stretched and walked around a bit, still talking. "And I don't know. There was somethin' about seeing those big mountains that just got at me a bit. I looked at maps again and headed east. Mountains it was gonna be. Maybe a bit of homesick in me still, I don't know. I got to the Cascades there in Washington and they were real nice, but I had in mind that I wanted to see the Rockies, you know, the real mountains and all.

"So I dropped down after that and kind of headed a bit over into Montana and I saw the Rockies, like real and up close, and that was going to be that. It was June then, and down below was all green and everything was comin' to life, and then up above, well, you know, you kind of think maybe God lives up there or somethin'. And if that was true, then there wasn't any place left to go, know what I mean?"

"Well, wait a minute," I said. "Why'd you stop here?"

"Ran out of money, like I said at the start," she said with a grin.

"Okay, but then what? I mean, how did you open your shop here and everything? You haven't said anything at all about cutting hair and such."

"Well," she said, kind of rubbing her hands together and sitting back down again, very thoughtful now. "That's a bit of a story.

"So, I gotta take you back to San Francisco for a bit...."

I settled back in my chair and made myself comfortable, my notebook ready, and Kenna looked at me and said:

"Put that thing away. Nobody else knows this, okay?"

I shut the notebook and put it on the floor, and Kenna eyed it like it might be a snake.

"Okay," she said, "here's the deal. I only just told you part of the story."

She took a deep breath then, eyes focused on something far away.

"When I was in San Francisco it's like I said: I'd go out to the beach and just sit there for hours lookin' out at the ocean. It was real nice and peaceful and you could just relax and think for a bit."

That was something I thought I could understand, and I was just nodding my head through that part.

"Anyway, one of those days a young fella came and sat on the bench with me, and we got started talking and I told him what I was up to and so on, and he was asking what I was going to do next and all, and I said I wasn't real sure what, and we kind of met like that a couple of days. So, after a couple of days he says he wants to show me around a bit, and so he does, and that's when I saw all those clubs and stuff and ate all the wild food and such."

She stopped for a moment then and started walking slowly around her shop, her hand every once in a while resting on the main chair, or touching a hair dryer or picking up a comb and sitting it back down again.

"Anyway, one night he says to come on over to his place, where he and his buddy have a shop where they cut hair, and he gives me the address and I show up first thing because I'm curious what he does for a living. So, I get there and they have this real nice place down town, and they show me around, my friend Steve and his buddy, Alex. They show me their appointment book and you know what? It was just like packed for as many days as you flipped through it! And I said that was really something how they'd done so well for themselves and all, and I asked how they got together and how they got started."

Kenna was still standing, sometimes wandering through the shop, but now she came and sat down nearby once again.

"So this is a real hoot. These two guys, they met at some bar or something and said maybe they should open up a hair place, but neither one of them actually knew anything about cutting hair or anything else. So Alex said he went to the library and got a book about it, and then him and Steve watched a couple of videos on the internet and then they said to each other we are good to go! Ha!"

Kenna smiled a bit then, thinking back on it, I guess.

"So they get this place and open up and they start getting customers and they don't really know what they're doing, but Steve says 'We just faked it,' and they like put on a show of knowing what they're doing and people are getting these really strange haircuts, you know, like one side is longer than the other and stuff?

But it turns out people really liked that and they started telling their friends and then Alex says they started gettin' some of those beauty magazines and lookin' at hair styles and he says we figured we could do something like that, and so they just faked it 'til they sort of figured it out!"

Kenna stood up and began wandering around again.

"So these two guys don't take any of all this seriously at all, and they are just havin' a good time. So, they said, 'Let's have some fun,' and they got me a smock and I put it on and Steve says, 'You'll be my student-in-training today. Just watch for a bit.' And that's what I did all day. He'd have somebody in the chair and be cuttin' away and chatting them real nice and then he'd stop and turn to me and say, 'Kenna, take a look at this here. What do you think?' and I'd come over and say, 'That's real nice, but maybe a bit off here?' and I'd point or something and Steve'd say, 'Yes. Exactly,' and he'd make a couple of snips and Alex would be looking over trying not to laugh his head off!"

By then I was shaking my head laughing, and Kenna was too. She could hardly get any more out because we were both laughing so much, but then she managed to get going again:

"So anyway," and she took a deep breath, "anyway, we did that a few days in a row and then we'd all go out and get something to eat and go to these wild clubs and just get a table and talk for hours. So the next thing was, they said I was now all trained up and the next day they said to give it a go, and you know what? I did! Some young lady comes in and I don't even bother to ask her how she wants her hair done and just go cuttin' away and Steve and Alex take turns comin' by and lookin' and they'd say, 'cut a bit right there' or 'leave that bit alone,' and when I got done the lady was all excited about her new do and said she couldn't wait to show her boyfriend and all. Ha! It was great, just great."

Kenna laughed some more, but then she stopped talking.

"Okay, now I get it," I say. "That's how you learned to cut hair. But I don't understand how you went from doing that to ending up in Montana. Did you start to think about the mountains then, and getting back on the road? Sounds like it would have been hard to leave."

Kenna was standing, looking out the window now, and she turned and came back and sat down and let out a long breath.

"It was hard," she says, "or maybe not. Steve died and I couldn't stay any longer after that. He had AIDS, Al, and one day he was just fine and then not long after that he was real sick, and not long after that he was gone. And after that Alex says he doesn't think he wants to cut hair right now and wants to take some time off and so he closed up shop and I got back on the road again."

The air in the room was so still right then I thought I could probably touch it, and I said how sorry I was and some other things, but what do you say, really? Then Kenna leaned back in her chair again and said that was all right because she ended up here in Dobbins and said she liked it just fine.

"But," she said, "like I say, nobody needs to know about that last bit, okay?"

I assured her that nothing about it would come out in The Paper, and then she stood up and said she'd better get going.

I asked her where she was headed as I got my things together and Kenna stopped me and said, "Tonight I'm going after Hollis Granger. I decided after I read your story about him. I'm gonna give it my best shot because he's the best man in town and this time he's gonna pay attention, one way or the other."

I stood there with my mouth open for a moment, and I think I may have said something like "I see", and then Kenna showed me out the door.

DAYS AND NIGHTS

The other day I was sitting there at church when I became unpleasantly aware of how close I was sitting to an outside entrance. It made me anxious because if a killer walked in I'd certainly be among the first to die, but I didn't think I could change seats during the sermon and I had a hard time paying attention because I kept looking at the door.

Chapter Twenty-Six:
The Game is Everything

Y ou know that picture that's hanging in the hallway of your parents' house? The one you walk past, day after day, year after year, but never really look at? Then, one day, for no reason whatsoever, you stop and finally do, and it's kind of a surprise to you? That sort of thing just keeps happening to me.

.   .   .   .   .

When I finished writing up Kenna's interview I just set it on my desk and looked at it for a long time. I thought it was pretty good as these things go, but it was em- blematic to me and depressing. Before I knew it I would have the next eight months to go of winter, coming up with my column for the paper, and things were looking pretty grim, as if winter wasn't grim enough.

I had a little notebook on my desk for people I might call and do a phone interview with for the next few months, because even with Chuck it was hard to get around in, well, January to April, and the list in my notebook was pretty slim. When I started doing this it never really occurred to me that living in such a small town I would of course rather quickly run out of people to write about. It was that picture in the hallway I hadn't looked at, I guess. Didn't want to look at.

Wednesday came, and that was my day to take the column down to The Paper, and Chuck did the honors of course, but he was very, very reluctant to stop at The Paper offices. First thing he did after leaving our place was just let up on the gas and coast on down into the valley at twenty-five miles an hour while I had coffee and looked out the window.

Then, when we got into town, he stopped at Gil's to have the full to-do because I guess he was feeling a little needy or something. Gil and Simon and Theo came out and gave Chuck a good going over and a rub-down and he seemed perkier after that, but after we left Gil's he pulled into the Safeway and sort of meandered around the lot, and then he took me over to Daffyd's as if it were a suggestion and I told him I was good for flies, and then he drove real, real slow past Del's, suggesting I should get coffee, but I still had some, and then I guess he sighed and turned, and instead of making the usual right to go The Paper he took lefts until he got us going in the proper direction. Kind of joke here about how two wrongs don't make a right, but three lefts do.

And so he turned around and headed down to The Paper anyway. So I guessed this was it. When Chuck finally pulled us in I kind of gripped my column in my hand so that I noticed that I was doing so, I guess, and then made my way in and down the hallway past all the things forgotten and came into the office where Chip and Jeff were sitting at their desks.

"Hey!" Chip said. "We were just about to have a game. Wanna watch?"

"Sure," I said, "but I just wanted to drop off the column and see what you thought. Kenna is featured."

Jeff whistled at that.

"Boy. Bet that was a good one," he said. "I'd get my hair cut there every week if I could. She knows every-thing, and is natural-born story-teller for sure. Want to get a scoop on something? Ask Kenna."

Chip chimed in at that. "I did that for a few weeks, actually," he said, looking down at his desk and moving some papers around. Jeff perked up at this.

"You did? You rascal. Why'd you stop?"

"Oh, well, there were some stories, you know? But nothing we could ever print, if you know what I mean," and he grinned sheepishly. Jeff and I laughed at that.

"I know what you mean," I said.

And, that being said, Jeff and Chip got up from their desks and the familiar routine began, during which Chip picked up some newspaper and wadded it into a ball and tossed it to Jeff for his approval, and then Jeff got out a quarter from his pocket and said, "Call it," and Chip did and he lost and Jeff had the "ball" and then the game was on, but I said, "Wait a minute. Just wait a minute!" for a reason I hadn't yet quite under-stood.

And Jeff and Chip stopped and looked at me and I said, "Can I just have a couple of minutes? I mean, just so I can understand what's happening here, because I never have understood and I'd like to," and I rubbed my forehead with one hand because it felt like a head-ache was coming on.

Jeff and Chip came over to me and pulled up chairs and looked at me, concerned, I guess, because Chip asked, "What's the matter? Are you okay? Is everything okay?" and he leaned in, looking me over a bit.

"No. No. It's not that," I said. "It's just I don't under-stand what you guys are doing. I mean, you put out The Paper each week, and...I don't know."

I got up and wandered around a bit, and then I came back and said, "Well, you know, right? I mean you guys are always screwing around playing this game and stuff and what the hell is that all about anyway? I mean, I'm sorry and it's none of my business, but you are both grown men and why are you doing this all the time? Shouldn't you be out on a story or something? Writing something? Doing some good for somebody somewhere?"

Then I sat back down and said, "I'm sorry. That was stupid. I guess I'm kind of worried I don't have any more columns left is all and I'm a bit strung tight. That's all. I'm sorry."

I think I was looking down at the floor when I said that last bit, because when I looked back up, both Jeff and Chip were looking at each other, and just grinning like mad men.

"Tell him," Jeff said. "Go on, tell him."

"The game is everything," Chip said. "I mean really."

He looked at Jeff and he was nodding and had his hands on his knees like he might jump out of his chair at any moment, and then he did and started to sort of circle the desk.

"This all got started when we were kids," he said.

"Bikes," Chip said, and then he got up and started wandering around too.

I just sort of looked bewildered and decided I wasn't going to ask any more questions unless absolutely necessary.

"When we were nine, Chip, if you can believe it, was bigger than me."

Chip grinned and said, "Yeah. I used to wax his tail in bike races all the way until junior high, and that's when Bean Pole had his growth spurt."

"It didn't really matter, though, because by then we were both on the track team as distance runners, and we'd just about die to see who could run the longest without passing out. Remember Missoula?" Jeff said.

"Puked my guts out that time," Chip said with a fond smile.

Okay, at this point I was a bit confused, but I think I got it. The two guys were nuts, and I'd never caught on before, because they always struck me as so very normal somehow.

"And then we joined the swim team and I won the state tri-meet in freestyle, so we had to move on from there," Chip said.

Okay. Now I really wasn't getting it, so I had to ask:

"What do you mean you had to move on from there? You mean you got older or bored or something?"

"Oh no," Jeff said. "It's just that there was no way I was going to beat that, so we both dropped the swim team and then in high school we did track for a year, and I won that one," and Chip nodded solemnly, as if remembering something unpleasant, "and so we went out for the tennis team junior year and Chip just smoked me there, and then we got crazy and played football senior year and I think we called that one a tie because neither one of us got to play very much."

"I had an interception once!" Chip said, and then Jeff

stopped his meandering around the office and said, "I had one field goal."

Chip nodded. "Yep. Guess that was it for us there."

"In the summers we went fishing," Chip said. "We always wanted to be the one who caught the Big One. One year, we went out for six days and camped on the Upper Missouri and fished all day every day, and then one day Jeff caught a Brown that was only, what?" He looked at Jeff. "Maybe three ounces off the state record? Something like that. Anyway, that was it. No way I was ever going to beat that, and so we moved on."

"It was like this," Jeff said, with his arms apart, smiling.

"No way I could beat that," Chip added matter-of-factly.

"So, yeah, we had to move on," Jeff said.

"Went to college," Chip said.

"By the time we went to college, we both thought about being newspaper guys, and so we got to take classes together," Jeff said.

"Kind of had the same grades, though, so that was kind of boring," Chip said. "So we started looking around for stuff to do, because at UM the competition was pretty stiff for regular sports. Had to find *something*, you know?"

"We roomed together for four years, and only played newspaper-basketball in the dorm room when there wasn't anything else to do," Jeff said, "just kind of between studying and classes and stuff."

"So we bought a ping-pong table and put it in our room," Chip said with a grin.

"What?" I said. "How'd you manage that?"

"It wasn't easy," they said together, and they both laughed hilariously at that.

"But all along, we always found something kind of fun and different to do," Chip said, sitting down now and reflecting a bit.

"Street hockey," Jeff said.

"Badminton," Chip said.

"Did drinking there for a bit in college," Jeff said.

"I think I won that," Chip said. "I think." And they both laughed just a little bit, kind of sheepishly maybe.

"Anyway, we found games to keep playing and it's been great. After we graduated we got the job here because we made it up ourselves. No paper in our part of the county, or anywhere else for that matter, so we bought this place and set up and that's about that," Jeff said.

"Well then what," I asked. "I mean about the game and all?"

"Oh, that's going on all the time," Chip said.

"It's why we went into journalism," Jeff said. "You know, who can get the scoop first and beat out the other guy for the Big Story." I nodded with understanding then.

"But what about the other games? Are they still on?"

Chip and Jeff both stood up then and said, "Come on. Back into the warehouse."

We went down the back hallway and came out into the warehouse and Chip flipped a switch and the fluorescent lights lit up about an eighth of a mile of stuff piled everywhere. It reminded me a bit of the left-hand side of Wiley's place. It was nearly impossible to tell what all this broken-down machinery and, well, just "stuff" actually was at some point. I felt like maybe I was witnessing some secret museum of days gone by, but it was awfully hard to tell what those days might have been, or what the heck people were doing during them.

Everywhere, except for little aisles going this way and that at random stretches, were piles of almost anything you might imagine: chains, and gears, and iron rods and hair dryers and things that were so nonsensical they should have been in a Lewis Carroll story or something. Near the hair dryers was a pile of what looked like giant rubber balloons, like old Army surplus weather balloons or something. Chip called us over to that pile.

"Remember these?" he said, grinning at Jeff.

"Oh yeah," Jeff said turning to me. "Broke my ankle with this one."

"What is it?" I asked, peeling back a layer of flimsy rubber with one finger.

"Army surplus weather balloons," Chip said. "We filled them with helium and then went over to the granary at Wheat."

"What?! That's maybe three hundred feet tall! That's crazy! That's just stupid!"

Jeff shuffled his feet a bit and said, "Well, we didn't go all the way to the top. They took us up, what," he looked at Chip, "maybe seventy-five feet is all to a little service door on the side."

"Yeah. I jumped first and did pretty good. Floated for maybe a minute and a half and then a down draft got me and that was it. Jeff was up for maybe five minutes, with me running after him. It was awesome."

Jeff beamed at that. "It was," he said, "until the down draft got me too and screwed me into a hillside."

"He won that one for sure," Chip said.

For a bit, all I could do was just look back and forth between them, and a thought flickered in my head that there was no way I was going to tell Joanie about this or she'd want to do this kind of crazy stuff too, knowing her.

"Come on," Jeff said. "Take a look at this!"

We meandered back through piles of machinery and things that might have been part of some conscious attempt to do something once upon a time, and eventually arrived at what appeared to be a currently occupied workplace, with a large, gleaming metal object occupying the space.

"Sled," Chip said. "It's crazy. We never thought of sledding before. Absolutely crazy. That ever happen to you when there's something so obvious, so just right in front of you, that you never even think about it?" I nodded at that.

"So here's the deal," Jeff said. "This is a design competition for speed, of course, and also survival. We'll be going down McMaster's Mountain in January."

I turned at that and looked once again from one to the other of them, searching for perhaps some outward sign of some kind of ailment, and both of them were just smiling away as if they were sane.

"No you aren't," I said. "We've all seen the mountain and there are no 'slopes' of any sort, only rocks and trees, and maybe a ten-percent grade. No, that can't happen."

"Oh, there is," Jeff said. "We made one. It took us two

years. We did a fly-by with a drone and mapped out the route and then we got permission from the Forest Service to clear a path, and then we got some guys to do that, and we've been up there off and on for months moving stuff out of the way. We have a slope that's twelve feet wide and six percent grade," and Chip was just pumping his arm at this pronouncement.

"It's going to be great," he said. I found something then that looked like it might support my weight and sat down on it.

"So tell me about this," I said, motioning toward the "sled", which looked more like a bathtub with a windshield.

"This one's mine," Jeff said, running his hand down an eight-foot-long aluminum tube that was sort of flat on the bottom, rounded on the front, and sported a windshield and some sort of seating contraption in it, maybe an old canoe seat. He drew my attention to the various straps in the compartment which were to presumably hold him in place should he become airborne.

"I've been polishing and waxing it for months. I'm hoping to get up to forty-five in it."

I kind of stood there just looking at him, words failing me until I thought to ask, "Can you steer it?"

"Oh yeah," he said, pointing inside to a system of foot-operated pedals which he assured me controlled a metal rudder in the tail of the contraption.

"I'm impressed," was all I could say.

"Take a look at mine!" Chip said, and we all moved down a few yards to where Chip's death-sled awaited. When we turned on the overhead light, and Chip removed the canvas tarp, you could tell that Chip had taken a completely different tack when it came to designing a sled.

"It's a flying saucer with fins," I said.

"Yes, it is," Chip said, all business now.

Jeff smiled, "It's very cool, but no way it's going faster than my tube."

I was stunned, however, at the sheer audacity of it. It was a disc maybe six feet in diameter with some sort of windshield affixed partially around it, and a rim of maybe two feet all the way around, and had a metal bar that looked like something to maybe hold onto. It, too, contained a seat and various safety straps and harnesses.

"That's pretty slick," I said, "but how do you steer it? Or do you?"

Chip beamed. "You just lean is all, side to side. My body weight should be enough to direct me, and so I should be able to make it down all right."

"What do you mean 'all right'?"

"It's not a straight run," Jeff said. "We have to be able to steer in some places or you can't go on down the half-mile-long slope. We've been planning this for two years, and that's the best we could get. So, each sled has to steer, at least a bit, all the way down. Otherwise we'd just sit on toboggans and sled, and what's the challenge in that?"

I had to look back and forth at Chip and Jeff then, in order to ground myself in the familiar simply by comparison of one reality to another.

I stood up then, dusted myself off, and said, "These are mighty fine. Yes they are. You will be spectacular in these..."

And I said some other things, I suppose, as we made our way back to the office and had seats once again.

When we sat again, I said, just so I really understood, "So the game is everything, is that correct?" Jeff laughed and Chip didn't.

"Yes it is," Chip said.

"I understand now, and I thank you for letting me know. Would you mind if I did a column about this, because it is of course very interesting."

And Chip stood up and whooped at the ceiling and Jeff stood up and handed him some money which Chip laid down on his desk and said, "I told you! Told you he'd write about it!" and Jeff sort of looked at me and said, "Sorry. I didn't think we were very interesting, you know, after all this time."

These were, perhaps, the most disjointed, crazy, silliest two guys I had ever known, and they were my employers. I didn't know what to say.

"With your permission, I'll run the column two weeks before the event? You know, get a little press out there?"

"That would be awesome," Jeff said. "Wish Wide World of Sports was still going."

We sat a couple of minutes after that, while I got up and made a pretense of leaving, because I wasn't quite sure about this, and then I walked to the door, because I knew Chuck was there for me, always my Chuck, waiting to take me away from what I couldn't understand and toward what I wanted, always, somehow.

At the door I turned around and Jeff and Chip sat behind their desks, and I said, "So which one of you is getting married first?"

Their mouths opened to say something, and then they looked at one another for a moment. Chip's eyes strayed to his phone, and then his hand. He picked it up and punched in a number.

"Hi Jill, it's Chip," he said. "Hey, I was thinking maybe we could have some dinner and see a sunset if you weren't busy. Yes? That's great! Maybe Friday, around seven? Awesome! I'll pick you up!"

He sat his phone down, looked at his desk, then turned to see Jeff's expression, which was open-mouthed awe.

"I was thinking ahead," Chip said.

"You little weasel," Jeff said.

DAYS AND NIGHTS

I am talking to myself quite a bit these days. I used to do so when I was practicing lectures for students and maybe just trying them out, sort of articulating out loud what I had in my head so I could get it right for the next morning. Now I just seem to be talking about anything and everything, and it's rare when Chuck interrupts me, though I wish he would sometimes say more.

CHAPTER TWENTY-SEVEN:

DEL'S

ONE THING I've discovered as I've gone along is that philosophy is best left to philosophers, those professional thinkers who don't seem to get out of the house very much. Philosophy is fun to read as a mental exercise, but it never really seems to be much use as a problem-solving tool, or as a form of comfort or inspiration.

Maybe it's because it always wants to address the largest of issues concerning the existence and purpose of life, which I can't help but think the average person doesn't ponder so much each day, as opposed to one's more practical and day-to-day experiences. Boethius felt that philosophy should console a person, but really, when your truck breaks down most people don't start out with philosophy.

·　·　·　·　·

Del's is our local eatery, and it's probably the only place in town, other than the Safeway, The Office, our local bar, and maybe Kenna's place, where you're bound to meet people you know whenever you go in. Even during tourist season, Del's normally packs in a majority of us townies, and so most of the booths and tables will be occupied by people you know. It pretty much doesn't matter if you're there morning, noon or night, you can always expect to shake hands, slap backs and pass the news as you make your way to a seat. Whenever we come in we can rest assured that we'll hear, "Hey Al, how's it going? How's Chuck these days?" or "Hi Joanie, how're the dogs doing?" That sort of thing.

Even the tourists get a heavy dose of this with the regulars around, and it seems to bring out the best in them, holding doors for others, chatting with the two waiters, and not whining if their hash browns were maybe just a tad on the crispy side of paradise.

Del's is decorated in what I might describe as Post-Modern-Lumberjack. There are bears on the walls, and two-person saws, and the sort of podium that the cash register sits on is an upright varnished log, and the paper place mats have bears on them, which, if you have a pencil, and I do, you can fill in a maze to get the bear from a starting point to a pot of honey, which I do every time I'm there, and sometimes just in bits, here and there, in case Joanie sees and frowns at me, but when I'm there by myself for coffee or something I pretend that it's a new puzzle and look at it for a long time before I fill it out. There's a name for that, but I forget what it is.

In the summer, there are fresh flowers on every table, and the windows are open. In the winter, there's like a blast furnace or something that keeps the place toasty and your coffee hot.

Joanie and I have eaten through the menu about two times by now, and we have found our favorites, and then of course the Things That Must Be Avoided. Among the latter are things like Fettuccine Alfredo, and

I don't know what Del and Alfred fell out about, but Alfred is obviously not welcome in Dobbins any longer.

There are also the fried oysters, and even though you live in Montana and should realize that you're pretty far from the coast and the Safeway doesn't have a direct line to Seattle or Portland, you still want to try them, at least once, in order to learn one of life's simple lessons. Upon having them, I believe Joanie said something along the lines of "My mouth will never feel the same again," and I believe I added that I would do something with my tongue involving a band-sander.

Describing Del herself is somewhat difficult. This is not because Del is so very plain that she defies description, but rather the opposite, and Dickens is likely the only person who might do her justice, but I'll give it a go, even though one of the real problems in describing Del is that she is a thing in motion, first and foremost, and so it's difficult to get a good long look at her so as to define her parameters.

Typically, one only sees Del as something in pale blue, as if one were somehow just glimpsing a summer sky, briefly, from the corner of one's eye, as she moves from place to place, never very long in one location, and almost always across the expanse of the room. Those tables that she might have actually visited likely remember something blue and then perhaps the breeze left by her vacancy, as if the air itself was an obstacle to her movements and her sudden absence allowed it to somewhat grumpily return to its former environs.

Del is perhaps forty-ish, though I'm not good at guessing age, and I suppose is what one would describe as being medium height. Perhaps her most striking features are a mass of sandy-brown hair which is somehow kept preternaturally neat, done up in some sort of elaborate weave upon her head, and her perpetually tanned features, even in the depths of winter.

I once overheard someone speculate that she had a tanning bed at home, and someone else said that she had ancestors from Spain or some other sunny climate, but I always imagined that she merely spent a good amount of time somewhere near the inferno of a heater in the back in the winter time.

As far as I know, there is no Mr. Del, or at least Kenna is unsure about this, and so I cannot make an accurate report. If there is a Mr. Del out there, he is probably exhausted with having to keep up with his wife, and this is why we've never seen him.

Del's is a predictable place, and as such it is comfortable and reassuring. I usually just order things by number, unless there's something new on the standing chalkboard that sounds interesting and doesn't involve oysters. One morning I called Joanie on my way back from doing an interview for my next column and we decided we'd meet for breakfast, and I arrived first and got a table by the window and ordered for us. Actually, I didn't really "order" because I only answered questions when Ricky came to the table.

Ricky is one of two very young men who work at Del's, and as far as I know they must live there because I've never been in when they weren't there. Ricky is dressed in jeans and sandals and T-shirt because it's summer. I think this changes over to flannel and boots in winter, but he, too, is a constant at Del's, in every way.

He said, "Hi Al, just you or will Joanie be coming along?"

Just to say, nobody in Dobbins is "mister-this" or "missus-that". You always refer to people by their first name.

Anyway, I said that yes, Joanie would be coming along before too long, and he asked, "Then that's a number 3 and a 6, right?"

I responded by saying that he was correct.

Ricky did not in fact whisk away to the next table, but instead put his hands in his front pockets and said, "Number 8 is looking pretty good today, Al, even though of course you're pretty happy with 6."

I looked blankly at Ricky for a moment. Is this true, I wondered. Should I maybe not have a number 8 this morning? Could I be missing out on something partic- ularly good? But now I was second-guessing myself, trying to remember what a number 8 was. I couldn't remember, and for some reason I didn't want to ask what it was. Was it the one that comes with ham and pancakes, and if it was, did that mean you didn't get hash browns? Or maybe it was the one that has gravy on the side? I couldn't recall!

I decided instead to use the Socratic Method to hide my ignorance: "What's so good about it today?" I asked.

"Oh," Ricky said, and unfortunately countered with Zen, which seems to provide only glimpses of solu- tions without revealing anything, thus negating my Socrates: "Gene is out sick today and so Johnny's doing the cooking and that one is sort of his specialty. So, what do you think?"

I looked down at the bear on the place mat and couldn't see at all where the poor bugger could possibly get to the pot of honey. I suddenly had Kierkegaard in my head, informing me of the possibility that every-thing in life could simply be a misunderstanding.

"Mmmm," I said. "That sounds mighty tempting, but I sort of already had my taste buds ready for the 6."

Ricky smiled weakly, perhaps disappointed in some vague Jungian way, judging that I've merely behaved in some safe and archetypal manner, but conceded by saying, "Right you are. Comin' right up."

Hegel informed me that I'd been completely rational in my decision, but now I had this nagging feeling that maybe I'd made the wrong choice, which could very well affect the entire rest of my day. Honestly, I don't need philosophical dilemmas at breakfast, especially when the result might be the tearing of your soul or possibly missing out on hash browns.

And just as I was about to pull out my pencil and ponder the intricacies of getting the poor bear back on the road to salvation, I heard somebody a couple of ta-bles over say, "Stacy," and then someone else said, "A bad bunch, them guys," and then, "Walter," and a few seconds later the name, "Hollis".

And as if to summon him, that's when Hollis came in.

The first thing you notice when Hollis walks into a room is that everyone looks up as if the temperature has suddenly changed, and then the next thing you no-tice is that everyone finds something else to do with their eyes. Hollis looked around, under the brim of his hat, and made his way over toward the window seats.

He passed by and I said, "Hey, Hollis. Joanie's coming. Want to join us?"

Believe it or not, there were actual sort of sideways

glances at this, people wondering how this might play out I guess, but Hollis turned, looked down where I sat, and parked himself on the other side of the table.

"Morning," he said, somewhat grimly, and by "somewhat grimly" I mean a bit more than usual.

"How's it going?" I asked. "Everything okay?"

"Uh-huh," he said.

Ricky magically appeared at that moment and put down two cups of coffee, and a third empty one for Joanie. Then, Del herself appeared out of thin air and asked if Hollis was having his usual. Hollis didn't seem to hear this or notice Del, because he was staring at his coffee, as if it might have some answers in it or something. I do that too, and sometimes it does. Del, however, merely looked at me, then at Hollis, and cleared her throat meaningfully, if you know what I mean.

Without looking up, Hollis said, "Yeah. The usual. Thanks Del," and Del vanished in a collapse of air.

Now, my way of playing out a morning in my life is to take it very slowly if at all possible, and more so recently. Don't get me wrong, I'm one of those Morning People and all that, but I usually don't care to have any philosophical dilemmas before lunchtime, and I certainly don't want two, and now I had the second one and I just despaired of getting the bear where it was supposed to go before Joanie showed up and then I'd have to hide my pencil.

But there it was again: Hollis was obviously feeling pretty low about something, and I should try to at least wheedle a bit of it out of him if for no other reason than just to commiserate, but on the other hand I was just dying to find out about Stacy and Walter and everything and apparently Hollis was in on it too! And there was no way I was ever going to ask Walter, and who knows if a human might actually see Stacy again in this lifetime, so, I decided on Direction A, wheedling and commiseration, and I was looking down at the bear and the little maze and I thought I remembered how it's supposed to go now, but what came out of my mouth was, "I understand you and Stacy and Walter finished up those fellows who'd been poaching. How'd that go?"

Hollis looked up and stared at me as if I had just come at him with a knife and he hadn't been expecting such rudeness at breakfast.

"Um, that is, I think that's what I heard, and of course I work for a newspaper and all," I finished lamely.

Hollis looked back down at his coffee a little longer, picked it up and drained it, and Ricky once again appeared and filled our cups and then Hollis said, "Okay," and looked meaningfully at Ricky who hadn't in fact magically disappeared and who was standing there looking at us both.

"Uh, sorry," he said. "Orders. Gotta go."

Before I could ponder whether Ricky meant he needed to get orders from customers or he had been under orders, Hollis said: "So, I've been following Stacy around."

I, well, I gaped at that. I have to tell you that on most days, and especially at breakfast, at Del's, with my place mat comfortably in front of me, a cup of hot coffee readily at hand, that I am not much surprised by anything too very untoward in the world. Normally the bear gets where it needs to go without any problems.

I did my very best Bland: "Oh. You've been following her around. Um, can a person even do that and why would you want to?"

Hollis didn't answer right away, and for some reason looked at his coffee again in a way I could somehow imagine was actual embarrassment, except that wasn't one of the possible emotions that Hollis had, as far as I know.

"Okay," Hollis said, and he rubbed his face with both giant hands and then he took his hat off and put it on the table! Hollis had an upper part of his head that I was completely unaware of and actually quite a lot of hair! Now I knew I was in for something, and I couldn't help myself and I put my elbows down on the table and kind of leaned in, and so did Hollis.

"Okay, the deal is I once saw Stacy and I thought she was kind of interesting, you know?"

Yes, I knew, and I asked him if he wouldn't mind if I interrupted him there for just a bit, and he sort of squinted at me and said okay, and so I told him about Grip and me on the river, but it took ten minutes, and Hollis was riveted on every word I said. When I finished, Hollis had a sort of glassy look, like he wasn't focusing on anything, and I asked him if he was all right and he slugged down his coffee and then Ricky appeared, again, magically, and Hollis gave him a particular look that I was now familiar with and Ricky vanished for good that time.

Hollis rubbed his hands together a bit, and then said, "Okay. Let me tell you."

And then he did. He told me he first found out what her truck was and any place that she'd hang out, and he started to follow around to see where she'd go, out in the mountains, and try to be on the real down-low about it.

"And she'd ditch me every time! Every time! I'd be maybe a quarter-mile back on some road she was headed out on, and then I'd keep going and lose her and nothing but a dead end and there's nowhere to turn off to! I know it! And she did it, like maybe five times and I know she didn't see me. I've done this before, following the Bad Guys in Iraq, and they were way spookier than anyone you'd ever run into here, and especially here. In the middle of no place!"

Del suddenly appeared then. She had a pot of coffee, and smiled. It was an odd smile I guess because she just stood there and didn't even ask if we needed more coffee.

Finally, Hollis looked up and said, "Can I have some?" and it took Del a couple of moments to realize she'd been asked a question and so she kind of just stood there smiling at us, and then something must have triggered because she said, "Yes. Of course. Ha! That's what I'm here for, after all!" and she filled our mugs and then I heard a vague 'snap' and she was gone.

So, Hollis was back to staring at his coffee as if he was expecting mist to rise off it and spell out words or something, and by this time I couldn't help myself and I was really trying to make a good go at Socrates again, because the guy was really more nosy than anything else I'm guessing, because otherwise why ask so many questions, right?

So I said, "Okay, I get it. But why were you following her and what about the Bad Guys and Walter and all that?"

Hollis picked up his hat absently with one hand as though he might put it on and with his other hand picked up his coffee and looked back and forth and I was just about to tell him not to pour coffee on his head when he put both down and sort of looked at the table again.

"It's like I said," he said. "I kind of find her interesting and so I wanted to uh, you know, see if maybe she and I could meet sometime."

"You thought that you'd kind of stalk her a bit and then ask her out on a date?"

Hollis stared at me and I could feel the heat burning through my cotton shirt.

"Oh," I said. "Oh...I think I understand. You just kind of wanted to be informal about it is all. Didn't want to look pushy or anything. Hoped you'd just kind of run into one another sort of coincidentally?"

Hollis sighed and unclenched his coffee mug enough so that I was no longer in fear of it breaking.

"Yeah. Like that."

Well, that was interesting, I thought. On the other hand, this wasn't telling me what I wanted to know, and the bear on the place mat obviously wasn't going anywhere soon.

"Okay," I said. "But what about Stacy and Walter and all that?"

So Hollis sighed again and put down his coffee and laid his hands on the table. This was going to be good. He said that he'd just been headed down 81 and saw

Stacy's truck turn up the Crescent Creek cutoff, and he decides he'll see where she's going. He hangs well back, maybe half a mile, because he knows this road and there's nothing on it but one little run-down shack out there and the road dead ends twelve miles out. So, he gets a ways up the road and just pulls over and waits, thinking this time he'll just say hello to Stacy when she comes back down.

Apparently, he's sitting there for about fifteen minutes when suddenly Walter's truck appears and blasts by him. Well, now he can't figure out what's going on, but he sure as heck is going to find out. He follows Walter as fast as he can, and manages to get close enough to just see him turn off the road. He slows down then, and turns off too, and sees both Stacy's and Walter's trucks parked outside this little shabby cabin. He sits in his truck for a minute and then decides what the heck and gets out and comes up to the little cabin and just opens the door.

So, he is standing in the doorway and sees three guys all sitting on the floor with their wrists zip-tied behind their backs, and Walter has his pad out and writing something down, and Stacy is sitting in a chair with her legs crossed, just all comfy-like, and is saying something to Walter about how she finally figured out who had killed those bucks the summer before.

So, Hollis says he's just standing there like an idiot and Stacy says, "Hollis Granger. Seen you around."

And then he says he realizes that he's just standing there like an idiot and so he can only manage to say, "Just thought I'd see what was going on. Sorry to interrupt," and Walter gives him a funny look and then he gets back in his truck and heads back to town.

He concluded all this by bemoaning the fact that he probably had no chance at all with Stacy now, or something to that effect.

And at that moment I heard Hildegard of Bingen say, "We cannot live in a world that is interpreted for us by others," but then I remembered what Immanuel Kant once said, that "Happiness is not an ideal of reason but of imagination" because that's the only way I can explain it, and so I said, "Well, what about Kenna?"

Hollis looked at me with a blank stare.

"Kenna? The pretty girl at the hair place? What about her?"

"Well, she told me she was sweet on you and was going to make you pay attention to her."

Hollis processed this for a couple of seconds and then whooped with laughter. Hollis laughed! This caused considerable consternation in the diner, however, and now every head was turned our way.

Hollis looked at me and grinned. "That's a good one, Al. She wouldn't look at me twice. I know."

"Even so, it's true," I said, and Hollis just stared at me with his mouth open while I pulled out my pencil and quickly drew the line that finally got the bear to where he needed to be.

"What's so funny, guys?" said Joanie, just reaching the table and sitting down. "Wow, Hollis. You have nice hair," she said. "I don't think I've ever seen it before."

Joanie turned to me. "You're not doing that stupid puzzle again, are you?"

I just smiled and put my pencil back in my pocket.

· · · · ·
DAYS AND NIGHTS

Someone may ask "Why are you angry? What are you angry about?" and you cannot say. They might ask after your feelings or how you're doing, and you cannot say. Words are very important, deep and rich as earth, and yet like the earth they can turn to dust and blow away. To say it in words would be a betrayal of your mind and heart.

CHAPTER TWENTY-EIGHT:
SUSPICIONS ABOUT HOLLIS

O NCE, early one morning as I was headed out fish-ing, Chuck's path took us through town on our way out. As we passed the Safeway, I saw Hollis's truck parked over at the side of the building, and I thought that was odd, because it wasn't light yet and the store wouldn't open for hours. I wondered if he'd had en-gine trouble or something and maybe had to walk home. And then it occurred to me: I didn't know where Hollis lived. I'd never asked him. I always saw him around town, it seemed, so I was pretty sure he lived somewhere nearby.

When I came back through town later I saw his truck was gone from the Safeway as I pulled in to get a few things on the way home. When I went through the check-out, I sort of casually asked Jill if she knew where Hollis lived.

"No," she said, "I'm not sure. Sometimes I see him coming down 81, so maybe out that way."

Amy looked over from her check-out lane and shook her head, as if to verify Jill's information.

Because I had nothing to do, and because I'm a real nosy sort of person, I drove out 81 a ways to see if I could spot his truck somewhere. I went up and then down, for quite a few miles, and pulled down the only side roads to look, but nothing.

So why was I even doing this? I have no very clear idea. I hoped it wasn't the stupid one I'd had before about maybe "fixing" Hollis and then, so, somehow, "fixing" myself, because I knew just how insane that was. And let me tell you, I didn't need any more crazy in my life. I just really didn't. And yet, I got back to town and drove around a bit before I went back home.

When Joanie got back home I said, "Joanie, do you know where Hollis lives? Have you ever heard anybody say? Has Kenna ever said, or anybody?"

Joanie thought about that and said, "No, I don't believe so."

"Okay. I need to know. Don't ask me! I don't know. I just need to find out. Like quietly."

Joanie was interested then.

"Can we wear black and balaclavas?" she asked. "Because if we can, then I'm all in."

"I don't think that'll be necessary," I said, having an idea already, "but I wouldn't mind seeing you in those black leathers again."

Okay. So we came up with our plan. It would be a stake-out. We would surveil the Safeway first. We got ready: Joanie got into all black and put on her shoulder holster with her Browning. I was watching. I was dressed as always, in jeans and flannel. Joanie asked if she should do some camo on her face.

"If you'd like that," I say.

This was the craziest thing we'd ever do. Well, no, not exactly, but that's for later. Even so, watching Joanie getting all Secret Agent on me was sort of exciting. As we drove into town in the wagon (Chuck was too conspicuous, we thought) I said, "Why didn't you ever get into martial arts? That would be really cool."

She looked out the window.

"Who has the time? The job, the dogs, life? Besides, who needs Kung Fu when I've got my Browning?"

I couldn't disagree with that, running that scene from *Raiders of the Lost Ark* over in my head. I had almost forgotten what this was all about.

"Joanie, if Hollis is, you know, without someplace to live, or if he's in some sort of bad way, then what do you think we ought to do? Because I haven't thought that far yet."

"You're ruining the atmosphere. Let's find out first."

So, we pulled into the Safeway lot and parked way over on the opposite side of where I last saw Hollis's truck. Then we waited. And then we waited some more. I was bored.

"I'm going to go in and buy some cookies."

"No you're not," Joanie said. "You'll blow our cover."

Okay. I didn't watch television any longer, but that sounded reasonable to me. So, we waited. Without cookies, which would have been really good, I was thinking. This was getting dumber and dumber for me now. What was it that I ever imagined might come out of this?

That's when Hollis pulled in.

"Bingo!" Joanie said. "Well, let's see what he's up to."

Hollis had parked over at the far side of the store, and then stayed in his truck.

"So, what's he doing?" I said.

"Maybe nothing," Joanie said. "Maybe it's what you thought. He doesn't have anywhere to go, and this is where he parks at night and just sleeps in his truck."

"Well, what the hell does he do during the winter then? He'd freeze to death."

"Don't know. Maybe he goes someplace else in the winter."

I didn't think so, but then again, I didn't really know much about Hollis when it came down to it.

"Now what?" Joanie said.

That was a good question. I didn't have a good answer.

"Do you want to go over there and see? You know, talk to him?"

I didn't know about that either.

"Maybe we just found out what we needed to know. Maybe now we should just go home and think about what we should do, if anything."

"Okay," Joanie said. "But let's wait a bit. I got all dressed up for this and everything."

So, we waited twenty more minutes, and then we headed home. After we got back from the "stake-out", I was as depressed as a person could be in a Montana summer in the Rockies, for about a week. Joanie and I talked about Hollis off and on, but neither of us had any bright ideas.

"I'm assuming he has some sort of pension or something, right?" Joanie said.

Neither of us knew even the least little bit about service men and women, and what life was like after one left the military.

"I don't know," I said. "But if so, it must not be enough to pay a mortgage. What I don't understand is why

Hollis isn't permanently employed with someone. You said that after that first column came out you'd heard people talking about hiring him for things."

"Maybe they did," Joanie said. "Maybe it was all temporary stuff."

Maybe it was. I hated not knowing anything.

·   ·   ·   ·   ·

I continued to see Hollis here and there, in town, at Del's, driving down the highway. I passed him in the street once and we said hello to one another. I asked if he wanted to go fishing again sometime, and he said he thought he could in a couple of weeks, but was taking a job for a bit with a rancher. I wanted to just flat out ask him what his situation was, but I just couldn't. And so that was that. Hollis wasn't going to offer any information willingly, and I figured there was likely a reason for that and it would not be welcomed for me to pry. So, Chuck and I headed back home, but then for some reason I turned off and headed out to Wiley's.

When I pulled into the Wreck-A-Mended, something seemed odd to me. I couldn't quite place it, though. Chuck parked, and I got out and wandered around a bit. Then it struck me: where were all the cars and trucks? There were only a few here and there. Wiley emerged from the office in a few minutes, decked out in his usual coveralls, wiping his hands with a shop cloth. What in the world does he do to get so dirty in the office? Another of life's mysteries that I had no intention of pursuing.

"Wow," I said. "It looks like business has been good. Like really good."

Wiley grimaced a bit, and his perpetually sad face looked out at the empty wasteland of his car lot.

"Yes," he said. "It is the Yin and Yang of life, the boom and bust, one's youth and springtime and the inevitability of age and winter and tired joints."

"Um, Wiley? What are you talking about?"

Wiley looked around the pasture, sucked in a deep breath, and let out a very long sigh that sounded like somebody strangling an ailing canary.

"Well, after you wrote that piece in the paper about me, and then when Chuck became famous, well, people started coming by and buying things. All the time," he lamented. "And now, now I have hardly anything left to sell and I can't fix cars fast enough to build up any stock that might attract future buyers. I am now down to the very dregs of existence."

"Somebody bought Carl?" I asked.

"And Fred and Richard too. I already told you about Festus," he said.

"Wow," I said. "That's amazing. But you made some money, right? Couldn't that be parlayed into getting some different vehicles on the lot?"

"Maybe," Wiley admitted. "But I've always liked just repairing things that people have thrown out for whatever reason. I'm not sure this old dog can learn any new tricks at this point in life. Besides, I don't actually like selling cars. I just like fixing them. You know?"

Yes, yes I did know. I wanted lots of things fixed. There was satisfaction in doing so, for yourself and for others. Yes. I wanted to fix things. Just, how do you do that? I walked around the pasture for a bit, kicking metallic debris out of the way here and there. And I was so damn angry suddenly that I didn't know what to do. This just seems to come on me for no reason whatsoever. Joanie can say something about nothing and then I just snap, and it's nothing. It's nothing at all. Grip wants to jump in my lap on the couch, all fifty-some-pounds of him and I just can't take it, or Delmer is shooting a gopher and I can't sit on the porch because I'll die, or whatever it is and I just get so angry and it makes my stomach hurt and I feel ill. And then I have to go into the garage or outside and stomp around, or go sit in Chuck for a while until it stops, and I wish I had just one more box to put it in, and it always seems like there are no more boxes left.

Then I walked back to Wiley who had now parked himself on a couple of what might once have been tires.

"Wiley," I said, "what about this. You still have some profits from your sales?"

"Mostly all of it. I live rather humbly as it happens."

"Okay. Hire a flatbed from Bobby and go out and get a couple dozen throw-aways. Then, hire a second hand. You can repair faster and sell faster that way. Save out 20 percent from each sale, and go get two more wrecks. In no time you can have both stock and vehicles in the wings. Then you can stay busy repairing and selling at the same time."

Wiley looked at me. He smiled.

"You know, I knew there was something about you when I first saw you. I could just tell it."

Then he looked sad once again, and the smile disappeared, like mud smeared over a chrome hub cap.

"But there's no one I can hire. Everybody's some

ranch-hand of some sort around here. Where I can I get a real live mechanic?"

I sat down on another pile of tires.

"Wiley," I said, "did you know Hollis was an engineer when he was with the Rangers?"

DAYS AND NIGHTS

It makes no sense to me that of all the emotions that have been purged that I would be left with nothing but anger, the thing most alien to me. Of all the things in this world that one can survive without, that would be on the top of my list. Maybe this isn't surviving after all.

Chapter Twenty-Nine:
Grasshoppers

I WENT DOWN to Daffyd's shop probably every other day, just to talk and maybe I'd buy a fly or two, just to be neighborly. This time of year, his shop was always busy with the tourists, or "transients" as Hollis called them, and it was fun for me to people-watch a bit, and hear fishing stories.

This one had been on the Yellowstone, and another had just come up from the Madison, or somebody passing through talked about the Big Hole or the Beaverhead, or someone else had a story about the one that got away on the Clark Fork. To me, this was the literature I wanted to hear anymore.

Pretty much everyone in the shop was dressed in expensive shirts that were presumably designed specifically for fly-fishing, or so I supposed from the various brand names they bore. In fact, Daffyd had a nice stock of these himself, along with "fishing slacks" and the like. The slacks in particular were much nicer than what I had to wear to church. He told me they were quite an item with tourists.

"But how does one admire these very nice slacks when one is wearing waders?" I asked him one time.

"Dunno," he said. "Maybe they just make you feel good about being encased in neoprene."

. . . . .

It was now somewhat later in the glorious summer, and the heat came on fast at that time of year. The tiny insects that might alight on the water in the wee hours of the morning faded as quickly as the sun could rise over the Rockies. Because of this, I had learned to have some really large hopper flies with me, because after the heat was on, it's pretty much grasshoppers everywhere at this time of year for insect life, and thus trout food.

I happened to be picking up a couple that morning when someone nearby was buying tiny little midges.

He looked over at me and said, "You're never going to catch anything on those, buddy, unless it's your ear," and he laughed loudly at his joke.

I couldn't help but notice that his shirt cost more than my monthly budget, and yes, he'd apparently gotten the matching slacks.

Two of his friends came over then and looked at the hoppers in my hand, and one asked with fake and exaggerated interest, "Wow! Where'd you catch those? I bet there's a limit on them."

I laughed a bit and said I never buy anything smaller because I can't seem to thread the eyelets on those smaller flies, and then I headed to the counter.

One of the three called out to Daffyd then, "Better help this fellow out to his car with his purchase! Those look kind of heavy!" and they all laughed.

Daffyd looked at me and rang me up, and smiled a bit.

"Tourists," he said. "What's a fellow to do?"

After that, Chuck and I headed to Del's because it was time for mid-morning coffee and then later I wanted to drive over and see someone about the tractor collection they had for my next column. As it happened, Hollis was there and so I asked if he'd mind if I sat and had my coffee.

"No," he said.

That's about what you might get from Hollis at pretty much any time of day, but I figured it beat sitting at the counter by myself. Hollis was reading the paper.

"Anything interesting, that is, in The Paper I mean?"

"No," he said. "Nothing going on."

I saw he was checking the classifieds, for his next job I assumed. I just drank my coffee. When you sit with Hollis, it's sort of free-time where you can just meditate on something without being interrupted by something mundane like someone else's engaging conversation.

So, I meditated on my coffee until I heard, "Hey, look guys! It's Dennis Hopper!" followed by some loud laughter. I looked up and saw the Three Stooges from the fly shop looking at me and laughing. Then they meandered to a booth and sat down, talking loudly and laughing even louder.

Hollis, without looking up from the paper said, "What's that?"

"Just tourists," I said, "who apparently didn't like my choice of flies this morning over at Daffyd's."

Hollis looked up, then looked over to the other booth where the others sat.

"Want me to talk to them?" he said.

"What? No! I mean, I'm good, thanks."

I could sort of imagine the carnage of Hollis "talking" to someone on my behalf, and I didn't have the money to repair Del's tables and chairs. On the other hand, I was sort of flattered he'd offered, in the same way one might be proud of knowing a hit man, just in case.

"Well, gotta go," I said. "Good luck." No reply to that, but I didn't expect any.

. . . . .

During the summer, Joanie and I do whatever we want, whenever we want. We don't have to ask each other for "permission" to do something we want to do, or anything like that. Summer is too short to not be doing what you want.

Yes, of course we ask one another, "Do you want to go into town tomorrow and get the meat for the freezer? Or do you want to do that trail with me and the dogs in the morning?" Of course we do. But, it's understood that if you want/need to do what you want to, well by golly it's summer so you'd better do it. Before you know it, it's winter and then you're just down to Scrabble, television and ice fishing.

For me, I pretty much only do a handful of things in the summer: go fishing in the mornings, head out to meet somebody once a week to interview for my column, write my column one evening and then take it down to Chip and Jeff, and hang out with Joanie and the dogs on the deck, unless Delmer is "mowing".

Yep. Summer is what you're born for, and I know I whine a lot and have more than my share of self-pity, but I have it pretty good, I'll confess.

So, it is dark-o'clock and I don't wake up anyone any-more because they're all sleeping in the other bedroom, and so I don't even need to sneak out with the thermos, and Chuck and I head to the river to cast a bit.

Today Chuck had in mind a stretch of the Clark that I hadn't gotten to yet that summer and I was really looking forward to it. Chuck pulled us off at a spot and I told him I'd be back in a bit and I opened the door and got my gear and turned around to see what was in front of me, and I wish I could say it so that you really saw it.

I could do it in ways that made sense to me: the beginning blue as darkness faded, which was just the color of the Mediterranean that the ancient Greeks could never say. Or that when the sun crested the first ridge it was like the dragon-fire that Beowulf bore down on, to fight for the sky. I could say that the water that passed me down below was a poem by Hopkins, and all was alive and striving to speak.

And of course you'd never see what I saw, because I don't write as well as I'd hoped I would. I'm sorry about that. You'd ache to see it the first time, just trust me. I'll give it another try later on.

The first bend in the river was still in shadow as I stepped into the water. It was perfect. I have cast rather badly for as long as I've been fishing, but the Clark is pretty forgiving in places. I cast out, watching the water slip by in eddies around submerged rocks, and missed my first fish because I wasn't really paying attention. Then I caught one, maybe five minutes later, and another five minutes after that. They went back to their dream world, and I did too, just further upstream.

There was a place maybe half a mile further up I wanted to get to by the time it got hot. A favorite place, where the water was deep and the fish weren't so easy to coax, but it was a beautiful place to stand and cast and lose yourself for a while.

I made my way upstream, trying to time the rising heat to when I'd get to the big pool I had in mind. But, as I rounded a bend I saw the guys from the fly shop were there.

This was bad in all kinds of ways, and I was already imagining the various ways this might ruin my morning. First, I had really wanted to fish that pool, and though I was willing to wait my turn, I really didn't want these guys hanging around because I am a sort of so-so caster, and wasn't fond of the idea of these guys watching me. Second, they were jerks. On top of all that, they were jerks.

I don't know why, but I continued on down the river, sat on the bank waiting for them to leave, and tied on a gloriously large hopper. It was green and red and yellow with rubber legs and it was so ugly it was beautiful.

Sort of on cue, all three of them seemed to pull in at about the same time, and began to wade out of the river, just about where I was sitting. As they got closer, the one guy with the expensive shirt spotted me and said to the others, "Whoa! It's Mr. Hopper himself! We should get an autograph!" and he and his buddies laughed quite heartily about this.

"Any luck?" I asked in the traditional greeting of one angler to another.

"No," one of them said. "Tried six flies and nothin'. No fish here."

"Watcha got tied on there, pard?" Expensive Shirt said. So I showed him.

"Man! That thing's like a B-52! If there's a fish in there you might stun it with that! Bet that's illegal around here!"

More laughs.

And then I went fishing, like I intended, and the three amigos stood on the bank to watch. Oh, good.

I waded out about as far as I could go, but I knew from previous experience that there was a ledge I could stand on next to the deepest water because I'd seen it in late summer when the water was low, and I think the onlookers were perhaps surprised that I could get out so far. I only did this because, as I said before, I'm not that great a caster.

I stood there in the middle of the river, with the Rockies at my back, and my mind just wandered off to where it always goes when I'm fishing. I'm not sure why that happens, but it does. And all I can see is the beauty of the water, and tiny little yellow flowers covering the boulder I'm aiming for. And I let some line wander down the current for a bit, and lifted it up in a back cast, and laid it out toward the boulder. And I lifted again, and I put the line out a bit more. And then one more time and that was going to be my cast.

My enormous hopper dropped onto the water twenty feet above the boulder and meandered downstream. Just about when it reached the boulder, the trout came up in a big swirl, and the battle was on.

I finally pulled the fish alongside, and it was a beauty. I took a moment to admire it, and slipped the hook and back it went. I cast again and again, admiring the water and the mountains, and the bluest skies you can ever have, and caught and released two more nice fish.

And then it was getting a bit hot, and so it was time to call it a day. I turned and waded towards shore, and there were the three guys, still standing there watching. I had forgotten all about them, and everything else.

They met me at the bank, and one said, "Wow! That was awesome!" and Expensive Shirt said, "You sure know this river."

I unzipped a pocket, and drew out a fly box, and handed them each a really gloriously ugly hopper.

And then I said, "Good luck, guys," and headed back up the bank to reach the trail for the long walk back to where Chuck was waiting for me.

When I finally reached the upper bank, panting, I passed a boulder and said, "Good morning, Stacy," and paused on the trail.

A voice said, from somewhere very nearby, "I see you kept no fish."

"I rarely do," I said. "They're far too beautiful to keep for yourself."

"Nice gesture with the flies," the voice said, "especially because they seem to be real jerks."

"Thanks, Stacy, and nice 'seeing' you. Grip is doing fine, by the way."

I sat on a rock to catch my breath for a moment, and Stacy emerged from somewhere, dressed all in gray, with a pair of binoculars around her neck.

"Did you spot me somehow?" she asked.

"Not really. I just saw the sun glint off something and made a guess. If you weren't really there, then I'd just be talking to myself, which is sort of normal for me."

"Hmm, these are rubberized," she said, touching the binoculars. "Must have had the visors back too far."

I sat there for another minute, then stood up to go.

"I like your articles," Stacy said. "I read them every week."

I thanked her and she said, "Liked that one about Hollis. He's kind of an interesting guy."

"Yes, I guess so," and I made sure I didn't say anything else.

And I walked back to Chuck, and I couldn't help but think that it was good to be alive, and to know that you were.

DAYS AND NIGHTS

Joanie told me a good joke the other day and we laughed so hard tears came to my eyes. It was the first good laugh I could remember, and later I just about cried about that.

CHAPTER THIRTY:
THE FIRE

THERE ARE so many things in this world that happen all the time, everywhere and all the time, that you know happen on an intellectual basis, but not an experiential one. I suppose on the one hand, this can be a bad thing, and on the other, a good thing. All I mean is that you know such things as toucans exist, of course you do, because you've seen pictures of them or eaten Froot Loops, but you've never actually seen one, and that's kind of too bad. It would be really something, wouldn't it?

Sometimes I lie awake at night imagining all the things I've never really seen: Machu Picchu or the Eiffel Tower or a celebrity of any sort. Sometimes I imagine all the amazing things I could possibly have eaten, like sesame-coated oysters, grilled on a beach in Fiji, while watching the sun set over a forget-me-not-colored sea. Other times I imagine Jerusalem, or a place in Croatia or Turkey, and think, "Wow. I bet that's astounding to stand where the photographer is." And yet, I never have, and so that's a little too bad.

On the other hand, there are all those other things that happen all the time, everywhere, that you really should take time out of your busy day to thank God that you have no experience of them. There's no need to wring your hands about such things, and the litany of evil things in the world doesn't bear mentioning here, but honestly, we just don't really 'know' such things until we do.

And of course, not really 'knowing' such things is a good thing, in my opinion. I mean, why in the world would you wish to experience hurt or pain or tragedy or injustice or anything along those lines? And yet, I will have to admit that such experiences can, at times and in certain places and circumstances, be an enlarging part of one's life.

When I was in high school in my tiny town in Nebraska a tornado devastated the town thirty minutes north of us. My summer job was working in this big irrigation head and engine place, and when we got to work that Saturday morning at seven, the Big Boss came out and told us all to head over to Grand Island and see if we could help in some way, and that we'd get paid as usual. And we did.

We all drove over, maybe fifty of us, and we all went around all day, helping in any way we could: bringing water, helping people carry their treasures from their destroyed homes, looking for pets...anything. At the end of the day, I drove home exhausted, but glad I'd been there.

And so these things, whatever they might be, they leave a mark on you, good or bad, that you carry around, whether you want it or not. That's all I can say about that for now.

·   ·   ·   ·   ·

That beautiful, absolutely gorgeous day in August came upon us like a kiss.

Joanie stood in the kitchen looking out the window and said, "What's that you always say? 'Another darn beautiful day in Montana?' Something like that? I guess it probably has to be, huh?"

She watered the Purple Loosestrife on the window sill, which had survived all winter and was now eighteen inches tall. I looked out the window with her.

"Yep. But I hear there's thunderstorms later today."

And so there were. You could see them boil up on the western horizon and then come racing down the valley toward us. This was a good one, too. Finn and Tan didn't like all the crashes, but Grip looked out the window as if it might be something worth his interest.

It was later that afternoon when we saw the first big plume of smoke go up. And really, it was big, as if maybe a bomb had gone off, a huge one, and you were just now seeing the smoke from over the next ridge. But the plume didn't die down, like smoke from a bomb would. It got larger and larger.

Our little place is up a prominence at one end of the valley, and Dobbins is maybe a couple of miles or so away and down below. Delmer's place is of course about ten acres away, and so are our other three neighbors who make up our "development".

On a clear day, which is all summer long, really, you can see Dobbins quite well, and with even a cheap pair of binoculars you can see people coming and going. With Joanie's spotting scope, you can see anything you'd care to. From our place then, you could see that huge plume of smoke, now mushrooming into the sky, and it didn't look too far away at all, and Dobbins seemed as if it was almost right in front of it. The smoke was white-gray at first, and then got blacker and more ominous as it grew. We stood in the front yard and watched for a bit. Then we got some lawn chairs and sat in the front yard to watch because, really, what were you going to do?

Delmer and his wife, Dorothy, dropped by a bit later, and we got them a couple of chairs too, and some iced tea. Then we sat there and watched for a bit.

"Bad," Delmer said.

"Too close," Dorothy said.

Joanie went inside and brought out her laptop. She turned on a little device that she set on the ground, and bingo, she had internet, just like that. She typed and scrolled, and had satellite of Dobbins...real-time.

"How'd you do that?" I asked.

"Nevermind," she said. "Look," and we all came over and looked, and there was the big fire, just right over the ridge from town.

Delmer stood up and looked down the valley. "Wind's coming this way," he said. And it was.

"I'm calling the Forest Service and the freaking National Guard if there is one," Joanie said, and she went inside.

Delmer, Dorothy and I stood and watched. What can you do? Yell? Play Johnny Tremaine? I don't know. There's nothing but Dobbins for two hundred miles. There's no cavalry to call in.

And then the siren went off and I just froze to the ground. And then I needed to run just run, but there was nowhere to go. This is the sound that I grew up with in Nebraska in the spring and summer, when we'd spend nights in the basement hoping and praying that the tornadoes would somehow miss us, miss us all, and that come the morning all would be well once again. And now it was not a tornado, but a cry sent to the heavens to get out of harm's way as fast as possible.

"What do we do?" Delmer said.

"Where can anyone go?" Dorothy asked.

Half an hour passed.

"There's an evacuation notice going out right now," Joanie said, emerging from the house and picking up her laptop with one hand with her cell phone in the other, "and fire crews have been notified. They say maybe forty-five minutes, because apparently they're already stationed here and there at this time of year."

"We should do something," Dorothy said, looking down at her clasped hands.

Joanie and I looked at her. Like what? What should we do? What could we do?

"We're safe up here," I said. "Maybe we should just tell people to get up here? There're no trees or anything, and even a brush fire can't hurt us this time of year, with no grass to burn."

Everyone stood and looked around.

Delmer and Joanie said simultaneously, "We're safe up here."

And Dorothy said, "Why don't we just go down and tell everyone who can to just come on up here? They can just park on the road and we'll wait and see what happens."

"That's a good idea," I said. "Joanie, can you call Walter? He's probably who set off the siren. Tell him what we're thinking?"

Joanie typed on her keyboard, then punched in numbers on her phone. Delmer and Dorothy and I stayed standing, watching the smoke cloud go higher and higher, and seemingly bigger and bigger.

"Forest comes right on up to town, you know," Delmer said. "It'll make its own wind. Seen that before. It gets one house going, and then that's it."

Joanie spoke to Walter. We waited.

It seemed a long time, but from where we were we could see the first line of trucks were coming up 81 and heading for town.

"That'll be the first line, just to check things out," Delmer said. "Smart folks, brave folks every last one of them."

We watched them as best we could see, and then Joanie went and got her spotting scope and set it up.

Delmer said with a bit of a grin, "I guess we'd better put the shades down from now on."

And then we just kind of stood around, taking turns looking through the scope, but not seeing much except an enormous amount of smoke coming up and getting bigger all the time.

"I told Walter to start sending people up," Joanie said.

"We need food and water if people have to hang out here for any amount of time."

"We should have a barbecue," Dorothy said, brightening a bit. "That'd be nice. Delmer, go down to the Safeway and get some things and I'll get the grill set up."

Delmer looked at me with one of those 'I'm not going to say "no" to my wife' kind of looks, and so I said, "Let's just take Chuck and we'll be back in no time."

It took us about five minutes to get to town, and we waved at four maybe five vehicles that looked like they were headed up the valley to our place, but when we got to town, it was chaos, and you could see why. The fire had crested the ridge a mile away and it was enormous. It filled the horizon with black smoke and vortexes of flame like something Dante could never imagine.

Vehicles were headed quickly in all directions. People were running, scared. Chuck took me and Delmer just sort of along and we had our mouths open pretty much so I was glad Chuck was doing the thinking for us.

We got down to the Safeway and it was still pretty quiet. People were busy doing other things right now, like dashing back into their homes and grabbing things: kids, pets, televisions...the kinds of things that instinct tells you to get. Delmer and I hurried into the Safeway and found Jill and Amy.

Delmer took the lead, because he's a banker of course, and told them: "Look. We're getting out of town. Everyone. We're going up to our place. Everybody. Got that?"

Jill nodded, and then she was just about to start crying or maybe yelling or both and I said, "We need you and everyone else here to help us load up food water and ice as fast as possible. Call everybody!"

Delmer looked at me. "Good idea. Let's grab as much as we can and get out of here. I'll pay for it, Jill," he said, looking at her.

Jill looked at us then, trying to come to grips with it, but she could see the smoke out the front windows.

And Delmer and I turned around and looked too. It was a thing from the times I try to keep all of that in the box. Except it was right here and right now and thinking was difficult. It was going to be on top of us in an hour at best. I was not in a good way, but adrenaline does things for you.

Jill picked up the PA and said, as loudly as she could, "Everybody get up here right now! Right now!!"

In thirty seconds we had ten people because the Safeway was the largest employer in town.

"We need everything," I said, "as much as Chuck can hold and more. All your cars and trucks filled too."

Delmer shook his head. "No, this won't be a barbecue after all. We need everything, really. For everyone, and we need it right now. What are we going to do?"

One kid, I don't know his name, said, "We've still got the truck in the lot. The delivery truck. It's empty."

Delmer slapped his hand on the counter. "Call your friends right now. Anybody you can get. Let's get loaded up."

Amy picked up her phone and tapped a button and walked off, talking to someone.

Dobbins is mighty small, and when ten people call on their cell phones, it only takes two minutes to get someone in front of you when it's an emergency. Yet another of the beauties of living in a small town.

In no time at all, we had twenty people loading everything into a huge truck: meat, water, canned goods, ice, Styrofoam coolers, charcoals and grills, and flashlights, and whatever we could lay our hands on. It made me think of the tourists I like to watch in the store, not knowing what they want, and sort of figuring it out as they go along. That's what we did, and I know we missed something, like the can opener you always forget on the camping trip, but that was how it went.

"Camping trip," I said to myself as we hauled things into the truck. "Delmer, can you get in touch with Walter?"

"Got him on speed-dial," Delmer said with a question in his look.

"Maybe, if it's possible, have Walter tell people he can find to bring their camping stuff? Anything they've got? Tents, stoves, sleeping bags, that kind of thing?"

Delmer just sort of made an "O" with his mouth and then got down out of the truck and dialed. He went around the parking lot talking to Walter—I assume—and then came back to the truck.

"He's going to try. He sent Veronica and the triplets already, and he's one of those people who'll go down with the ship if you know what I mean, but he's going to try."

Jill said, "That's it. That's all we can get in."

"I'm glad," Delmer said, "because I'm too tired to haul anything else."

Jill and three guys got in the big cab of the truck, and got going, with Chuck leading the way. Amy and a caravan of cars followed along. We honked our horns and there were five other cars and trucks behind us from the Safeway, and we got out on the road and yelled at people we saw and headed on up toward home and safe ground. In two minutes we were twenty vehicles. Along the way something occurred to me and I called Joanie and she answered immediately.

"We're on the way back now. We have lots of stuff. What's it like there?"

"There are two hundred people here!" Joanie said, and she doesn't use exclamation points in almost any situation.

I tried to breathe and not worry or say something sappy because I needed, for once in the past two years, to stay focused.

"I need you to do something for me," I said. "Listen. Make sure the way in for us is clear, and then call Hollis. No, I don't know his number either. Find him, okay? Tell him I need him. I need him now. Wherever he is, tell him I need him now."

When we got back to our place, it was chaos. There were already maybe forty vehicles that lined the road up the hill, on either side and in the ditches, and everyone was carrying something or someone. Joanie had done her part, and the driveway into our place was clear, and Chuck took us into the garage as he always does and the big Safeway truck pulled in behind.

I got out and hugged Joanie who met us, and she said, "He said he's on the way."

I turned around and looked at more vehicles coming up the dusty road, and all I could think was, this is going to get bad for us if Hollis doesn't show up soon. My own mind was just about headed off to that oh-so-familiar-shut-down mode, the one I had become so satisfied with, the one that when faced with the overwhelming just snuck into the back seat, and then on into the box, and that looked so good right now.

I tried to rouse myself, and shook my head, and said to Joanie, "I wish I had a megaphone or something, and then we could get a bit organized. I wish I could get things organized just a bit."

Delmer and Jill and Amy came over then, and asked the million-dollar question: "So what do we do now? We have all this food, and the fresh stuff won't stay good all that long."

Delmer looked back down the hill at the smoke, and within the smoke, giant spouts of flames headed toward poor little Dobbins.

"Listen," he said, "we did our best. I have no idea how many people Walter was able to contact, but obviously everyone's leaving even if they didn't get the evacuation issue."

That's when Joanie said, "It went out half an hour ago, didn't you guys hear the siren again? It was on the net and radio and TV."

Delmer and I looked at one another. Maybe we were in the truck or something, but we hadn't heard anything.

Jill said: "That's 3,000 people then, and some of them will have places they can go, but if what you said to Walter is what he's doing, Delmer, then they're all coming here. Maybe thousands of people."

Delmer looked around at Joanie and Joanie looked at me and said, "Between these four lots we've got twenty acres, which is pretty big for a camping spot. We've got food for two days I bet, no matter how many show up, we can figure it. Let's camp. Let's get everybody settled somehow."

"That's a great idea," I said. "Where should everyone go to the bathroom, though?" And Delmer and Jill turned and looked at Joanie.

Joanie looked back: "I took care of that. Bobby is bringing twenty porta-potties on a flatbed in a couple of hours, he said."

Joanie is the most important and amazing thing on this earth of ours, and Delmer hugged her before I even had a chance!

And so we turned again and looked around, at a scene from a movie maybe, where our little town down below was on the edge of being swallowed by flame and smoke, and more and more people were arriving, having parked their vehicles farther and farther away, and walking to the top of the hill with whatever they could carry. We had no idea how the firefighters were doing, or even what they were doing, and we stood and stared and then tried to just get going and make things okay as best we could.

We had 300 people now just crammed in what we thought of as our front yard, and that wouldn't do because many more would be arriving if we guessed right. You could see the plumes of dust kicked up by vehicles down in the valley, and they were headed our way.

"We need to get organized," and so I started walking around to groups of people and asked them if they would pull back more so that we could make room for more people coming, and some did and some didn't, riveted in place to watch the spectacle down below and to wonder about their homes.

I was wishing I had a bull horn or something. Maybe I could get their attention better like that. I didn't have the energy to start shouting at anyone, and if I did, I doubted I'd have much authority, even though it *was* my yard they were occupying.

I went back to where Joanie and Delmer and Jill and Amy and Dorothy were standing, and Delmer said, "I guess we still better figure out pretty quick what we're going to do. We can't just let all this stuff in the truck melt or spoil. I don't even remember what all we've got in there."

"Put it in the garage?" Joanie said. "I don't see how moving it from one place to another would do much good. We need like the National Guard or something to get things set up, because otherwise tonight is going to be a disaster, even with toilets."

And more and more people were headed up. There was one dust plume, however, that didn't stop down below, and as it got closer I could see blue strobe lights flashing and wondered if it was finally Walter, arriving at last. But it wasn't, I saw, because it was a black pickup with heavy-tinted glass, with the lights flashing from behind the grill.

It was Hollis. He pulled up and parked so as to block the remaining driveway, and then extricated himself from the cab. He was all in black. His wide-brimmed hat was angled down over the front of his face. He closed the door of his truck, which had no name, and made his way up the drive. I went to meet him.

As I got a bit closer, close enough so that he could hear, I said, "What's with the lights?"

He looked up at me then, his face as grim as the fire down in the valley. "Came with the truck. Never used 'em before."

And then we stood in the driveway, looking at each other, and then him looking at all the people there, and then he turned back down into the valley.

"It'll be bad, from what I saw," is all he said. "I saw Walter, the idiot. Still down there, I guess."

A pang went through me then, because Veronica and the triplets were already here, I'd heard, and I hadn't found them yet.

"Chuck and I will get him in a bit," I said. "For now... listen. Joanie called, right?"

He turned then to look at me full on, and even though we had gotten to know one another he still had that look that made me want to shift my eyes away, like maybe he was waiting for me to say something more.

"Yeah," he said. "She called."

And that was it. That was it. He was waiting for me to say it, for whatever reason. So I did.

"I need you," is what I said.

I don't know why that was so hard, but I almost gritted my teeth when I said it. I don't know why. We'd been through a lot together already, and it should have been easier. But Hollis pushed back his hat with a thumb, and stuck his hands into his front pockets and leaned sideways a bit and said with a flat face:

"That's good. That's really good." He pulled down his hat then, and looked me over a bit, it seemed.

"I know how you got me hooked up with Wiley. He said so. I saw you and Joanie watching me one night at Safeway. I know why you did. I know you now. There hasn't been any way for me to pay you back, and I've been waiting. So, maybe this is it?"

And he looked at me then in a way that made me want to either run away or shake his hand, and I wondered how he looked and I'll say instead there aren't words for that. Stern? Expectant? Ready? Relieved. Yes, I suppose all of those things if one can do them together.

So, I closed my mouth, which I'd just then noticed was hanging open, and when I opened it again all I said was, "Take charge."

Hollis opened his mouth enough to show his teeth, and I had come to know that just a bit better, and then that went away, and then one hand went to the hat and snugged it down in a certain sort of way and he looked around for a bit.

"Okay," he said. "What've we got?" I told him. He looked at the crowd. He got to work.

I watched Hollis walk over in front of a big bunch of people and I sat back in the lawn chair to watch what would happen. The first thing that happened was that everyone gave him room, and there was no way they were going to crowd him, as if they'd just discovered a landmine a few feet away.

Hollis looked down on everyone and bellowed: "People! Come forward right now! I need your absolute attention!" And they did, even those folks who were sort of milling around an acre or so away, when they saw everyone else heading toward Hollis.

"There is a crisis as you know," Hollis shouted. "We are safe here, and we may need to stay here for some time. We are awaiting official word." People looked at one another, but no one doubted Hollis-By-God-Granger.

"Further assistance is on its way. For now, we must organize ourselves for the night."

And now people started looking at one another and talking back and forth to family members, because naturally, almost everyone thought they were likely just going to hang out here for a while and then head back home.

Hollis lowered his head, but just as loudly said, "No one will be leaving to go into town until the all-clear. We must stay out of the way of those who are protecting us."

He let that sink in for just about a second and somebody asked a question, and instead of answering Hollis shouted, "I need a show of arms! Right now! Men! How many men are here as the heads of families! Right now!" And arms went into the air. "Women! How many women are there here who are heads of families!" And more arms went up. "Men and women with families. You will now move a hundred paces to the rear, and a hundred paces to the right!" People stood and looked. "Right now! Get moving! Night will be on us before we know it and we have much to do!"

And they moved. And it went on like that, and he got groups separated and set down in the pastures, and then he got the single guys and girls separated too ("No funny business tonight," he told me later), and then he called out men to volunteer to unload the truck and they separated out everything we had. And so we began.

An hour later Bobby showed up with the porta-potties and we had those taken off to one side of the property. Hollis cut some sections of fence between properties and we moved people and porta-potties into as many places as we could on twenty acres. We had only six picnic tables between us all, and we put them all down along the driveway to do the cooking and serving of food.

Hollis got everyone who'd brought a tent to set them up all in the same place, and we started assigning the oldest people into those. He told singles and couples that he had "appropriated them" in the name of the greater good, and stared down anyone who might think otherwise, and yet explained the greater need.

Delmer and I and the other two neighbors took infants and their parents into our homes. We had Veronica and the triplets in our place, after Joanie had finally found them, and another young couple and their toddlers in the front room. By the time the sun was headed toward the ridge, we had fired up the grills and were cooking. And down in the valley, the fire burned on, and more and more vehicles went in that direction, and more and more came the other way, up the hill, to sanctuary. By nightfall, we had hundreds of people up on the top of the hill, and more arrived every hour.

Days and Nights

All of us have heard the phrase "senseless violence" before. I think about this and I try to understand what might be sensible violence, and I suppose that must somehow be understood as that which has a "purpose", something where somehow someone could find some sort of meaning in it.

When the killer shows up in the classroom and then is dead along with others, everyone quickly seeks for meaning: the parents must be responsible; the "disturbed" person, and was he bullied? (It's always a "he" by the way, something that seems to go unnoticed or un-discussed, as in how the Hell are we raising our boys these days?), and we ask and we ask and our news media makes sure to find something to tell us about, in order to provide us with "meaning" and "sense": Bullying. Not very stable. Troubled home life. Easy access to anti-personnel weapons and body armor.

No, I'm sorry, those are not explanations at all. Those are just things that we say so that we can make sense of senselessness. Those things make as much "sense" as comfortably bombing civilians from miles away where you don't even see their wrecked bodies and homes and children. No, it's all quite senseless. But in my life, meaninglessness is not an option. I must make sense of things. Somehow.

You have no idea how angry this makes me. If you ever met me you'd probably think me a quite pleasant person, I believe. However, we are human, and that means that we seek out meaning for everything, absolutely everything. We do it constantly, if you'd ever sit still long enough to let yourself notice. It is the absolute nature of science to explain everything to us, everything, so that we know about pollination and bacteria and disease and what just might be happening on Io, circling Neptune, in the ceaseless stars that surround us all.

But there is no meaning here. None. You cannot explain it away and say, "If only this...or if only that..." No. We always seek meaning, all of us, all the time. If we didn't, there would be no reason whatsoever to keep on living. Meaning is everything. Understanding is everything. And then there is none, and everything you thought you knew is shattered.

I'm sorry to have to remind you of that. Just go on about your day.

CHAPTER THIRTY-ONE:
TO FEED THREE THOUSAND

WE MADE IT THROUGH, but it wasn't easy. We set up and started cooking burgers and beans and potatoes and then all the other fresh meats went to freezers among the four houses in case we had to do it again tomorrow. We got everybody lined up and had the town's biggest barbecue it had ever seen, though not by choice. We got everyone fed, and it was a miracle. It really was. There wasn't enough food, there couldn't have been, and everyone was fed. I know you don't believe that, and I don't either, but it's true.

Later, as the sun went down over the ridge, we got everyone settled as best we could, but there was still a good sized crowd up at the front of our place and Delmer's place, looking down below, watching. And the fire had not stopped.

Joanie and I sat in our lawn chairs with blankets and watched as well.

Joanie put down her binoculars at some point and said, "There are buildings burning now. You can't tell what they are. I'm trying to remember if there's more than just the Duds and Suds and The Paper over there."

That reminded me that I hadn't seen Jeff and Chip around, though they could be over at Delmer's place. I kind of doubted it, though. They were likely down below, snapping photos and interviewing exhausted firefighters.

"I haven't seen Walter yet," I said.

"He's probably prowling the streets, looking for looters," Joanie said.

"Looters! Here?"

Joanie just looked at me. That did worry me then. If there were any bad guys down there, there was only one Walter and no backup. I wondered if I should drive down and see, and I said so out loud.

Joanie said, "Not a chance. What would you do anyway? Write down people's license plate numbers or something?"

"I don't know. Just find Walter is all and tell him Veronica and kids are okay so that at least he doesn't have to worry about that too."

"That's a good idea," Hollis said, standing right behind us looking out over the valley at the fire and smoke that you could still see in the dark now, and Joanie and I both jumped.

"Sorry," Hollis said, tiredly, distractedly, quietly. "But I'll drive, Al. I know the roads better than you."

Joanie sort of stared at Hollis then, and then she looked at me with a frown that said "bad idea" but all she said was, "Don't be gone long. We've got things to do up here too, and I won't make it by myself before I have to sleep."

"It might take a bit," Hollis said. "I need to find Kenna too, and I don't know where she is."

Joanie and I looked at one another then, realization settling down on the both of us at the same time, and no little surprise either. But in all the day's madness we had never once thought where Kenna might be, and now we both suddenly knew that she and Hollis had maybe been seeing one another.

"Oh Hollis," Joanie said, "we didn't know or think. It's been so crazy here..."

"We'll get her, no doubt about that," I said, and we got into Hollis's truck and headed down into the valley.

We passed Wiley's and then Gil's place in just minutes, but down here in the valley it was hard to see much. The smoke was heavy and from here, the only thing that illuminated the way was the fire, still up ahead, but obviously closer than when I was in the Safeway just hours earlier. We went slowly through town, because it was hard to see anything clearly. I'd already asked the obvious questions at least twice:

"Where are we going? Where's Kenna live?" and "Where did you last see Walter?"

Hollis was Hollis: "End of town. Up ahead. Side neighborhoods."

We drove on and got to the Safeway. We slowed and saw just one red truck in the lot, up front, and three guys standing near a broken window. I couldn't believe it. There really were looters. In Dobbins! Hollis slowed and then stopped.

He pulled out a pair of binoculars and said, "There's a pad in the glove box. Write this down," as he eyed the guys and then their truck. He read off the license plate number and I wrote it down and put the pad back.

"I know these guys," Hollis said grimly. "Bad bunch. Walter can take care of them later." But two of the three of them were now looking at us as we pulled away.

We drove on, dodging strange things in the road: somebody's garbage can, a stroller, a box of books, a television. Even going slow, it didn't take long to get to the end of town, where the fire was.

There were crews all over the place here, and for good reason. Coming around a corner, we were full-on for the show. Several homes were on fire just two blocks away from us. You could only make out vague outlines of the homes, and through the smoke you could see firefighters hosing them down as best they could, but the real problem was still out front: the forest that comes all the way to the edge of town, and that was a firestorm scene out of disaster movie. It was so large and so violent it simply didn't look real. An army of men and women were battling it the best they could.

Hollis and I sat completely quiet and just watched for a minute or two. For my own part, I was simply stunned by the enormity of it. Finally, I roused myself to remember why we were here.

"Where's Kenna's place?"

"We're parked next to it," Hollis said. "She's not there."

"Then where is she? She's not at our place. Where did she go?" I asked, stupidly, since of course that was what we wanted to find out.

"I don't know, but I've got an idea," Hollis said, looking ahead at the fire. He turned to me then and said, "If I'm not back in ten minutes, get back to your place and we'll meet up later. Stay here so I know where to find you, but after ten, head out. Maybe keep an eye out for Walter."

And all I said was, "Be careful," and Hollis got out and headed toward the fire.

This is probably not the time to break the suspense, but I'd like you to take just a minute to analyze what I felt like just then. There I was, sitting in the passenger seat of the truck, no use to anyone, and it was pretty darn obvious. I sat and stared ahead for a bit. I should do something, I thought. I got out of the truck and looked around. Yes. I should be keeping an eye out for Walter. Uh-huh, that's what I was doing. I felt the heat of the fire on my face and arms and I was standing sentinel, watching other people's homes burn.

I was obviously not helping anyone. I was a stupid spectator to the inferno. A mere tourist in Hell. It was time to take action. I got into the driver's side of Hollis's truck and waited.

And then, up ahead like some scene from a movie, here comes Hollis striding through the smoke and Dear Lord! He's carrying Kenna in his arms!

I got out of the truck and rushed up the street. "Kenna! Kenna! Is she okay?"

Kenna had an arm over her face, and Hollis set her down on her feet and Kenna doubled over. Hollis's expression was the one I was used to: as grim as the fire behind.

"Kenna! Are you okay?"

And then I realized she was not hurt or sick, and instead was laughing her head off!

"What the hell?!" I said. "Why were you carrying her?"

I looked at Hollis, but Kenna said: "Told him to. You know, 'damsel in distress' and all that."

Hollis frowned, and we all got in the truck, with Kenna in the middle. Hollis's knuckles were white on the steering wheel.

"Kenna, just what the hell were you doing out there?" I said.

"Watching the fire," she said, and then with a grin she added, "Well, watching the guys fighting the fire. They were pretty impressive," she said, half looking at Hollis. "Why, there was this one guy with a hose like this long," and she spread her arms out and laughed.

Hollis put his head on the steering wheel, and he was making strange little sounds that I couldn't interpret, and Kenna elbowed him in the ribs and Hollis lifted his head and he was laughing so hard there were tears in his eyes. But then the door closed up, and he gave a long look at Kenna.

"Don't ever do that again. I was worried about you."

Kenna looked at him a bit, as if assessing him, and patted Hollis on the leg. "Yeah, sorry about that. But, you know, no harm no foul, right?"

Then she looked at me and said, "'Bout time you two showed up. Guess damsels in distress are a dime a dozen in Dobbins."

Hollis said nothing, but just started up the truck.

I looked at her house and said, "Anything we should get first?"

Kenna looked at the house, then said, "Nah. Couple pairs of nice scissors, but no big deal. I put my leavin' shoes on before I left the house."

We drove back through town and saw no sign of Walter or anyone else. We drove through the dark, lit only by ten thousand fireflies of sparks, drifting, sometimes spraying across the hills, laying down somewhere and maybe causing more, and I had this feeling that once again I'd seen Evil, and once again there was nothing I could do about it. Perfectly helpless. We headed back up the hill to sanctuary, and the uncertainty of morning.

DAYS AND NIGHTS

I know what guilt is and what it can do to you, eating you alive, bit by bit, from the inside out leaving you empty like a dry pea pod. Guilt plays this game with me. It's a very simple game. If I say a three-letter word, "yes", then that means you die. If I say a two-letter word, "no", it means I die. That's it. Do you want to play?

CHAPTER THIRTY-TWO:
WE MAKE IT THROUGH TO ANOTHER DAY

W HEN WE GOT BACK, Hollis wandered through the endless line of cars and trucks and up the driveway and we found Joanie asleep in a lawn chair, covered in blankets. I leaned down and kissed her forehead. There were people out in front, looking down the valley, who would likely not sleep this night.

I told Hollis and Kenna that there were blankets in the house, and where to find them, and that their best bet was to get a couple more lounge chairs from the garage and bring them out with me and Joanie. Eventually, the four of us were lined up, side-by-side, re-clining in lawn chairs, looking down the valley. Hollis's chair wasn't nearly long enough, so eventually he just lay on the ground with his jacket rolled up behind him for a pillow.

"We'll figure something better tomorrow night," I said. "If there's a need."

The stars and the fire were our night-lights, and we watched both the heavens above and hell down below.

We slept for I don't know how long, but when I

opened my eyes there were still a few stars and Joanie was awake.

"We should get going. We need to feed people because there's been no all-clear."

I got up, sore, tired still, cold, and pulled the blanket around me like a shawl. And then we just got going. We started pulling food out of the garage and coolers and more people wandered by to help, and we just got going.

"Hi how ya doin and there's still a lot of smoke and well we'll just have to wait and see and how did you sleep okay? yeah same here and the bathroom's that-away and can you pour me some coffee thanks and you can do the potatoes over on that burner" and like that.

By the time it became truly light enough to see, people started to come by to the smell of food and coffee. People lined up to help and eat, taking shifts. Veronica and the triplets came through the line, and everyone got orange juice and sausage links and scrambled eggs. There wasn't a lot of banter except here and there.

Hollis and Kenna came through the line and we talked quietly and they moved on. Others took over and Joanie and I sat and ate. Eventually, people started lining up for the porta-potties, and that took a while, as you might imagine. And then everything was cleaned up and there was nothing left to do.

Hollis and Kenna came by then, and Hollis said, "Today is likely going to be some trouble unless we jump on it first."

I hadn't thought of that yet. Hundreds of people, maybe even thousands, being stuck on a hill in a field for a night was one thing, but to be stuck up here, in the sun, all day with nothing but worry, yes, things were likely going to get bad. And the food and water would run out soon.

Two hours later, as people were expectedly going to their vehicles to drive on down into town, Walter showed up. His truck sent up a plume of dust that showed his urgency. He was coming fast. However, there was a somewhat smaller dust trail in his wake. Something much smaller and slower. In about three minutes, Walter was finally here, and he sagged out of his truck.

Joanie and Hollis were there to meet him.

"Where is she?" was all he said.

Joanie took over then, and told him how Veronica and the kids had been housed and fed, and as she led him to the house he looked back over his shoulder at Hollis and me.

Hollis didn't turn to address me, he never does, as if speaking to himself perhaps, but he said, "Last night I called him an idiot. I was in a different way of thinking then. I don't think that way now. He's more the We Never Leave Anyone Behind type. Met a few of those in the past."

He turned then and just walked off. And I just want to tell you, I don't know how to do that. I don't know how to sort of switch things off like Hollis seems to be able to do. I'd like to be able to do that a little better when it's needed. I mean, switch things off that really should be switched off. But then, Chip and Jeff showed up.

I went over to meet them and they were both bent over dragging their gear out of whatever that pillbug was that they drove around in, and Chip was setting up a tripod and said, "Hi," and Jeff was pulling out a video camera and smiled, but didn't say anything yet, and so I said, "Hello," and they turned and said, "Just a sec," at about the same time and then presumably they'd gotten everything out of their little caravan of tricks and were ready to go because Chip turned around with his camera and said, "Hear you fed three thousand on forty loaves of bread, and where do I shoot?"

"Um, what?" was all I could manage because I'd just woken up and hadn't had but three hours of sleep and what the hell did he just say?

"All the people," Jeff said. "Fed and housed, right? Right here? Whole town, right? Stand over there. Where's Joanie?"

And as if on cue Joanie came down the driveway, wrapped in a blanket, and asked what this was and then they started taking pictures and Joanie was looking for her Browning.

It isn't polite to say here what she said, and she impressed me once again with her knowledge of dead languages, but Jeff and Chip moved off then and did whatever it is that they do when they're not tossing wads of newspaper into a basket.

I shouldn't tell you this, but I guess I have to because I understand that someone might read it, but that's why I kind of hesitate, because Walter and Veronica came out of the house then and Chip and Jeff had been walking that way, carrying their cameras, and when they came out, surrounded by the triplets, all holding Veronica's skirt, Walter turned around and kissed her in one of those sort of *Life* magazine kisses that describe what a kiss really ought to be and anyway Jeff and Chip whipped around and took pictures, and I looked at Joanie, my best friend for thirty years, and she looked back at me, and we kissed, and there were no pictures, and we laughed and laughed and we were so very tired.

DAYS AND NIGHTS

Things became so fragmented that after a while I found it difficult to piece things back together again in some meaningful way, just so that I could remember how things had unfolded.

It was very confusing for me and broken up in a way I didn't understand or even realize for a long time. Everything was out of place. I haven't yet been able to tell you about what really happened because of this, it has all just been little pieces coming to me here and there, and that is what I have said so far. I don't think I can tell you about That Day, not yet, but I think I will try to tell you now, as best I can, as best I can remember what has happened.

I remember that there came a morning when I got out of bed—I can't say that I woke up because I don't remember if that was a time when I actually slept at night, I don't recall sleeping any longer—and something had happened to me and I knew it but I didn't know what it was.

I walked out to the kitchen and Joanie was there and she looked at me and asked how I was and did I sleep all right and I said I was fine and asked her how she had slept and she said something and then I went outside because I wanted to see if I could understand the thing that I now knew had just happened.

It was summer now I remember and so quite some time had passed since the killing, or killings, or murders, or mass shooting, I don't know what to say. But I hadn't been aware that time had passed but it had, and the air was warm even early in the morning and I went outside and I walked around for a while and looked out at the pasture and the barn, and back to the house, and then I walked over to the garden and looked at it for a while, and I sat down and looked out as best I could but then I stopped looking because I think I knew what had happened.

I think I must have known then that I had somehow emptied myself, that I had emptied myself completely. There were no emotions left anymore, none, and I was safe.

But I remembered the words that you had to say when you spoke to someone and the things that you had to do with your face, which always had to go together for some reason, and that they had to match one another, and that was kind of difficult, but I remembered it as best I could.

If Joanie said something was beautiful or awful I knew what to say and what to do with my face. Sometimes there might be a bit of a lag before I answered, because sometimes I had to try to think a bit in order to remember the right words, but I usually did, most of the time, and then I could get along with things. I was inside myself looking out, and I would not come back out because in here I am safe.

CHAPTER THIRTY-THREE:

AFTER

THERE CAME A TIME THEN, when the smoke became less, and we all of us looked down the valley.

Have you seen such things as a mass of starlings in the fall leap and jump and call and say to one another the same thing and move in one direction and then another, all in concert, flowing one way and then folding back against themselves, perhaps passing pleasantries as they do so, fire-ashes against the sky meaning something to someone somewhere, shifting as with a hive-mind and moving again in another direction? That was us. It was time to see, no matter what.

I am so very tired now that I can't explain it, and somewhere there is fear about what has happened in town, but I am almost dead to it. Has that ever happened to you? You know, when something really bad happens and you can no longer feel it or even see it? I ask because I wonder any more if that's just me and maybe if there's something more wrong with me than I know, or is that just normal somehow? Can I still see and feel what's bad and good? I don't know. All of it just seems to wear me out any longer, all this thinking and seeing. Clearly I don't know the answer. It just makes me tired. Makes me want to sleep and try over again later.

But now, now it was time to go and see, and we all of us felt it, calling and pulling and down we went, a flock of us, descending on the town all at once.

Joanie and I went down with Chuck, and Kenna went with Hollis. We were all just part of a slow-moving line down the valley, and then when we got a ways past Gil's, the traffic split up a bit until we at last came to a barricade across the street where a lot of us pulled over and got out.

A bunch of us headed over toward the end of town, because we'd seen at least some buildings on fire, and naturally we had to see. The crews were still active, and we weren't allowed to get very far, but even from where we stood you could see that the Duds and Suds and a number of homes had burnt to the ground. Kenna's was one of them.

Both Kenna and Hollis just looked on, not saying any-thing, but there were plenty of teary-eyed onlookers in the crowd. Joanie and I went and stood by them for a bit, and eventually Hollis looked down at Kenna and said, "Now what?"

Kenna rubbed her face with one hand and said, "It's okay. There's plenty of room in my shop."

DAYS AND NIGHTS

I was so very afraid of everything.
Riding in the car with Joanie.
Noises.
An unexpected shadow.

Inside looking out was the safest place I could go, but the fear never went away. I shut everything down and emptied myself, I just bled out, but even in this new gray world the fear was there like a June bug clamped onto your screen door, unmovable.

There was a time that came, and I don't remember how long it was after I had shut everything down—time really didn't seem to matter very much, nothing seemed to matter very much—when the only thing I had left was fear and anger.

I thought about buying a gun for some reason. I looked into it. Joanie had two. Maybe I should have one.

CHAPTER THIRTY-FOUR:
I MEET DEATH AND LIVE TO TALK ABOUT IT, AGAIN

I SUPPOSE BY NOW you've come to understand what I said in the beginning, about being screwed up and all. This isn't something I can help very much, at least for now. Yes, I get frightened or confused by things, and yes, if maybe I opened that little box in the back of my head I'd maybe, maybe, face some things and well, maybe get "better" in some appreciable way, somehow.

But I also should mention in my own defense that life is in fact a threat on most days and that many of us just don't see it face-to-face very regularly, unless you're just sort of paranoid, or your occupation is one of those that qualify as "hero" on a daily basis.

Anyway, all I'm saying is that yes, of course, you could die at any time and in any place and so that's that. We usually understand this, somewhere, maybe in a box in the back of our heads that we just keep shut all the time. I'm not saying that you have one. I wouldn't want you to think that not thinking about your eventual death is somehow a bad thing.

For my own part, I'm kind of hoping that this will be something I see coming, like, hopefully, being a hundred and eight years old and then just sort of getting tired of the same-old same-old and then, you know, move on. Thanks for the good life, and all that.

. . . . .

The previous winter, Joanie, in our utter boredom with Scrabble, asked: "So what do you think the worst way to die might be?" Oh boy. There's my favorite thing to ponder.

"You first," I said.

She thought about it for a bit and then said, "I don't know. I suppose being burned alive at the stake would be awful. I was just reading Hawthorne."

I had to imagine this, briefly, as my mind sort of just did its usual skittering away from such thoughts, and then I said, "Being eaten alive. Yes. That would be the worst. Alligator. Thank God we don't live in Florida. 'Just when you thought it was safe to go in the water!'"

Joanie, introspective, said, "Yes. You're right. That's maybe worse by a smidgen."

Now I'm going to have to stop there for a minute because what I've come to understand is that once you know something there really isn't any effective way to stop knowing, or at least that's what's happened with me so far, and of course knowing things can be good or bad, so I guess you have to just live with that.

Along these lines, one of the things I know is that once you name something then you'd better watch out. It's actually a very ancient idea, all caught up with magic and such, just like Othin hanging himself on Yggdrasil the World-Tree and traveling into death as a sort of third-rate deity and then returning with rune knowledge and becoming the king of the Norse gods.

It's a persistent idea, it seems, and that's what our old saying "Speak of the Devil" actually means, of course. You know, you're talking about somebody and say their name and then there they are. The rest of the saying is "Speak of the Devil and he appears," and so we came up with all kinds of names for Lucifer so that we'd never speak his name, because if you did... And I have to tell you that on 364 days of the year I'm pretty much not superstitious, but just kind of naming your own ending in your living room made me wish I'd learned more about how people back when used to divert the Evil Eye or something.

However, there are no alligators or giant anacondas in Montana, so that's pretty safe, I think.

I have to leave that line of thinking for a bit because I'd better instead tell you about what I was really thinking about in the first place, which was yet another foray into the mountains, fishing, the summer after that conversation, where I'm pretty sure now begins and ends what I have begun to see as the second, maybe third most important thing in my life.

For me, going fishing is a trip to The Otherworld, or perhaps Fairy Land, not merely in terms of 'escape', whatever that might mean to you in your own world that I don't know anything about, but rather *potential*.

You see, when people in the old stories go over into The Otherworld, things can work out just one of two ways. They can either return from The Otherworld changed in some positive way because they've inter-acted with the magic of the place or they've slain the ferocious beast and eaten its heart or perhaps the Fey-folk have bestowed a blessing or favor of some sort. That happens a fair little bit in the old stories.

The reason it does is because it's a kind of testing process of the hero, to see if he or she is made of the right stuff to return to their own world and maybe do some kind of good there. They've returned to life because of the trip, and now they're more powerful or wiser in some way.

Of course, the other thing that can happen is that they fail the test. That happens too. They get eaten by the dragon instead of slaying it. All I'm saying here is that going fishing for me, crossing over into that dream world, is risky business. You come back better for it, or maybe not.

.   .   .   .   .

That morning, when Chuck was taking us out, was just all wrong. I got going later than usual because I'd forgotten to put the coffee on the night before, and then halfway down the valley I remembered I'd forgotten my hat and I drove a little farther deliberating whether or not I wanted it, and then I told Chuck about it and he thought I'd probably want my hat and I agreed and he turned us around and back we went and then finally we were going again and it was a bad start. Portentous, I guess.

The place I wanted to go was not a place I'd been before but I'd seen it on the map and it was kind of "out there", if you know what I mean. Then again, this is Montana, and so by "out there" I don't mean like way over to the other side of town or something. I mean "out there" and, well, also "up there" because it's the

Rockies and that's how that is, most of the time, and it's why you absolutely always have a spare five-gallon can of gas with you, as well as other necessities. Did you know that if you plunked down Montana on a map, over by Jersey, it'd stretch to Ohio? It's like that. They say "Big Sky" and all, but really they mean: pretty much anywhere you might go, anywhere, really, is nowhere near what you might fancy as civilization.

So, Chuck was taking us along and then we hit a thunderstorm and I was already thinking about how if we drove into that here then probably the river would be out for hours with all the new rain and I told Chuck that maybe we should turn around, but he felt it was fine to at least go ahead and see, no harm, you know, and I couldn't argue with that.

We finally got to where I assumed we should be, given the map, but I didn't actually see the river yet and so Chuck kind of meandered along while I looked out the window through the trees and eventually I could in fact see a bit of a gap down below where maybe the river cut through a bit of a canyon and so this looked like a good enough place to stop and take a look and so we did.

I got out and looked around and sure enough I could see water down below and so I got into my gear and said my goodbyes to Chuck. Before I headed down, however, I looked for a path. There's always a path. Always. If there's a place that you might conceivably get down or across to a river and fish it, someone has found it before you have, and there's a path.

Even if other people haven't made one, then deer and elk and antelope have. They all want the same thing as you do: get to the river by the easiest way possible. So, you follow their paths. But there was no path. That was odd. And so, because I had to get to the river, I made my own path, and walked into the deep-dark woods which are the threshold to The Otherworld.

Surprisingly, with a little scrabbling here and a bit of climbing over blow-down there, I got down pretty easily and was confronted by the most beautiful stretch of river I had seen in a while, and that's really saying something out here. The river lay out in front of me in smooth, boulder-filled pools that made you imagine unicorns drinking at the edges. It rushed down in white parkways of water and around the rounded monoliths of stone as though a river-goddess had formed a colonnade as entrance to her realm. Mosses and ferns adorned the stones, and a kingfisher sat sentinel on the tallest of them, gravely watching my approach.

I saw him and said, "May I enter?" and I laughed a bit and he chattered and shouted and went his way to bring tidings of guests. And so I had made my hellos, and waded into the water as this repeated baptism that I do, and felt myself slide away into that place that is just me and water and nothing else.

I'd tell you about the fish, because some of you at least would like to know about that I'm hoping, but I have to tell you instead about the bird. The kingfisher came back as I was standing in the river next to an enormous boulder where I was just trying to stand as close to it without being fully in its sphere of influence and so get swept away when I looked up and there he was, resplendent in his blue surcoat. He was about two feet above me, looking down.

Well, he looked at me and I said, "Hi. What's up?" because he was really looking at me, like maybe the way Hollis does that just sort of unnerves you, as if you were being calculated somehow.

The bird looked a bit longer, and then just chittered and chattered at me as if it were a long sentence. Now, you have to listen here for just a bit so that you don't think I'm completely nuts. The human brain wants to make sense of things, always. That's how we are. That's why, when you hear someone passing, who's speaking another language, your brain just automatically tries to translate it. The Portuguese was one version, but your brain made some sense of it, even though you might have wondered why that couple who just passed you were remarking about underwear. That's how it is.

Okay. So what the kingfisher just said was: "Make way for the Queen and the Prince!"

Just like that. I'm not making this up. I reeled in after that and walked back to the bank and came out on dry earth, the thing I live on all the rest of the time. And that was when the grizzly came through the trees, directly in front of me. Fifty feet away.

She was strawberry-blond and enormous. Not as large as the male of her kind, but still, a giant predator who had no threats to her dominance of the world. She ruled this world as no mere human could ever hope to do. She walked through this world in complete and utter command of it, at all times.

She paused, and lifted her head to smell me, still a bit of a ways off, and she had an enormous grin on her face. I know what you're going to say, that people anthropomorphize animals in order to relate to them, and you're an idiot. No, it really does go that way, where you see pain, joy, love, sadness, and all of the other emotions that God made us all with, and if you haven't figured that out yet you need to get out more.

And this gigantic bear, this huge thing just walking straight toward me, was extremely pleased with life. Maybe even my own? I had a fleeting hope of it. That if I just stood really still, and there was certainly no problem doing that, then maybe she would just go on about her merry way and not kill me? And then I saw. She was trailing a blond cub, and I knew right then I was dead.

The worst feeling I've ever had? It's being frozen. What one literally means by being "petrified", a quaint way now of once referring, back in the 1700s, to the new and in-vogue idea of the scientific fact that something could actually turn to stone, that was once alive. It was a lovely metaphor, I'm sure of it, three hundred years ago.

It was no longer a metaphor. It is the absolute worst thing that can ever happen to you. I couldn't think, move or even breathe. I stood as still as a stone even though I wanted very much to at least attempt to turn and run and dive into the river because drowning and still maybe having a chance of not drowning was far better than being confronted by the giant furry monster with eight-inch claws and six-inch teeth that was coming toward me, no matter how nonchalantly.

I thought: "Run!", but couldn't. I thought: "Pick up a rock or something!", but couldn't. Frozen. Just frozen and waiting. Stuck to the ground utterly, rod in hand, I couldn't even drop it. And on she came.

I don't really know how I was standing right then, be-cause things were somewhat jumbled in my head, but I recall I wasn't exactly like on a "path" of some sort, though there was level ground here along the river, and perhaps I was standing just a bit out of the way, if in-deed there was a "way" that the folk of this place passed by on any sort of regular basis. And, I really don't know, but that might have been all that it was that saved me that morning in The Otherworld, and that that was the only test to have passed, but it seemed as though, maybe, I was just merely out of the way, as any by-stander might and should have been.

Because when the grizzly was ten feet away from me, and I stood there watching, she raised her heavy head at me and smiled. And then her cub came to her side and she nuzzled him, and looked up and met me eye-to-eye, and just smiled. No, I'm not making this up. She was so very pleased. So happy. And she opened her enormous mouth and yawned a bit and snuffled and moved on, cub in tow.

I don't know how much time passed, but I know I fi-nally melted and fell to my knees.

"Long live the Queen," I said aloud, and a kingfisher chattered.

DAYS AND NIGHTS

The thing I eventually came to be most afraid of was Joanie. My words didn't seem to be working any longer, or maybe it was because I just sat in my room and stared at the computer a lot. I could see it in her face, I was losing her, but once I went inside myself, into the box, I couldn't get back out again. I don't know how to explain this to you, but that's the way it is. I never went looking for the box, I simply got up one morning and found that I was there. I didn't know how to get out of the box, even if I wanted to, because I never understood how I had gotten there in the first place. But somehow I saw it in her face that she had no intention of living with a dead person.

This made me unspeakably sad, even though I thought I had purged myself of grief. It was a kind of sadness I hadn't known before, and in that empty space inside myself with only my fear and anger beside me, the sadness came in and pushed out even them. And then it was just us two as companions, alone to-gether.

I began to see how it was going to go for me then, and that if I couldn't have Joanie I'd have lost every-thing, absolutely everything, and so there really wasn't much choice except to kill myself, and find true emptiness and absolute release, because this new grief was something that could not be borne.

CHAPTER THIRTY-FIVE:
A BRIEF MEETING WITH EXTREME FALL

SOMETIMES I WONDER about rules. I'm one of those rule-followers for the most part, and they have always been rather comforting to me, and yes, I've bent and broken some along the way, for whatever passing reasons, but more and more, the older I get the more I like rules. They help me get my bearings, I guess. They're something you can count on. In a way, they're like a person's routine, where you get up in the morning and put on the coffee and take a shower and get dressed and eat breakfast and then get to work and like that. I'm okay with that.

Over time, I have come to discover that there are Big Rules and Little Rules, and depending on who you are, the ones you follow may go under either of these categories. There are also the Rules You Didn't Know Were Rules, but those of you who are not married will not understand such things, so I'll only try to explain the first two.

The Little Rules are of the sort that can be broken from time to time when a pressing need obstructs you from following the rule. This might range from things like Pet the Dog in our house, but your hands are full or the dog has just rolled on a dead elk's carcass, to things like Never Buy Eggrolls at a Gas Station, but you know, you just sort of had to that once because you hadn't eaten in hours and that was pretty much what they had. Among other Little Rules are the familiar ones like: Brush Your Teeth Before Bed, and You Never Forget Daylight Savings Time, no matter how foolish the whole thing might be.

It's the Big Rules that sometimes trouble me. These are the inviolable ones, the ones that you break only in the most dire of circumstances, if you know what's good for you, and maybe even if you don't. Just as an example, Never Flout God. Really. That's just never a good idea, and you have to be very, very careful about this, I've come to understand. Look what happened to Oedipus and Jonah. You want to end up like them? I mean, sometimes it's just not even a good idea to say out loud something like, "Tomorrow I have some plans and I think I'll..." because you can't be so very sure about tomorrow. Just trust me on this one. Anyway. There are quite a few Big Rules, but just to explain one of my troubles I will mention Sacred Places and why you don't—or shouldn't—fool around with them.

First, understand that by definition Sacred Places abound with Rules. Sometimes these are of the man-made sort, but usually they are of the unspoken type, which may or may not fall under the heading of Natural Law, depending on who you are. Thomas Jefferson, for example, had the crazy idea that the whole world was a Sacred Place, governed by such rules, and came to the conclusion that certain things were inviolable "truths" and were thus "self-evident" and needed no further argument.

Sacred Places as well can take on many forms, and some of us may consider something sacred while perhaps another will not. That's the way it is. For me, a walk in the woods is a Sacred Place, and so is the river I'm standing in, or the first avalanche lilies in spring, and so you don't step on flowers that give beauty to the world and you don't trash the living waters, and you don't burn down the woods and all the things that live in it. You do not kill. Why would you? What's wrong with you anyway? That's pretty straightforward, I hope. And yet, I will admit, sometimes breaking the rules helps you stay sane.

.   .   .   .   .

On September thirtieth I mowed the lawn one final time and even though it was 70 degrees I placed the lawn chairs on the back deck in preparation for storing them in the garage. Tomorrow was "fall", and would be twenty degrees cooler than today, and in four days it would be winter, again. Joanie said we should celebrate fall, all three days of it if possible, and to that end we invited Chip and Jeff over for dinner and Scrabble. We figured if anyone could muster a good game of Scrabble it'd be a couple of journalists. Chip said they were bringing dates, and Joanie wondered who they might be, but I wondered if maybe I might have inadvertently touched off another competition. Who knows, it might be interesting to see.

When they arrived, I was only somewhat surprised to see Jill and Amy with them. Joanie greeted everyone and we all headed to the dining room, where Jill sat down next to Chip, and Jeff set down a large leather case he was carrying and pulled out the chair for Amy to sit in and Chip slapped himself in the forehead and looked at a grinning Jeff and made a mark in the air with his finger as if to say "score one for you". Obviously, the game was afoot.

We got seated at the dining room table, and opened a couple of bottles of wine, and exchanged the news with Jill and Amy while the dogs milled around introducing themselves, or at least parts of their anatomy. Meanwhile Chip and Jeff looked like they were just dying to say something, and so I asked. Jeff smiled.

"We wanted to show you how to play Extreme Scrabble. It's great. You'll like it."

"Really," Chip added. "It's fun. You never get bored playing. We'll show you."

Joanie looked at me, and I just said, "Sounds great. Let's play."

Jeff pulled up the leather case and opened it up, pulled out a large folded square, and then proceeded to unfold on the table the Frankenstein Monster of Scrabble boards. Joanie and I stood up to have a look, and Jill and Amy just laughed.

"We've played before," Jill said. "It's a hoot."

"What have you done?" Joanie asked, and poked a finger at the board.

"It's my creation," Jeff said, with his right hand over his heart. "It's four boards cut and pieced together at strategic points and extended so that the triple-word scores aren't just at the corners where everything gets all clogged up."

"But what are these penned-in squares that say 'A' or have arrows on them?" I asked.

"That's where if you can make an anagram you get a triple-word score," Chip said.

"And the arrows are when you can reverse the letters of an existing word, or scramble them, to make a new word," Amy added.

"And there are extra letters," Jill said. "Four times as many as usual. You need them."

Joanie sat down and had a sip of wine. "Okay. I think I get the 'extreme' part." Everyone laughed except me and Joanie.

"Not yet," they said.

Jill and Amy said they'd be score-keepers and judges for the first game, and so we began.

As luck would have it, I had to start, and even with the nine letters we got to pull instead of seven, the best I could do was "goth" for a score of five.

Oh well, lots of game left, it seemed. Joanie was next and she made "ostrogoth", and sat with a smile while the rest of us sat in stunned silence for a moment and then everybody said at once, "Wow...That was...Holy..."

Then Jeff said, after looking at his letters, "I have another word, but I want to show you right away how this goes, and then we can talk about the rules." So, he laid down "icus" on the end of Joanie's word and then looked at us. We looked at him.

"Go on," he said, "ask me."

"All right, I'll bite," I said. "What the hell is 'ostrogoth-icus'?"

"It's the archaeological discovery of an Ostrogoth," he said.

"Good one!" Amy said.

Joanie and I looked at one another while Jill wrote down a score.

"So here's the deal," Chip said, putting his elbows on the table. "You can make up new words, but you have to justify their meaning. You know, Shakespeare used to make up words all the time, right? Why can't we? As long as you've got a decent definition for it, the judge rules in your favor. The only thing you can't do is the old lame thing of making a plural or maybe adding an "ist" or "ism" or past-tense to something. Okay? That's how it goes. Have fun!"

Joanie finished her glass in one gulp. Set it down. "Okay. Pass me the bottle."

Chip went next and had "poultry", which in any other setting was a pretty darn good word, in my estimation, but he said that was an easy one. Jill put her arm around him then and said something in his ear and Chip smiled. I looked at the board, now that it was my turn, and I might have made something here and there, but instead I just figured I'd go ahead and get fully into the spirit of things and so I added onto to Chip's word.

Amy said, "What's that? I can't see it so well upside down."

"'Poultrygeist,'" I said. "The spirit of a dead chicken."

"Good one!" Chip said. Joanie gave me a look.

Jill wrote down the score. The wine went around.

After a while, we weren't sitting; we all stood around the table shouting and pondering if "volanger" really did describe the dissatisfaction of voles, and then that led to discussions of whether or not animals might have such opinions and then Joanie asked Grip if he would ever like to sleep in the snow, and Grip lifted his head from his bed by the fireplace and stayed put and so Joanie got that one.

Jeff had "peanutbetter" and described that as being when you get a jar of mixed nuts and how there really aren't very many cashews and pecans in it, and that you really should get them, because of course they're the better ones, and we all nodded in agreement about that, obviously. Still later Amy whispered something in Jeff's ear and he spelled out "flabbergusted", which is when the wind is so strong that it ripples your belly.

I'm not real sure what transpired after that because there was a bunch of shouting and the judge had to weigh in and once Amy said, "Really? That's the best you got?" and I think what we had for our store of wine for the winter got used up and finally so did the board and then we all sat down and laughed and looked at the words we had made and laughed some more and then somebody, maybe it was me, said, "Weren't we supposed to be having dinner?"

And then we ate, and it was serious business, and nobody bothered to say, "Gee, this roasted duck is really good" or "I like Yorkshire puddings a lot," or "what did you roast those carrots with? Is that a harissa and yogurt sauce?" because it was all about eating. You don't need rules for that.

Later, after everyone had gone home, Joanie and I sat on the deck with the dogs, watching the stars.

After a while Joanie said, "I'm going in and ordering three Scrabble games from somewhere."

I laughed and she went inside, the dogs trailing along in her wake. I looked up at the inviolable stars and smiled a bit.

DAYS AND NIGHTS

I don't feel any pressing need to tell you about the ways in which I contemplated killing myself. What would be the point? Even so, the more I thought about it, the easier and easier it seemed to me. Each time, however, I think I somehow just got distracted, not being able to think very clearly anymore, and so I never really just managed to get around to it.

I think Joanie tried to help me in some way at this time, I just don't remember it very well is all, but I think there were ultimatums made, and there was just enough fear left in me, hanging around somewhere near the door, that I could see Joanie just a bit again and I said I would see someone on Monday.

This proved to be a complicated task. Before I could have my health insurance pay for seeing a counselor I had to first be seen by a physician. I hadn't been to see a doctor for maybe twenty-five years, and so I had no physician I could see. Someone told me I could see one at the emergency room, and so I finally did.

He asked me a lot of questions about the shooting and the dead and where I was and how I was sleeping and suicide and eating and drinking and I said whatever it was that I said because I wanted to see this through for some reason.

He left me for a while and came back maybe a half an hour later with a little piece of paper, and the paper said that I was not all right and needed help, and I could have told him that an hour earlier.

A week later I started to see Linda.

SECOND WINTER

CHAPTER THIRTY-SIX:

JEFF AND CHIP HIT THE SLOPES

(AND OTHER THINGS)

THERE ARE SO MANY unexpected things in this world, and some things that you might expect, that cannot be understood or reckoned with. I think I am just now beginning to see a glimpse of this, and am trying to understand it. For one thing, it is true what Hollis said back then, about trauma following us around. There's no escape, and I suppose that's how it must really be.

I think back now about how Gil had to make tough decisions, and about Dorothy and Delmer losing their only son, and how even Wiley might have had his ups and downs and worrying about his future. And then Kenna. Losing her friend like that? And then her house? And Hollis? He's so busted up I have no idea what might be the cure, though I tried to find out. And I guess that's the way it is.

We all live through some sort of trauma because we're alive, and we lose things that you can never get back, and I have this very bad feeling that if I looked for a moment at the box in the back of my head I'd discover what I've cost Joanie these past two years. I don't think I can bear to see. I have this very bad feeling that it might have to do with my ability to not think about things, which I have so very carefully cultivated.

There are also those things I've discovered that simply defy any sense of the world you may have experienced before. I could go on about a few of these things, and have shared a few before I think, but it's time I tell you about this other one. I know you'll think I'm making this up, but I'm not. It's a very funny world, just full of things you can't explain, or don't want to. I mostly like it like that. Do you?

· · · · ·

In November I went down to The Paper to turn in my latest column. Jeff and Chip were not in fact in the office playing "basketball". I had come in what I now thought of as the "front" door, and so wandered back into the warehouse to see if they were there. After navigating several large columns of refuse I spotted the overhead lights and made my way past some splintered crates and found Jeff and Chip lifting Jeff's "sled" onto some saw horses. Chip was pointing and saying something about the rudder on the back and Jeff was frowning.

"I don't think it's down far enough to actually let you steer," Chip said as I got close enough to hear.

"Hi guys. I just stopped by to drop off my piece."

"Al, take a look at this and tell me what you think," Jeff said. "Chip thinks my rudder isn't low enough to steer, but it looks okay to me. What do you think?"

"I think you guys are crazy and are probably going to kill yourselves. Are you really going to do this?"

They both looked at me then, sort of dumbfounded maybe.

"Of course!" they said in unison.

Chip and Jeff wrote their own copy and published an announcement about the upcoming "event" in The Paper, complete with photos of themselves and the things they'd be strapped into while hurtling down McMaster's Mountain to their certain deaths.

When the issue came out I showed Joanie, who merely said, "We're going, right?"

The announcement of all this foolishness hit Dobbins as the most exciting thing since Veronica's triplets, and a great anticipation began to build. By the middle of January, after the snow had really gotten some momentum going, people at Del's could be heard talking about where the best viewing places might be along the chosen route, and whether or not any food trucks would be there. Meanwhile, I put in a call to the hospital in Great Falls and quietly arranged for a paramedic truck to be on hand.

I slept somewhat more fitfully than usual the night before the big day. It seemed to me a premonition of unpleasant things ahead, though it may have been nothing more than my old nightmares. I woke to a bright and sunny yet very cold Montana morning. Joanie and I went through our usual routines, and then bundled up as best we could, and with a thermos of coffee we headed out.

Chuck meandered the lonesome road out to the mountain, and as we got closer we discovered many, many vehicles already lining the road. There came a point where we figured we weren't going to get any closer, and so Chuck pulled over and we hiked in the rest of the way. When we got within view we saw several hundred people all dressed as if they were headed out for a brutal day of ice fishing, but there was definitely a festive quality to the atmosphere.

To my not-so-very-great surprise, there really were vendors here, selling hot dogs and beer at eleven a.m. The hot dogs were being called "sled dogs" which I just didn't think was funny, but I imagined the beer was frosty cold. About midway down the half-mile long run we spotted Hollis and Kenna. It was easy to pick out Hollis, given that he was head and shoulders taller than anyone else, and Joanie and I exchanged looks as we saw Hollis's arm around Kenna's shoulders.

"Mind if we stand with you guys?" Joanie said as we came up behind them.

Hollis and Kenna turned to meet us and Kenna said, "Guess you can freeze your butt off here just as well as anywhere. Hey, you know these guys, right Al? So what's their story anyway? This is the craziest stunt I ever heard of, and I've heard some crazy things."

I was going to reply something along the lines of yes, these are probably two of the stupidest men I've ever met, but I thought that this might be a bit inappropriate as an elegy in case something dire did in fact happen, and also because it wasn't true.

So, instead I said, "Yes, I've gotten to know them. It's a long story, but the short version is this sort of thing seems to mean everything to them, and they've been doing it for years. I can tell you about some of their other stunts if you like, but the bottom line is that even if they don't know what they're doing, they're going to have a great time no matter what happens."

Hollis looked at me and nodded. "Yeah. I think I know what you mean."

"I think it's great," Joanie said.

Kenna said, "Well, I guess we'll see, huh?"

There really were several hundred people up and down the slope now, and as I looked around I even saw a camera crew or maybe two, though I couldn't tell which outfit they belonged to. The sun was well up now, but it was very cold, and we all had some coffee from the thermos. Further down the slope I saw Jill and Amy, pouring from a thermos as well, but it looked like they were having something a bit more warming than coffee.

I'd have loved to have trudged up the slope to say something to Chip and Jeff, but it was too far to go now. I knew how this was supposed to go: at noon they'd both get a shove from a few guys they'd lined up, and they would head down the slope at the same time. The path they'd made was supposed to be roughly twelve feet wide, and they'd made berms along the really dangerous places to keep themselves from flying off the mountain, and they'd piled up snow walls in the curves. The three boulders on the way had to be navigated or else.

"What time is it?" I asked, getting kind of nervous.

"Three minutes 'til," Joanie said.

Just then, up above there was the screech and beep of a loudspeaker coming alive, and you could have knocked me down with a single finger, because Delmer's somewhat solemn voice came over it!

"Ladies and gentlemen," he said. "Thank you all for

coming out and braving the weather to witness the first annual McMaster's Mountain Run!"

A large cheer went up then, but I could only think 'First Annual'? Oh Lord, if they survive this one then that should be enough.

Delmer went on: "Jeff and Chip want to welcome you all, and hope you have a good time watching them blast down the slope. They've put a lot of hard work into this, covering almost two years, and they hope you enjoy the competition!" And then that was it, and it began.

Joanie and I had binoculars, so we could see that each sled had four guys to get them off to a good start. Both Chip and Jeff were wearing some sort of head gear, and they appeared to be harnessed in pretty good. You could see them both smiling and talking back and forth to one another, and then from some unseen signal the pushers started pushing and down they went.

Chip must have gotten the better push because his saucer jumped out ahead, but Jeff quickly came along beside him, and the first straightaway was now becoming the first curve around a boulder. Jeff seemed to have a bit of trouble steering and veered one way and then the other, but made the turn, and Chip, coming along just a couple of yards behind, seemed to easily bank around the rocks and they both gathered speed in the next moments. It looked like they were going really fast as they got down about midway through the run, almost to where we were standing. The crowd was cheering, and I noticed I hadn't been breathing for a bit.

It happened very quickly—later Chip said he merely hit a bump—but as they passed us the edge of Chip's saucer seemed to dig into the snow, and then flipped, speeding along upside down and then off into a tree. Just a moment later, I saw the rudder snap off of Jeff's sled and he hurtled down the mountain, with no way to steer, and crashed into a boulder.

A gasp and then a cry went out from the crowd, and a bunch of us hurried toward Chip and another bunch toward Jeff. Hollis and Kenna and Joanie and I found Chip upside down against a tree. His sled looked like a crushed pie tin. We bent and as carefully as we could we flipped him over, and there was Chip, strapped securely in his harness, his head gear askew and his goggles shattered.

"Ow," he said, and passed out.

A paramedic arrived and told us to move aside and so we hurried down the slope to where Jeff was. Nobody had touched him yet and when we got there we saw that his face was twisted in pain. His tube was about one-third shorter than it had been, and his knees were bent almost up to his chest.

"My leg," he said. "Get me out of this...carefully."

The paramedics were as careful as they could be, but Jeff screamed once and then he too passed out.

"Good," one of the paramedics said. "Let's get him onto a stretcher."

The aftermath was a bunch of people milling around while the paramedics loaded Chip and Jeff into the truck and whisked them away to the hospital in Great Falls. Amy and Jill followed along behind, but Joanie and I went on back home to the dogs.

Later on we watched the news and sure enough there was a segment on The Dobbins Daredevils, as they called them, showing the big crowd and the race, and the crashes and the medics and a few close-ups of people with shock and concern on their faces. Then the scene shifted to outside the hospital in Great Falls, with the reporter standing outside telling us that both men had suffered injuries—Chip a broken arm and Jeff a broken leg, in addition to multiple bruises—but were expected to make a full recovery. We went to bed. I didn't sleep very well.

The next morning Chuck took me over to Great Falls. I had already looked up the hospital's visiting hours, and got there an hour or so after they began. I checked in and then wandered down a hallway and saw Jill and Amy just coming through a doorway.

I said my hellos and asked how the guys were, and Amy said, "Idiots," and Jill said, "Not so bad, considering," and so I went in.

There they were, two beds and two busted up journalists. Chip was sporting a cast that covered his right arm, and his face was pretty much a bruise on one side. Jeff's left leg was in a full cast, and suspended from a wire. Otherwise he looked to be in pretty good shape.

We talked a while and I admitted that it was a pretty exciting race for as long as it lasted, and they both smiled at that, and I told them about the news story and their new nicknames and they practically beamed.

I also mentioned that I supposed basketball was now out of the question, but Chip said, "I figure if I sit in a wheelchair and Jeff uses just his left hand, then it should be pretty even." Jeff agreed, but noted that it was likely going to be quite a few weeks before either of them got back to the office.

"So what about The Paper?" I asked.

Jeff and Chip looked at one another and then Chip said, "We're glad you asked."

Chuck took me back home later in the day, and when I got there Joanie asked how the guys were doing and I passed along the news.

"What's bugging you?" she asked. "You look like you've had some really bad news. I thought you said Chip and Jeff were going to be okay? Is there something you're not telling me?"

"Guess who's going to be running The Paper this winter?"

DAYS AND NIGHTS

I don't remember how many sessions I had with Linda. At first we just talked and talked, and I really couldn't tell you what we said, but at some point Linda said she wanted to do a little something with an array of lights, this rectangular row of lights that moved left to right at an adjustable speed, and she said what she wanted to do was to help me remove some clutter from my head and maybe help me put certain things back where they once were at the same time.

So we did this thing, and she asked me some questions that I don't remember, and when we were done I was exhausted and wanted to lie down on the floor but instead I think we were done for the day and so I left and drove home not seeing anything at all. When I got home I slept.

The next week I was due to see Linda again and because the sessions I'd had with her made me very tired I decided to lie down on the bed for a short nap before I had to head out, and so I stretched out on the bed and closed my eyes but I couldn't sleep.

I cannot explain this next part to you. I do not have the capacity to correctly explain such things. I will have to only say that suddenly I sat bolt upright in bed, more afraid than I had ever been before in my life, because I was very suddenly no longer in the box, and everything I had ever known, seen, done, touched or breathed in, in all of my life, was now all in my head, all at once. It was beautiful and it was terrifying, and I couldn't turn it off, I couldn't get away or run away or escape.

I left the bedroom and found Joanie and said something incoherent to her and I told her to call Linda and I left the house and some while later I found myself in the parking lot outside Linda's office, crying and crying, and she came out and brought me inside.

There are only just a couple more things I have to tell you. The next several weeks were some of the most beautiful days of my entire life. After the floodgates had opened I saw everything, everything, and I remembered everything, all at once like a symphony in my head, all of the life I had had, and it was the most glorious thing I had ever seen, a giant panorama of life, and all and every mote and brush stroke were all interconnected and so was I.

I did not sleep for three weeks. Instead, I lay in the dark, and saw life like the great spine of the Milky Way washed against the night sky, uncountable stars that make up a whole larger than imagining. I laughed a lot.

Three, maybe four weeks later, Joanie and I took a little trip and it was wonderful, just beautiful, and I felt like that first time you know you are in love and it was like an endless river and I swam in it, moving with every current. I never wanted to ever feel any different, and in my joy I knew a new life had just begun, a new life in which the days and nights would never be the same.

And then on the way home I started to feel strange, almost like what I imagine it must be like after anesthesia and you realize you're about to become unconscious but yet are not quite wholly gone, holding on, holding out, refusing to let go. And that is when I went insane.

I will not recount that here. I cannot speak of it any longer, and I can only say that I was so very afraid again, so afraid, you cannot imagine it, this thing stalking your waking thoughts like an angry animal tearing you to pieces and sucking the marrow from your bones, tearing your mind away from the stars and love and life, afraid.

There was no other thing I could do. I had to run away, I had to. It was the only way to stay sane, to be safe. The box was there, waiting. You can see that, can't you? Please tell me you can see that.

CHAPTER THIRTY-SEVEN:

HUGGIN AND MUNINN

I WALKED OUT onto the deck in the back yard the other day, and it was so cold I was numbed in moments, and yet there were ravens flying overhead and they spoke to one another, and so I stood and I listened, and then they wheeled again over our place and you could hear, so close it seemed, as if in the crystalline air they were on your shoulder, and I had a thought then of Othin's ravens, Huginn and Muninn, Thought and Memory, which the story says sat on his shoulders and told him what he needed to know, and I smiled a bit at that. I have seen some studies done which showed that ravens and crows could learn tricks that people had taught them, to show just how intelligent they are. I couldn't help but wonder about these things, however, that after the people had taught the ravens a little thing, if ever the people stopped to listen to what the ravens had to say to them. I'm guessing a person could learn quite a bit from the right sort of bird if they ever stopped thinking about themselves long enough to listen.

I'd really like to continue telling you about what I know about ravens, but unfortunately I have to tell you about what happened with trying to run The Paper for a few weeks.

For one thing, I am still astounded at myself for having agreed to do this even though I knew perfectly well that I had no idea at all what I was going to do and that stress is definitely not my thing these days. Honestly, when I said "yes" to two guys lying in hospital beds I didn't do so just because they were all busted up and I felt like I couldn't just say 'no, you're crazy'; I think I actually thought that even though I didn't know anything about newspapers that I could sort of wing it for a couple of weeks and nobody would really notice all that much. I think that right there should give you the only insight you ever needed as to how stupid I can be at times.

. . . . .

My first three days down at The Paper were an exercise in despair. I quickly came face-to-face with what I already knew, which was that I had no idea how you put together a newspaper, or even what went in it, and even though I'd known this I discovered that I was in no way prepared to do anything about it. No, there wasn't going to be any winging it, and I spent two straight days just looking at Chip's and then Jeff's computers, searching for clues as to what I should do. The guys had provided me with their passwords, so I had access to all their files. Chip's password was "Paper-Lion77" and Jeff's was "Mothersmaidenname01". I found nothing useful in their files, however. There was no recipe that said, "First, collect some news items. Next, write things about the news items..." or anything like that.

Then I sat at a desk and looked at past issues of The Paper, seeing if I could figure out what sorts of things were usually included. I made a list of these things: 1) Local and State News; 2) Advertising; 3) My Column; 4) Upcoming Events (if any), and Photos. That kind of summed up what usually got printed. The problem, though, was that I had no idea where to come by any of this stuff in the dead of winter. This was going to be a disaster, and everyone would know about it too.

During the first two days I looked at their computers for awhile, then I'd stand up and walk around the room for awhile, noting various cracks in the walls and ceiling, and then I'd sit at a desk for awhile and maybe flip through past issues of The Paper, just sort of seeing what it looked like and all, and then I'd walk around a bit more and at some point I think I came to genuinely appreciate the basketball hoop they had on the wall. I'd sit, then stand, I'd walk around a bit, and then I'd sit some more. I made eighteen "basketballs" with wads of paper because I thought maybe that might help.

At one point I started to write something that began with "Local News", and then that was pretty much it because as far as I knew there wasn't any. I did another page and began it as "State News", but the same thing. I had no idea what was going on anywhere because I had made a point of not knowing what was going on anywhere because that is of course the safest thing you can do for your mental health. I didn't bother attempting National News. As far as I was concerned, who cares? I live in Montana. Just leave me alone. I made more basketballs.

On the third day I started to wonder if maybe I could just go back and reprint articles from past issues and if anybody would notice. There was a deadline approaching, of course, which I was only sort of vaguely aware of because The Paper came out on Saturdays, and I could feel the hours quietly and quickly ticking away.

About the time I started wondering if there were rafters in the back I could hang myself from, there came a tapping, softly rapping, upon my chamber door. Naturally, I got up and opened it and a woman of approximately my own age stood in the door and introduced herself as Maupsa, and mentioned the fact that it was damn cold outside and speculated that it might get colder still before it ever got warmer.

"Maupsa?" I said. "Like in Peter Rabbit?"

"No, that's Mopsy," she said, and looked around a bit at the office, sort of sizing it up.

Yes, it was damn cold outside and going to get colder and so I invited her in. Why not? She wore the usual coat that we all wear in the Montana winter, something that's made of leather and lined with fleece and stretches down your legs as far as you can get it, pretty much like everyone in Hollywood imagines what cowboys look like I guess, but she also sported a red stocking cap over a hairless head with a wide-brimmed hat over it sort of like what Hollis always wears, and she had an eye patch over one eye, under her glasses.

As you know, I'm not real quick on the draw with most things these days, and I sort of stood there foolishly looking at her without saying anything during what people often refer to as pregnant pauses, which really doesn't apply here because my thoughts were rather sterile at the moment. In any case, she stopped looking around then and looked back at me, and there I was just looking at her and wondering if God had somehow sent me a pirate for reasons I was yet to fathom or if the day was going to merely go from bad to weird.

She came to realize that I was in fact merely standing there looking at her and then she said, taking off the wide-brimmed hat but not the stocking cap, touching her head, "Oh. It's just the chemo. Nothing to concern yourself about. I'm here because I understand you're trying to put together a newspaper."

I believe I merely stared at that.

"Kenna told me. You want any help? I used to work at the paper down in Cheyenne."

I nodded, kind of thinking maybe God had heard me whining again and had decided He'd had enough and sent my salvation, again, just to get me off his back for a few hours.

"Great! What have you got so far and when's the deadline for printing?"

"Printing?" I said.

She sort of looked at me then, kind of the way Hollis does, or maybe it was just the eye patch, but I have to say that it had the same effect on me, and I don't quite recall things here but perhaps I looked around the office for a bit then, searching for answers, but all I had was twenty-fours wads of newspaper on my desk.

"Okay. I think I understand the situation. Where's my desk?" she asked.

I made a kind of motion with my arm and mentioned that I had no idea what I was doing and that I was merely trying to help out my friends, and she nodded and said, "That's okay. Don't worry about it. We can do this. Let me just get settled for a bit and I can tell you how to help."

She sat down at Chip's desk and I told her the password for his computer and Maupsa muttered, "Oh brother," and started clicking away.

"While I'm doing this, see if you can find out who the printer is and what the deadline is," she said. "Just start looking for invoices from somebody. You'll find it. Trust me. If somebody has a contract from which they make money, they'll be in contact."

That was a good idea. I got busy while Maupsa flipped through a few back issues to see what the standard fare was.

"Where's the coffee?" she asked. "We're going to be here for awhile."

"Um, that's a good idea. I'll go get some at Del's."

She looked up from a past issue. "Not yet. Find that printer and then go get coffee."

Okay. I was motivated. I found it ten minutes later and saved the info to Jeff's desktop.

"Good," Maupsa said, smiling and then returning her attention to Chip's computer. "Nice work. Now, go get coffee. Enough for hours."

I got to Del's as fast as Chuck could take me, and called Joanie and said I might be late for dinner.

When I got back with something like a gallon of coffee, Maupsa was leaning in to Chip's monitor and she said, "This newspaper is called what? That's the stupidest thing I've ever heard."

She turned to me and asked, "What do people around

here actually call the thing? I mean, they don't actually say this Beacon-Bee-Herald-Whatever stuff, do they?"

"Everyone just says 'The Paper,'" I said, setting down a cup of coffee for her.

"Okay. Good. These issues we'll just call 'The Paper.'"

This announcement seemed to wrinkle something in my soul, somewhere in that area that I think of as Me-Not-Wanting-To-Screw-Things-Up.

"Is that a good idea, though? I mean, Jeff and Chip are kind of expecting me to make sure things sort of continue smoothly here. I mean, you know, as smoothly as my incompetence might allow."

Maupsa leaned back in her chair and looked me over.

"No, it's a better idea that we call it something else. That way if they don't like it, then nothing sticks to them and they can just blame it on you. Okay?"

That sounded like a good idea to me. I hadn't had any ideas myself thus far, so what the heck, and I sure wasn't going to ask, "But won't they blame it on both of us?"

The overhead light in the office was dim, and it hurt my head and so I shut it off, and it was getting dark outside with our Montana sun just about having it up to there with this place and wishing to get on to somewhere a bit easier to navigate, and most of the illumination seemed to come from our computer screens, and desk lamps, as if we were wrapped in halos. I sat at the desk and looked at Maupsa mostly, because I didn't know what I was doing, and just waited.

I did what I always do, and just drifted away into I have no idea where, but still I was watching her in that light, and she looked deeply into the illumination in front of her, and tapped away at the keyboard, recording—I had a flash of that thought—information and knowledge that I was not privy to and would be allowed to know at a date when the universe saw fit to reveal it to me. I hate being helpless, but even so, I was mesmerized just watching. She was sort of this darker shape, sitting in a halo of light, searching and searching for something.

There came a time, and I don't know how long a time passed there, when Maupsa began to print some things and when she had she put them down on my desk and said, "Rewrite these. Be there. Give credit where credit is due, but rewrite them for The Paper. They're stories from here and there, and are appropriate for The Paper."

I flipped through the pages.

"Rewrite them? Like take somebody else's work and just sort of re-do it?" I was lost again, or maybe still.

Maupsa suddenly asked, "What do you know about philosophy? Do you know Plotinus? You know, the Greek philosopher?"

And, like starlings in the fall, sweeping one way and then another, as if with no possible orchestration, my brain just shifted over to comfortable and familiar ground. "Yes, I sort of remember. Third century BC. Maybe in Alexandria, or maybe just his writings showed up there."

"That's the guy. They say he invented the Western idea of souls. They say that maybe Hebrew scholars in Alexandria got the idea from him, and the whole idea of an afterlife."

I laughed a bit about someone maybe inventing the idea of my soul, and said so.

"It is a bit odd," Maupsa said. "Even so, I like to think I'm creating my own soul day after day, just a bit at a time. Someone else's labor is in those pages, but information is fair game, got it? Have you got a few minutes to recreate your soul?"

I nodded. I hoped I could.

I rewrote those stories so that I felt they were my own writing somehow, and said so aloud, but Maupsa was very busy now and didn't hear me, and so I sat at my desk in a pool of light in the darkness and tapped my fingers on the desk, just absentmindedly, not thinking that it might wake anyone else from their reverie, and just about before I drifted off back into the same old place I usually go I said, "Do you like flowers at all?"

She looked up at me then and swiveled in her chair: "Flowers? Yes, of course, I adore flowers. What made you think of flowers in the dead of winter and in the dark?"

I didn't know why I'd said that, in fact, but I tried to remember for just a bit, and I said, "I don't know. I think I remember flowers and that I like them. They're harmless, you know, except this one that we have in the kitchen window which, what I hear, would destroy everything if we set it outside or something. They're nice."

I rubbed my face for a minute and said, "That's all. I think I like flowers is all."

"Good," she said. "That's real good," and returned her attention to whatever it was she was doing.

It was a little while later, or I think so, and then Maupsa suddenly stood and said, "That's it. Done for the night. Have to meet someone shortly now."

She quickly went to retrieve her coat and then just as quickly was at the door and she opened it to the wind and snow and said, "See you tomorrow, okay? That was fun," and out she went and closed the door, and I sat there in a pool of light smothered by the darkness.

There would be no more tappings at the door, and so I went out into the starlit darkness where if you waited long enough you could hear the reverberation of the stars and told Chuck it was time to go.

The next morning I came in early and found that Maupsa was waiting outside the door. I asked her how long she'd been waiting, and she said not so long, and I said good because it was about -5 outside, and then I asked her if she had much of a drive, because I'm a nosy sort of person, and she said not so very far and so I wasn't going to get anything more about that and we went in and got to work. We did what we did for the next day. I wrote up a piece on Chip and Jeff, and we got some photos from some other papers, and that was going to be the Big Story, and then I had my column as well on the third page like always. Maupsa wrote an editorial piece, which was something that hadn't happened before. Then we came down to putting things on pages and formatting and all the things I'd never have known how to do, and Maupsa took care of all of that.

When we finished up on Thursday night I was exhausted, and asked if she wanted to come over to our place for a late dinner, because I'd checked this out with Joanie.

"Thanks, but I've got some things I have to take care of."

So, we sent off "The Paper", and closed up, and I watched her walk off into the snowy darkness.

On Saturday morning I got down to the office early and Maupsa came by a couple of minutes later. The paper was being distributed by now. We sat in the office and waited, sort of looking around and waiting.

"Pretty cold again today, huh?"

"Yep. Probably going to be really damn cold tomorrow as well, don't you think?"

"Oh yeah. No doubt about it."

It wasn't long, though, before the calls and emails started coming in, some expressing consternation as to why The Paper was suddenly being called "The Paper", which was both expected and yet a sort of breakdown in common sense, which I really wanted to explain to some, but didn't. Even so, I reassured everyone that it was only a temporary thing until Jeff and Chip were back on their feet, and that explanation seemed to satisfy most people. Then, as expected, Jeff and Chip also sent emails asking about the new name for The Paper, and I responded with Maupsa's explanation, and they both wrote back to say that was very thoughtful and that they thought The Paper looked great and to carry on and so on.

After a couple of hours of this Maupsa stood and said she was done for the day. I asked her if she wanted to come by that evening for dinner because Joanie said she'd like to meet her, but she just smiled and said she had a prior engagement. Maybe next week.

"How many more issues until your buddies get back?"

"At least two I'm guessing, from the sound of things. Maybe three."

"See you on Monday then," and out the door she went.

I answered a few more emails and then Chuck took me home. I slept pretty well that night for some strange reason.

As it turned out, we put out the next four issues of The Paper before either Chip or Jeff were genuinely mobile enough to come into the office again, somewhere near the end of February. Each week seemed to go a little smoother than the one before, and after a while Maupsa didn't need to tell me what to do as much as usual.

About the time that maybe the third issue was coming out I felt pretty okay with all of this, even though I eagerly awaited Chip and Jeff's return so that my life could get back to normal.

At some point when we were putting together what we knew was going to be our last issue of "The Paper", Maupsa turned in her chair and said, "So what do you think of journalism now, Al?"

I said something along the lines of it being harder than I imagined it would be, but that I could see how a person could get to like it.

Maupsa nodded and said, "It sure beats nothing but Scrabble all winter, huh?" I had to agree.

I knew it was going to come out of me sooner or later, even though I tried my best to keep my mouth shut, but day after day of working with someone who has cancer eventually eroded away whatever good graces I might have possessed. And so I asked her: What was it? What is it like? Why the eye patch? How are you doing? She actually didn't seem to mind my asking, and instead turned in Chip's chair and folded her hands on the desk.

"It's in my eye. I may go blind before I die from it. It's supposed to be rather rare, so lucky me. Al, you know how you cure a cancer patient? You get dragged screaming to the edge of death, and you stand there looking out and wondering which is better, to fall down and fall off, or stand still and wait. That's what the chemo is: taking you to the edge and then hoping at the very end that you can somehow be snatched back again. Each day I look out over the edge and won-der how it's going to be."

Stupidly, the only thing I could possibly think to say was, "Why are you here? Wouldn't you want to spend this time doing, I don't know, something else?"

"No," she said, "it helps to keep me from looking back at the cliff edge all day long. Already did that for a bit."

As usual, I really couldn't muster anything useful to say, because saying something like "That's too bad" is absolutely worse than saying nothing. I only nodded.

Maupsa said, "My mother, as she was slipping away from me, merely said, 'Life is loss,' and while it's true, it doesn't help all that much to know it. So we would sit under the big maple with our wine and watch the evening creep in. And I would be wondering when the big hemlocks would finally give up and fall. I never told her what I was thinking. I never told her about the hemlocks and how they made me miss her before she was gone. I just tried to make her laugh."

I nodded again, and I think I did so with some under-standing.

During the weeks that followed we talked about

philosophy and the universe and poetry and dying.

Once, looking up from her desk she said: "Chemo is like the film *Groundhog Day* stretched over three weeks, six times, and I do find it harder to concentrate or to feel or think about much outside this monotonous spiral. Chemo brain is a lot like being in a required undergraduate lecture where you did the required reading when you were fourteen. Nothing but marginalia. It's an afterlife in this life."

Another time, from nowhere, she said, "Proust once said, 'We are healed from suffering only by experiencing it to the full.' Did you finish the piece on farm subsidies?"

I answered with, "Seneca said, 'Sometimes even to live is an act of courage.' And the farm subsidies piece is the most boring thing I've ever written."

"Sounds perfect," she said. And so it went.

The week before the guys got back I managed to find somebody who had a wheelchair they no longer had a need for, and brought it down to the office. I also adjusted the height of the hoop to be at the new "standard" for paper wad throwing.

"They do a lot of that, do they?" Maupsa asked.

"More than you might imagine," I said.

She shook her head at that.

"They sound like a couple of characters," she said, and I laughed, at everything.

"Don't forget to get back here and get paid after they come back next week. They owe you five weeks' worth, and probably two-persons' worth at that."

"I'll be around for awhile, I do believe," was all she said.

When Thursday night rolled around and we had submitted the last issue we were ever going to put together, we sat there quite still for a bit, and then as if by mutual agreement we stood and tidied our desks and put on our coats and closed up.

Outside I said, "See you Monday. Jeff and Chip will really enjoy meeting you."

"Until then," she said, and pulled her hat down a little more snugly, and walked off into the starry, frozen night.

On Monday Chuck took me down a bit early and I opened the office for the guys and had coffee going in the coffee machine I got at the Coastal, and Chip and Jeff made their way in, with Chip helping Jeff get out of a car and getting onto crutches, and then managing to get settled into a wheelchair. It seemed to me as if they had somehow done this before, and maybe they had.

When they got in and got settled there was a bit of catching up to do, and Chip was excited that I'd gotten him a wheelchair for basketball and Jeff laughed, and we talked about "The Paper" and they said how much they liked it and were very impressed by how professional it was, and they thought the opinion pieces were really good and I told them all about Maupsa and of course they said, "Like in Peter Rabbit?" with a laugh, and I said no and we kind of waited around, I guess, for her to show up.

But she didn't. She never did. That kind of hurt me in a way I couldn't quite put my finger on because it was a mixture of something selfish that I wanted, and then also some other things that just flitted away from my mind because I couldn't or didn't want to see them.

Later, at home, I told Joanie and we sat on the couch to think about it, and she said, "You have to admit that it was kind of odd that she said it was Kenna who told her you needed help with The Paper. I mean, after all, she obviously wasn't down at the shop getting a haircut."

I let that ramble around in my head for a bit.

"So, what then? High Plains Drifter? Blows into town and solves everyone's problems and then slowly vanishes in the heat waves of the final scene? Or in this case, is blurred by flurries until no longer visible?"

I was getting bad now for some reason, the same reason I never understand anymore, and I knew in advance that thinking was going to be a problem for awhile. Joanie put her hand on my knee.

"Listen. Sometimes it's like that. Something or someone comes along and helps you unexpectedly. You don't see it coming because you can't. It's like with Chuck. It just happens, that's all. It's one of those good things that can happen in life without any planning at all. Just enjoy it, okay?"

Later, I told Joanie that I wanted to run down to the Coastal for something, but I really just wanted to drive for a bit. I went and got Chuck and we headed down a dark road going somewhere, and there was something in me as we made our way and I could feel it and pushed it away. And there it was again, just sort of gnawing at me, and I pushed again and it wouldn't go away, and I could feel it coming and gritted my teeth as though I was outside in the deadly darkness and it would not go away would not go away, and I so much wanted it to go away: the anger, inexplicable, coming again. I looked out the window onto the snow and dark, and somewhere, unbidden, the idea of loss, the holes that can never be filled I think, these thoughts and feelings unformed in a way that I can't explain, came back again and there was just no pushing it away and the world was cold and dark and full of snow and why is that?

DAYS AND NIGHTS

I can feel it coming back again. I have pushed all things back into the box where they belong and yet they seep back out, reminding me, and what I can feel and see is that I don't feel or think or live, because I have put it all and all into the box, and there is such sadness in this I cannot explain it, and I have tried. I wish I could say. I wish I could tell you so that you'd believe me. Please don't go.

CHAPTER THIRTY-EIGHT:
THE CONSOLATION OF PHILOSOPHY IN WINTER

S O, THERE'S THIS GUY named Boethius. He was a Roman with a Greek name: One-Who-Helps, and he was another one of those philosopher guys who seem to have been crawling all over the place back then, but with a name like that you figure you should at least check him out and see what he's up to.

Anyway, he gets himself thrown in prison, which seems to happen quite a bit to those philosopher-types, and it makes you wonder if too much thinking about things can get you in trouble, or maybe it's because you start saying the things you've been thinking, which is often not a good idea even if you're not a philosopher.

So, the thing is, while he's sitting there in prison waiting to be executed, this woman named Lady Philosophy shows up and says she's there to comfort him. Now, I realize that you're thinking this is just another one of those of inmate fantasies, but let's keep in mind that he's a philosopher and give him the benefit of the doubt.

So, he has this long conversation with Lady Philosophy who tells him that all the things he thought were sources of happiness—wealth, influence, good health, security and so on—are really just things that always come and go from mere chance. She tells him instead to look to his soul and practice virtue and count his blessings, and to exercise his mind in his own behalf, or something along those lines, because everything else, all the stuff that just sort of happens to you, happens to everybody anyway and so it's not something to dwell on. In the end he is comforted by this and Lady Philosophy says, "My job here is done," and she leaves. I don't remember if he got executed or not.

. . . . .

The remainder of winter continued to grind on. Joanie and I went ice fishing a couple more times, but it was brutally cold and so we decided a break from the Great Outdoors might be in our best interests. We played Scrabble from time to time, and some other less threatening games, and read books and watched TV. I did some phone interviews with people and put out my column each week as usual. I just emailed each one to Jeff and Chip anymore because I didn't feel much like going down to The Paper if I didn't have to.

We didn't actually see many people that winter. We'd talk to Jill and Amy down at the Safeway when we went into town for supplies, but that was about it. I spent a lot of my time in my little study area, thinking about I don't know what-all, and as usual I wasn't sleeping very well.

Yes, I wondered about Maupsa and how she might

be, and I also wondered how Hollis was getting along. I wondered as well what Delmer and Dorothy did during the winter, and if they had any hobbies they pursued. I wondered about Gil, and what it was like at the Good Gas this time of year, and if he ever got bored or not. I wondered too if Stacy was somewhere out there in this weather, hiding behind a snow drift, or if she just hung out at an office somewhere, waiting for spring. I wondered how Kenna was getting along, and I supposed people still came in to get their hair cut as usual, but I wondered what it was like living at the shop all the time.

And I started to wonder about myself as well, which I rarely seemed to do, and why I felt the way I did, and just what was really wrong with me because something seemed all so wrong with me in some way I couldn't figure out.

For some reason, I typically turn to books for answers about many of life's conundrums. After all, everything that we've ever thought that was worth thinking has been written down for us these past five thousand years, and so you'd think that you'd eventually find something that helps.

When Joanie and I were students way back when at the University of Washington, we'd walk into the gigantic Suzzallo Library and wander the aisles for hours, for no particular reason. We just wanted to look at the books at first, I think, just to be amazed at what humanity had done and said. In time we would bring snacks and then a meal in a backpack with us, and we'd say, "Meet you back here in three hours," and we'd just go off somewhere and see what we could see.

Sitting alone in my little study it occurred to me that I had about three hundred books in boxes in the closet in the bedroom, and so I started pulling them out and going through them one by one.

As it happened, the first box I opened had Dickens and Victor Hugo in it, and I figured that was the last thing I needed. Then I ran across my old, battered Shakespeare but I reckoned I really needed something else. I kept digging around and then discovered my old *Encyclopedia of Philosophy* from way back when. I pulled that out, and got a chair and sat down with it.

I flipped through the pages for a bit, and there was old Boethius. I remembered him from somewhere long ago, something about his name and the idea of consolation. That sounded like a good starting point, so I read a bit of his stuff, and that seemed good in some way. I flipped ahead a few pages and there was Hildegard, and I remembered she was in my head for some reason not so long back, so I read a bit of that and to tell you the truth she was sort of beyond my reach with where she was headed, but I liked her because she'd had visions like some of my favorite poets, and so that was kind of good in some un-nameable way. For all my admiration of her, however, she wasn't what I was looking for, if there really was something I was looking for.

Then I came across the old familiar names like Nietzsche and also flipping backward there was Jeremy Bentham. No. Too dark, and way too utilitarian, breaking down our sorrows and happiness into what seemed to me either despair or slides for a microscope. Had neither of these guys ever smelled a flower?

On I went. Plato? Holy smokes no. This guy, when you sit down to read him at all, pretty much doesn't care for anything because he figures it's somehow threatening the purity of his soul and mind. The way I reckoned it, I was way past concerns like that. I read bits of the Book of Matthew. That was good. Hadn't read that in some time. Great beginning and middle, but as some of you may know, there's both tragedy and triumph at the end, and so you have to sort of be ready for that. I read some more.

After awhile, however, I sat still for a bit to realize what I was doing, just sitting still. I was trying, like good ol' Boethius, to find some simple consolation, just a little bit of something that I could sleep on for the here-and-now. No big fixes, no life-altering revelations, just a bit of comfort, that's all. And I couldn't find it, because too much else was crushing in instead.

I thought of Maupsa then, and wondered where she was and if she had made it, had lived, had survived to live again. I had waited for a message, a letter, an email, her showing up on the doorstep, seeing her at Del's, something, just something. I thought about Delmer and Dorothy, and how badly they must miss their son, and what it must possibly be like to wake to a certain emptiness that once was not empty. I thought about Kenna's friend who was there-and-then-not-there in seemingly the blink of an eye, just somehow snatched away.

And I thought about Hollis, seared and scarred and broken and angry. And, as if in answer to an unheard call, I heard that stupid voice once again in my head and this time tried to push it all the way to The Box if I could. I wouldn't walk that path, I knew it now, because I had no power to fix anyone or anything. Never did. Never would. I still had my own house to set in order. All my days and nights, stretched before me. Those had to be my only concern.

I walked out of my little study and into the front room where Joanie was watching a mystery show, and I sat down on the couch with her and wanted to say something about what I'd been thinking, but she said, "Shhhhh" because a good part was coming up and so I watched that. And then, about ten minutes later there was kind of a scary part, and I reached for her hand and she held mine and I held hers, and I realized in that little bit there that Joanie is the best philosophy there is.

DAYS AND NIGHTS

I'm going to have to assume that if you're still here you probably have some questions. If you've been paying attention you can see that we're getting to the end here pretty soon, and so you might want to know certain simple kinds of things. You might question, why did I tell you about Gil or Walter or maybe half a dozen other people in town when these people really don't have very much to do with this story? I think that'd be a good question.

I know you can't see it, but the reason I told you about them is because they strike me as normal people. They're just living and getting on and they seem happy enough to me, even though I don't know them very well. But the thing is, the thing is, when I meet them they're like sandpaper, abrasive, hurting me in some way that I cannot explain.

Spring

CHAPTER THIRTY-NINE:
THE HOPE OF SPRING

SOMETIMES what I pray for is simple clarity. It's not like I'm asking to know the future or something, but maybe just less confusion, or perhaps a bit of reassurance about something. I don't know, maybe it's not so simple a thing to ask for. I think by clarity all I really mean is just one's bearings, one's reference points. I think I ask for this because sometimes I don't see things very well anymore, or I don't understand them in the ways that I used to, and that's not how I used to be at all.

I seem to want answers that I never asked the questions to before. I seem to want direction, from within, telling me where to go, what to do and how it ought to get done, and now there seem to be many times when I don't have an answer or a direction, or a purpose. Maybe that's why I talk to Chuck all the time, like maybe he'd give me a straight answer for once instead of hemming and hawing all the time like he does. I think I'd just like to see things once again, see them like I used to, with all their colors and shapes and very, very fine details.

·　·　·　·　·

Spring arrived precisely on schedule; that is to say, one day it was winter and then the next day it wasn't, and everything pretty much thawed out overnight. And then, Joanie and I did our Dance of Life, as every Montanan must do, so happy, so excited, because we've made it through another winter and it was time to live again, I mean really live. Chuck was excited as well, and eager to get going, and so we did. The dogs jumped in the back, and Chuck happily took us down roads this way and that.

We saw flowers and rushing streams and blue sky revealing gigantic snow-covered peaks and it was all so glorious you could breathe it and drink it and never want for more. The dogs ran like wolves and ended with tongues lolling, full of all the world's scents and signs and sights, and were content again.

We got back into town and Chuck drove past Wiley's and beeped his horn to say hello. We passed Walter on main street and he nodded in our direction, and we stopped at Gil's to get gas and said hello to everyone there. We stopped at the Safeway and got some things and talked to Jill and Amy and how's it going and all that, and on the way home we saw Delmer and Dorothy out in their yard and we honked and waved. Ah. Spring!

I think maybe since about February I'd spent time and time again out in the garage getting my things ready for fishing. Sometimes I'd go out and go through my flies and sort of clean them up or fluff them a bit, kind of checking them out to see if they were still worthy of the adventure. Other times I'd tie new leaders or check out my waders or wax my fly lines, just once more. Other times I'd tie on a fly imagining that it was the very first one I wanted for the new season, and then later I'd go back and tie on a different one, imagining the upcoming water levels and where I might be and what the fish in their dream world of moving water over roundy stones might wish to wake to. Joanie would ask if I wanted to see some television and I'd say maybe in a bit but I wanted to check on some things and I'd wander out there and sit, waiting for winter to end, just waiting. And now it was time to go.

. . . . .

That first time out I'd have gotten up and left at midnight if I could, because I couldn't sleep again, and I was wanting so badly to just be away and in the river once again, just standing there casting, and so to be away.

The crazy thing was that when I finally did get up in the dark and made my way to the driveway and found Chuck waiting, I didn't know where I wanted to go. There were eight places I might have chosen, but I couldn't decide. So, I just let Chuck decide. He headed on down the driveway, then past Delmer and Dorothy's place, and he turned right and headed down the valley toward town and then through it, and up into the foothills and forests somewhere. He went on for a bit and then pulled over and I looked up to see where we were and was a little surprised he hadn't gone very far out of town after all.

"Here?" I asked, and he seemed to think so.

It was just light enough to see now, but instead of getting out and getting into my waders and vest I just sat there for a while with the window rolled down, breathing in the air and looking out. It was a new day, and I guess I wasn't in a rush after all. It had been such a very long winter and now it wasn't winter anymore and even though I knew summer flew by like it always seems to do, I sat and waited for awhile, wondering if I was really ready to begin, because once you started then that was the beginning and the way it goes is you can't go back.

I'm not sure how long I sat there, but eventually I roused myself from whatever it was I was thinking and told Chuck I'd be back after a bit and then got out and struggled into waders and boots and vest and picked up my rod and headed down a path through some scrubby willows, showing just the first hint of new leaves and new green, and made my way to the water.

Passing through the willows I came to a large stretch of meadow that ran on either side of the river for half a mile. Several paths led down to the water and I picked one at random and made my way through the grasses and tiny pink and blue flowers that edged the path, as if passing through someone's grand garden. The sun crested a ridge and the river arced away in both directions, running like a ribbon of crystal-gold. There was still some chill in the air, but it would soon warm, and insects and birds were already busy in their flight. A kingfisher chattered somewhere downstream, and I came at last to the river, the water rushing by, never waiting on anything or anyone.

The water was high and fast as I knew it would be at this time of year, but it didn't really matter. I mostly stood on the bank and cast out, but sometimes I waded just a bit into the river, just so I could stand in it, feeling it rush around me and past, to wherever it was headed in such a hurry.

Ahead of me at the edge of the meadow, the trees seemed to bend and rise again, though there was no wind. Dragonflies skimmed the quiet eddies of the water and swallows glided through the upper airs. The sun rippled on the river, molding its every swirl in golden light. I looked out and if you didn't look directly at it, but just maybe in the corner of your eye, in that peripheral vision that can't really ever fully capture something, I thought I could see the whole world breathing in and out.

I don't know how long I cast, but at some point I looked up and the sun was getting high and the air was warm and I had come to the woods at the edge of the meadow. I decided that maybe I'd wander into the trees for just a bit before turning and heading back.

I hadn't gone very far when I walked out into another little meadow, and there sat Hollis and Kenna on a blanket, having a picnic, and two fly rods were leaning against a tree. I'm not sure which astonished me more, seeing Kenna and Hollis together out in the woods, or imagining that Hollis had begun fly-fishing.

I actually didn't recognize Hollis right away because he was dressed in jeans and an orange flannel shirt, and he had no hat and you could see that his hair had gotten longer. Maybe even more so he didn't look like himself because he was stretched out on the blanket, propped on one elbow, and laughing at something Kenna was saying.

I just sort of stopped and stood where I was, and eventually Hollis noticed me and righted himself a bit.

He had been holding Kenna's hand and when he saw me he let go and said something to Kenna and she turned now to look at me too.

"Uh, hi," I said. "I was just passing through... I mean I was just headed back...uh, how's the fishing?"

Neither one of them stood, but Kenna waved me over and I couldn't really slink away now.

Hollis sat up then, and Kenna said, "You're just in time!" and I made my way over to where they sat, with some picnic food spread out and a couple of those little plastic bottles of wine opened up. I sat down with them and Kenna handed me a plate with some deviled eggs and ham slices and grapes on it.

I sat there for a moment not knowing what to say and feeling more than a little embarrassed for having spoiled what otherwise looked to be shaping up as a private and somewhat intimate outing for them.

Neither one seemed to mind, however, but Hollis, maybe sensing my discomfort, said, "We bought fishing gear this winter. We're going to learn how to do it together. Kenna's done it before a bit, so she's going to show me."

"That's great," I said. "How's it been going so far?"

Kenna looked at Hollis then and smiled.

"It's been going great, Al. This year I'm catching a big one," and she laughed and Hollis smiled a little at that.

"That's great," was pretty much all I could say, except that the eggs were really good.

We chatted a bit more and I finished my plate and got up to go, but Kenna said, "Hang on just a bit. We've got something to ask you. We want to know if you and Joanie will come to the wedding."

There are times when a person hears something, and they understand what the words mean, and yet they can't comprehend what's being said, even though they're perfectly certain they've heard the words correctly. I just stood there, blankly, looking at Kenna, who was just opening her little bottle of wine.

"Well?" Hollis said, giving me his old once over.

"What wedding?" was all I could say.

"Ours!" Kenna said with a laugh. "Who else?"

When it finally became clear to me what was happening I felt an inexplicable happiness. Something somewhere somehow had turned a corner, or maybe had begun again and I didn't know it had stopped, but I laughed and laughed I was so happy, and Hollis stood and I shook his hand and said congratulations and then I hugged Kenna and we all laughed. We all sat back down again and talked for some little time.

"But, but when did all this happen?"

"It's been a long winter, Al," Kenna said. "It's time to live again, just really live," and she clinked her bottle of wine against Hollis's.

Eventually I said my goodbyes and headed back up the path, out of the woods and into the open once again. I was maybe halfway back when Stacy suddenly appeared on the path in front of me.

"Hey Al," she said. "Headin' back?"

I said hello and that I was, and she said she thought she'd head out too. We walked along for a while without saying anything, and I thought that Stacy seemed a bit down. I hadn't noticed because I guess I was so happy right then, and I couldn't wait to get home and tell Joanie the news.

Finally I said, "I'm thinking you probably heard all that back there."

Stacy admitted that she had.

"I wasn't really trying to eavesdrop or anything," she said, and I reassured her I hadn't been thinking that at all.

A little further along she said, "I think I'm going to miss Hollis following me around is all."

We stopped walking then and she looked out on the river, going its own way.

"I never really had anybody follow me around like that before. I liked it, even though I always did manage to ditch him," she said with a wistful smile.

We both looked out at the river then, just looking. From where we stood the river ran through the expanse of meadow, and on either end was the forest, and you couldn't say from just looking where the river came from or where it went.

"Stacy, you ever do any fly-fishing?"

DAYS AND NIGHTS

For some time now I've been thinking about Linda again, trying to remember the things we talked about, what seems so very long ago now. I remember just talking, words, and the words had power. They were things that if you listened to them, or you said them yourself, they could change things. They could wake you up, draw you out, tear down walls, help you discover where the wound was and even heal.

Yes, I think I remember now, just talking, just the words and what they could do. I think maybe I'll call her and see if we can talk. Maybe we can start over again. Everyone deserves a second chance.

CHAPTER FORTY:
A CAST AWAY

"Many men go fishing all of their lives without knowing that it is not fish they are after."

—Henry David Thoreau

"Oh-oh, let's go down, down to the river and pray."

—Traditional American Folksong

SOMETIMES, just sometimes, I wonder why I'm fishing.
I just wonder is all. I'm not hoping for a revelation
about anything, I just wonder. That's all. I sometimes
think it's because I just want to be outside, and close to
the water and the trees and whatever else is going on
outside of myself. I sometimes think it's maybe how
clever I can be: fooling the fish with a little bit of something that could make no difference at all to anything
else but a fish. Sometimes I don't even pay attention to
fishing and I'm just standing in the water, bracing
against it, seeing, maybe, as it flows around me, and
turning my head to watch it come and go.

Sometimes I am not thinking very much about anything, and sometimes all my attention is on something
really, really tiny, like the fly or myself, flowing and
drifting along, so small I can hardly even see it or

myself in the rush of water, everywhere, all around me, drinking me in, and me it. And sometimes I notice that I don't notice and that the water and stones and the air in my face just heated to that warmth that you know is dawn and the day has just happened because the sun has come over the ridge and has fallen down in a way that I didn't understand or notice because I wasn't watching, and I didn't see it coming, and I didn't understand it.

And sometimes, when the fish haven't been what I have wanted them to be, or maybe something else hasn't, I keep thinking: Just one more cast. Just one more cast, and then maybe something, and then I can rest and be at peace. I am just one cast away. Just one more cast away.

CHAPTER FORTY-ONE:
ELEGY

"The light danced to the rhythm of the breeze on the water; it was all in one and magical, and that was what I dove into."

—Larry Levine

I have a four-foot Viking ship in my arms which has two valkyrie Barbies in it with gold lamé helmets and braided hair and I just can't tell you about that right now and so I should tell you first while you're waiting that it is dark like real dark and I am driving fast to get there because there's no way I'm going to be late and it doesn't matter that my night vision is bad and there are deer standing all over the road and I have my coffee in one hand and the steering wheel in the other and going as fast as I can without killing myself and trying to find one stretch of road straight enough to drink my coffee because I need it.

This road that follows the North Umpqua from my place to his is like a bad snarl in your line and is cutting up and then down the foothills following topography like a deer trail and then there are those whoa-times when even as slow as you're going you'd better hit the brake and then you gun the next hundred yards thinking there's a straight space but there isn't and all your attention has to be on the road but it isn't because you're already thinking of the river and that's the way that goes and there's really no helping it.

I'd give you some in-between but it's sort of secondary but if you had to have it because that's how you think a story has to go I'd say that when he had tossed himself and his gear in the truck we talked about the week before and what we'd been doing and how's your garden and what did you eat and man I'm not looking forward to school and I hated turning the calendar page to July and me too and that latest fire over the ridge and how hot and dry it is so early but the water is still good and he says he tested it and it's 50 degrees amazing for this time of year and like that and what do you think you'll tie on and he's thinking the purple leech and I'm saying yes and maybe I'll just do the green skunk-butt and that's pretty much it except do you have more coffee and yes of course I do.

And then we come to Cable Crossing and I ask here? and he says let's go on up and see Wright Bridge first because two days ago I pulled off and saw from up above at least one good fish there and that's good enough for me because he's been on this river thirty-five years as man and guide and man and so Wright Bridge it will be and as we pass the firs and cedars and pines and oaks and vine maples and ferns and moss and all of creation all in shadow on either side the road it's just a slice of light in front of my truck and it's like driving through a tunnel toward the other side of night.

It's at this point that I should tell you about the river because it's the whole point of a sort and we've stopped and gotten out and we've struggled into waders and boots and are tying on flies in near dark and I'm just about to ask him can he tie this on because I know he can do it with his eyes closed really while half the time I can't do it at all but I don't and finally cinch the knot and now down we go except to tell you about the river.

Where we stand about fifty feet above it swirls and runs through the canyon of first light and I don't have the words for things like that he would but I don't so I'll say instead that it was one of those things that if you were somewhere else you'd bow your head or say a quiet word before you approached it and I'm sorry but I'll have to leave it at that.

We make our way down twenty-five feet and there is the brass plaque for Dan who photographed this river for pretty much all his life and he's famous and Larry pats the boulder twice and says good morning Dan and we watch our footing and there is no water on these rocks and so we're the first ones there and that is very fine and my hand slides over Dan's rock with a gentle touch but all my mind is on the river.

I want to tell you about what we did and where we stood and how we cast and the water and the rounded red gold yellow green and shot through black and white stones that surround you and mending the line as it reached out into somewhere just caught for a moment against the flow and how you lift and realign and all your mind is focused on that tiny piece of yarn and feather that he made and how the water catches on a rock and foams pushing and pushing and then breaks and swirls and rushes downward and I just can't do it.

Some of you will know what I mean and the rest of you will need to trust your imagination.

And I would tell you about the other six places we stopped that morning before the sun could fall suddenly down between the rocks and ridges through which the river winds its way falling like an avalanche of light to crash on the water which means the day's fishing has to end but every place is the same there just another stretch of wonder and so I can't describe it.

Instead I can tell you about Larry in front of me as we made our way down the tree-shrouded path to Rattlesnake and the sun filtered down in ghosts onto the forest floor and how he'd suddenly stop and look up at a tree limb or down at a sword fern and had to step off the trail for about three minutes once to look at an old log and mentally mark it for mushrooms in the fall or a woodpecker lodge in the burn out from years back and just walking from sunlight to shadow sunlight to shadow.

And how when we reached the river half a mile later he sat on a boulder instead of leading the way and just pointed and said three lefts and two rights and go slow and then straight ahead about midway through the run and I knew what he meant because even in summer water you want to know where your feet are at all times and he knew every rock and you listened and he pulled out his pipe to light it for the first time that morning. And that's the way that goes pretty much every time just so you know and I can't tell you any more about that.

I had better tell you instead that I was sorry the day had ended and that I asked him what about Tuesday and he said he couldn't Tuesday and I said that was too bad because the water is so good right now and he said well you don't need me anymore and I laughed because I knew what he meant of course but it also struck me like maybe this was the first lie I had ever heard him say. And I knew what he meant because he had been teaching me for going on five years now and had shown me everything one could see and know in that amount of time and so I said yes there's that but it wouldn't be the same of course and I didn't say that out loud.

I started that next Tuesday and began those first forays on my own and it was still very beautiful in the ways I've already said I can't say. And another summer is passing and the calendar pages are turned.

I need to back up a bit here and say that Larry and I became friends on the first day we met and you can imagine there's a story behind that because that doesn't happen to pretty much anyone but I don't feel like explaining that right now and so I'll say that he asked me about myself about a week later there in our office and he said so you're a real Ph.D. and have been around and I said yes and told him about my studies and then he asked where I'd been and what I'd taught and that was twenty-five years worth and he sat back in his chair and looked at me and said, so you've been teaching all this Great Literature for like a quarter of a century and I said I suppose I have now you say so and he leaned forward and spread his hands and said I just have to say this and I hope you don't take offense but I just hate Great Literature because it's so boring. Ha!

So then we talked about it for an hour and I said you have a point but what about this and he said that's very fine but what about this and he pulled from his brief-case a paper that was titled the ten best opening lines from literature because he'd been dreaming about teaching a fiction writing class and had been putting it together for quite some time and I read these and none of them were of course Call me Ishmael or something like that and I was just screaming laughing at the first two and then thoughtful about the next several and then we had to talk about the last couple and I realized that I had never read any of these stories before and so I learned something very new just like that.

And this is how that goes. With a friend you never know everything all at once like looking at a landscape and instead it's much more like just seeing bits and pieces floating along and surely we're just at the head-waters of the stream and so it is with any stream that becomes a river and then what's added just here and there runs down and down and down until it finally meets the vastness of the sea and that's how it really is for anyone who'd care to notice.

I'm sorry I had to wait but I guess I have to tell you about that Viking ship now and get back to where I started even though I don't want to. It's Thursday the week before classes and Larry is there giving the copier its what-for so he can be ready next week and I am surprised and glad to see him, because we haven't met up for a few weeks because of the fires and the river is down and everything and so we've just been emailing and I have to go float a Viking ship and he has that expression on his face which is his usual grin like what the hell is that and why didn't you say something because I have a Viking ship in my arms with two Barbies dressed as valkyries because last year the guys from the Science Building had this real cool boat that won the annual regatta on the fountain before school starts and this year was going to be the Year of the Humanities if I had any say in it and Joanie and I are saying hello and then we have to go to play with our boat. You see?

I will say this just the once and never again: So after my ship sinks in the fountain and the valkyrie Barbies are recovered, Larry meets us and says would I mind switching classrooms with him so he can have the same one, Snyder 15, for both his classes so he doesn't have to move and even though I like Snyder 15 myself because it's the first classroom I ever taught in for UCC and I like it and am comfy there, I of course say well yes you can because that makes sense because Larry always has a bunch of stuff he wants to set up in advance for his students and I know this. Do you see? That is my classroom? Good.

So it is Thursday again now of our first week of classes and I am sitting in my truck and looking across the parking lot and Larry is walking in through the first light and he doesn't know but two mule deer are following behind him like about twenty feet, just coming along behind like he's their shepherd, and they stop to look around when he turns the corner to go to the office, and I'm still in my truck when he comes back around the corner to get his classroom set up before students arrive and the deer look at him and then trot to the fountain. I told him in the office and we laughed about who was stalking whom, and that the deer had the better of him.

We talk baseball again and who will be in the playoffs and how many games he will be watching simultaneously at home and yes I remember his uncle is famous and how he sat in the dugout at Yankee Stadium and all that and he smiles because it's baseball season and summer still. We decide to go fishing the next morning, but this is an effort on my part because I know this violates his schedule because he only fishes Mondays Wednesdays and Sundays, but he says that sounds good so we're all set and I can't wait for classes to end. Tuesday was so hectic that we finally have a chance to just sit and talk like always.

So I'm saying what Joanie and I did and it's his turn and we talk and he stands up from his chair and is looking out the window just almost leaning out of it if he could and tells me he saw a red dragonfly the other day and it was beautiful and he'd never seen one before though he'd known they were around and for decades on the river he'd never seen one and he said that last week he'd seen cirrus clouds piled up one on top of the other in big V's right on the river like he'd never before seen and about how you know how he hangs his watch up on this little branch when he sits on his favorite boulder along the river where he reads all day so that he won't forget that he's been reading all day long and how a damselfly sat on his watch and told him what time it was and he said with his grin that maybe Nature was trying to tell him something once again and we laughed and I made my joke and we laughed and we sighed because we had to go to class and we looked at the clock and said see you in a bit.

Those first two shots sounded like people fooling around in that room next door and I said to my students it sounds like they're having quite a time there because I could hear what I thought was laughter and that wouldn't have been at all unusual because we are a pretty fun bunch and like to whoop it up in the class-room and there have been many occasions where we've each walked next door or around the corner and asked can you keep it down a bit.

The next series of sounds though, one after another in rapid succession, dull thuds like bricks dropped on a carpet, I don't know. It was like a toggle flipped in my brain and I was shouting get out get out and follow me and some other words that you just don't use in the classroom and then there is running and fear and the feeling of something looking at your back.

And we are running or at least I am because by the time I pass the library heading for admin there are only a few with me and I am yelling at students to get inside and finally we are, in a dark little room where we slide a cabinet in front of the door and wait. There is the bizarre elation of being alive in me, and under that is an acid wash of fear and guilt and worry that burns the throat because I know what room that was. I see I am still carrying my coffee cup. There are others there, terrified, and so I squeeze shoulders and speak softly and wait.

And I am driving that dark road the next Tuesday be-cause I thought that was a good idea and I am doing pretty good and there are turns and deer and I am do-ing pretty good and I am doing pretty good and I pass by your house and slow and I am doing pretty good and I decide to go on and I am okay and just fine because I am doing pretty good and I am not asking what fly you want to have on or your opinion of what I should try or what the water temperature is or how you sat on a boulder reading yesterday and what it was you read and what you saw because I am doing pretty good. I am driving and I think I'm going to hit Cable Crossing first but I slow and then move on and I'm not real clear where I'll stop maybe Baker and try the upper run and see but I go by that too and I pull off at Wright Bridge because I think I want to say hi to Dan and the sun is just giving enough light that by the time I have my rod in my hand and my vest already on the river below is molten silver shot through with veins of the rest of night.

I make the careful way down because even though there is a path worn by many boots there are also many boulders sunk into the sides of the steep decline and you can see the cleat-scratches in them even in this light and there is no water on these rocks the telltale sign and I am the first one here.

I reach Dan's rock and I pat him twice and say hello Dan and it is just me by myself this time and then I cannot see or breathe and my knees buckle and I am slip-sliding down the slope and something hurts but I am stopped and on my hands and knees with my hands in the river. And the water is silver-swift and just keeps moving along and I can see now a bit and I realize now that it's all new water every moment and never the same because it can't be because it's always going on and by and you can never stop it even for a moment.

I put my hand in the river to touch it and it slides between my fingers and is gone.

LATER

"So, how do you feel now?" Hollis asked, sipping his coffee.

"What do you mean?"

Hollis looked at me a moment. "You know. Now that you finished that book."

"Oh. About the same, I guess. How about you?"

"Yeah. About the same." He looked at his coffee, then me again. "But don't you feel any better at all? Like maybe you learned something?"

"Sure, yeah, a little bit, I guess."

Hollis looked at me again without saying anything, and I looked down.

He said, "Are you going to call Linda now?"

I thought about that for a moment. "I don't know. Maybe. Maybe I'll just see how things go for awhile."

Hollis sighed and drank his coffee.

THE END